MW01295061

déjà-BOOM!

By

Wally Duff

A Hamlin Park Irregulars Novel:

Book 2

www.HamlinParkIrregulars.com

All rights reserved. This book or parts thereof may not be reproduced in any form, stored in any retrieval system, or transmitted in any form by any means — electronic, mechanical, photocopy, recording, or otherwise — without prior written permission of the publisher, except as provided by United States of America copyright law.

For permission requests, write to the publisher at:

Attention: Wallace Duff
c/o K, M & N Publishers, Inc.
Hamlin Park Irregulars, A Nebraska Limited Liability Co.
Suite 100, 12829 West Dodge Road
Omaha, NE 68154

© 2018 -- Wallace Duff. All rights reserved.

Visit the author's website: www.HamlinParkIrregulars.com

First Edition

ISBN-13: 978-1732465206
ISBN-10: 1732465207

This is a work of fiction. Names, characters, places, and incidents are either the products of the author's imagination or are used fictitiously. Any resemblance to actual persons, living or dead, businesses, companies, events, or locales is entirely coincidental.

To Bill Crozier, Dwayne Jelinek, and Perry Wickstrom:
Tim Newens and I will miss you three Benson Bunnies.

Just because it looks like a leprechaun and talks like a leprechaun, it doesn't mean it can't act like the little demon it is. ~ N.L. Gervasio, *Nemesis*

Part 1

Chicago, Illinois

August 2nd

1

"Dear girl, I am so delighted to meet you," Dr. Michael Doyle said to my cleavage.

He glanced at the *Chicago Sun-Times* business card I'd handed to him. It identified me as one of their reporters.

"Christina Edwards, is it?"

He had a patrician British accent. Mine was pure Omaha, Nebraska.

"Please, call me Tina."

We shook hands. Doyle put the card in his suit coat pocket. The aroma of sandalwood and something else, maybe jasmine, drifted over me.

I sniffed.

He caught me.

"Clive Christian No. 1, a gift from a grateful patient," he said. "I am told it is the most expensive perfume in the world."

"The scent goes beautifully with your suit."

The material was dark blue silk with a faint burgundy stripe which matched his burgundy-colored French cuff shirt and burgundy, patterned Hermès tie. The large diamonds in his cufflinks cost more than I made in a year.

"Bespoke Savile Road. My personal tailor does a fantastic job, don't you think?"

We were in his opulent, soon-to-be featured in *Architectural Digest,* four thousand four hundred and four square foot penthouse office on Chicago's Lakeshore Drive. He indicated where he wanted me to sit, nodding toward a matched pair of padded Queen Anne chairs across from his mahogany desk, which was slightly smaller than the deck of a nuclear aircraft carrier.

Following his silent instructions, I sat down. He moved behind the desk and settled into an ergonomically-correct black leather chair. "How may I help you?"

He still spoke to my cleavage, and being a twenty-two-year-old female reporter, I was about to take advantage of that. I'd worn a short, tight black skirt, five-inch black pumps, and a clinging, white silk camisole top, which displayed enough to keep his focus on my physical assets and off the questions I was about to ask him.

Dr. Doyle was internationally known as the "Fat Doctor." The European cut of the suit could not hide that he didn't appear to be using his own weight-loss pill on a regular basis. In his PR press packet he was listed as five feet nine inches and one hundred fifty pounds.

That was a total fabrication. I am five feet eight, and even without my high heels, I would have towered over him. He was no more than five feet five, including the lifts in his glossy, burgundy Italian leather shoes. His slicked-back, abnormally black hair contrasted with his pale facial skin, but even a well-trimmed black beard couldn't disguise jowls that proved his weight was north of two hundred pounds.

"Do you mind if I ask a few background questions to get to know more about you?" I asked.

That was a tiny fib. I knew more about him than he did. I was here because one of my Alpha Phi sorority sisters, Kelli Reischl, almost died from kidney failure while attempting to lose twenty pounds before our senior year spring break trip to Cabo.

Kelli was on renal dialysis for two months before her kidneys began functioning again. The end result was she missed that spring break and graduation. Her doctors never did come up with a reason for her near-death experience because she didn't tell them about Doyle's pills.

It wasn't until after our graduation that I found out she had taken Doyle's formulation right before her kidneys failed. I began sniffing around her story and discovered the real truth about Doyle.

2

"You received a medical degree and a PhD in biochemistry in London," I said. "Gosh, you're so young. That's amazing."

He arched his right eyebrow slightly. "I was gifted from an early age."

"And then you came here to Northwestern Medical Center seven years ago where you discovered the treatment for obesity."

It was hard to miss his glistening clear-polish manicure when he pointed at me with his stubby index finger. "I have to make one correction. I found the *cure* for obesity."

From my background research, I learned that Doyle's system worked. People did lose weight taking his supplements. But that wasn't why I was there.

"It is *not* a claim," he continued. "It is a scientific fact that my formula is effective."

"I'm not a doctor or scientist, or anything like that, but isn't something missing from those studies?"

He glanced down at his platinum Piaget watch and stifled a yawn. "Nothing, my dear. Absolutely nothing."

"What about complications?"

He straightened up in his black leather chair. "There can be rare idiosyncratic reactions from any formulation."

"How about kidney failure?"

"To my knowledge this has never occurred."

I took out a copy of Kelli's medical record from my briefcase and placed it on top of his well-polished desk. I slid it toward him. "Then how do you explain this?"

Out came his gold reading glasses. He glanced at her name on the record. "This interview is over. Please leave."

"Dr. Doyle, tomorrow, my newspaper — the *Chicago Sun-Times* — is going to publish my investigative article alleging that your formula has dire side effects. I am here to give you an opportunity to present your side of the story. I think it would be in your best interest to give me a statement."

"And I am certain my attorneys will disagree with you." He picked up Kelli's file and threw it in his wastebasket. "We are done here."

"Before I leave, there is one other related item that you might want to comment on. What is the Vakili Corporation?"

"Bloody hell! I have no idea what you're talking about."

"That's strange, because the Vakili Corporation provided the money for your two new Bentleys, your private jet, this office, and your Lakeshore condo, along with total financing of your entire operation. Isn't that correct, doctor?"

Tiny beads of sweat appeared on his forehead. "My CFO is responsible for these financial matters."

"Dr. Doyle, do you deny that your profits are being funneled through several off-shore shell businesses to the Vakili Corporation, a front for the Irish Republican Army terrorist activities in Ireland?"

Follow the money. That was the clue my bureau chief had given me when I first began researching Kelli's story. While doing that, I fell in love with investigative journalism.

The real issue wasn't Doyle's formula. It was the money that he made off the fat Americans using his pills to lose weight. And he wasn't British. He maintained that deception to mask his real country of origin.

From my background research, beginning with his birth, I discovered that "Mick" Doyle was Irish and his black hair was actually red.

Like a leprechaun.

Doyle's laundered funds were distributed to his relatives in Ireland who ran the IRA. His money also supported al-Qaeda and Hezbollah, which provided training for IRA members, including instruction in firearms, car bombing, firebombing, shooting mortars, and constructing IEDs.

Once I discovered this, I alerted the Chicago PD and FBI, with the stipulation that they would give me an exclusive on the story.

I stood up and took out my cell phone, preparing to hit a speed dial number to the authorities who waited in the hallway. The sound of a bullet being chambered in a handgun stopped me.

3

"Put that phone down!" Doyle screamed.

Yikes!

Doyle assumed a shooter's stance. He pointed the barrel of the gun between my eyes, something he might have learned at a Hezbollah training camp.

"Toss that phone to me," he directed.

My heart thumped against my sternum. A call from my cell phone to the guys waiting in the hall was the only thing that could save me.

There might be a better option.

My brother is a professional baseball pitcher with the San Diego Padres, but he has always said I have a better throwing arm than he does.

"You want this?" I waved the phone at him. "Here it is, buster."

Before Doyle could react, I threw the phone as hard as I could at his face, hitting him squarely on his nose. He dropped his gun and put his hands to his face. Blood from his nose squirted between his fingers. A new, metallic odor overpowered his expensive cologne.

I dove for the gun and landed on my stomach. He jumped on my back and grabbed my hair. He pulled back. The pain was excruciating.

I screamed and grabbed the barrel of the gun. I swung it backward over the top of my head. The grip made solid contact with his skull. It sounded like I'd thumped a ripe melon.

I kept swinging. He let out a loud groan. The pressure on my hair was released. I rolled out from under him.

He struggled to his knees. I swung the gun like I was hitting a tennis forehand and struck his left cheek and the side of his nose with the barrel.

There was a squish from his ripped skin followed by a crunch from his smashed bones. More blood flew out from his newly caved-in left cheek and increasingly deformed nose.

The force of the blow from the gun knocked him on his back. He sobbed, mingling tears with the blood surrounding him on his expensive wool carpet.

I reversed my grip on the gun and held it in front of me. In Nebraska, I'd grown up around guns and was an expert at shooting moving targets. If he tried to move, there was no way I could miss him.

And I won't hesitate to do it.

4

I picked up my cell phone and speed-dialed the cops and FBI agents in the hallway to alert them that I had a gun in my hand and not to shoot me when they entered the room.

The door flew open. FBI agents and several Chicago Police Department officers rushed in.

A young Chicago policeman pointed at the blood-covered, whimpering Doyle thrashing around on the carpet. "What the heck happened to him?"

The cop was tall and muscular and looked like an Italian movie star sent in from central casting.

"He messed up my hair," I said, shaking my long brown tresses to free up the tangles. "I'm all about my hair."

He smiled. "Good to know."

The cop put on latex gloves for protection from the blood streaming from Doyle's face and nose. He pulled the doctor's hands behind him and snapped handcuffs on his wrists. Jerking Doyle to his feet, he took out a white card and read the doctor his rights.

Doyle's swollen nose rapidly turned dark purple, and his left eyelid puffed up to a tiny slit. The skin over his newly deformed left cheek, his nose, and other facial lacerations continued to bleed profusely.

To see me, he had to tilt his head back, giving me a disgusting view of the fresh blood now beginning to clot in his nostrils.

"I will kill you for this, if it's the last thing I ever do," Doyle hissed, his accent no longer British aristocracy.

Pure Irish.

He tried to spit blood in my face, but the cute cop shoved him away from me. "Button it, slick," the cop said, as he twisted Doyle's arm a little harder for emphasis.

That attracted the attention of one of the FBI agents. "Ease off, Infantino. We'll take it from here."

He released his grip on Doyle. The FBI agent pushed the doctor into the hall. Two Chicago PD detectives followed.

"You seem a little shook up even though you just beat the crap out of the doc," Officer Infantino said to me.

"I'm okay," I said, with more courage than I felt.

It was my first big story, and there was no way I was going to be terrified by Doyle. But as the adrenaline surge dissipated from my system, I realized I had been scared out of my mind.

Infantino eyed me up and down as he watched me attempt to control my rapid breathing. His gaze stopped at the same place Doyle's did a few minutes before.

"How about having a drink with me after work to kind of relax, talk about the case, and so forth?"

I handed him my business card. "Call me."

He fingered the card. "Go off-shift at four. Can be ready by seven."

"Sounds good. I'll be done with my edit by then, but I would like to go home and freshen up too."

"No need, sweets. You look great the way you are."

This was going to be the perfect way to celebrate my first big investigative journalistic story.

And I couldn't wait.

Part 2

Chicago, Illinois

Saturday, August 12th

Fourteen years later

5

We traveled one block before I lost it.

"When were you going to tell me?" I asked.

I drove our blue Honda Odyssey "mommy van" home. My husband had consumed way more than his share of red wine during the Saturday night dinner party at Debbie and Rody Janzen's house.

I was furious, and I'd held my anger in as long as I could.

"Tell you what?" Carter asked.

"About the bombing of an abortion clinic in Chicago!"

"It was not in Chicago."

That stopped me. "It wasn't?"

"No, it wasn't."

Something's not right.

"Then why were you and Rody talking about it?"

"We discussed several of his stories that I'm editing."

Carter is an assistant managing editor for local news at the *Chicago Tribune*. Rody is one of his reporters.

"It's late, and I've had too much to drink," he continued. "Can we talk about this in the morning?"

I pulled the van to the side of the road and slammed on the brakes. "Where was the clinic located?"

"In Deerfield."

"*Deerfield?* You didn't think I would be interested in hearing about a bombing," I took a deep breath, "thirty minutes from our front door?!"

"Honey, it's late. Let's go home."

"Do the police know who did it?"

He shook his head.

"Was it the same M.O. as Arlington?"

He took in a deep breath before he responded. "The device was made of C4 and left in the men's bathroom."

C4!

Hearing that thrust me back into the hallway of an Arlington, Virginia, abortion clinic over five years ago. I chased a story about a bomber and nearly died when he detonated a C4 bomb hidden in the men's bathroom.

Just like in Deerfield.

Here it comes.

There was a blinding flash of light behind my eyelids, followed by the roar of an explosion reverberating in my head. The odor of broken medical bottles and cleaning solvents, and the stench of burned hair and skin, flooded my olfactory system.

And then a pounding headache gripped my head like it was in a vise.

Over the past five years, the PTSD attacks had gotten less intense.

Until now.

6

I kept my eyes shut and lowered my forehead against the top of the steering wheel.

"dèjá-BOOM! again?" Carter asked.

This was what he called the PTSD attacks I began to have after I was blown up in that Arlington clinic.

Taking in several deep breaths to center myself, I nodded but didn't say anything. He gently rubbed my neck and waited, knowing any talking would just make it worse.

The incident dissipated in less than two minutes, and I was able to drive home with only a residual dull pain in the back of my head.

We live with our two-year-old daughter, Kerry, in West Lakeview, an upscale North Chicago neighborhood. Home is a three-story structure with all floors above the ground. It faces West Melrose. The two-car, detached garage is on the cross street, North Paulina.

When I pulled into the garage, I was still angry, but at least my neck pain was gone. I didn't speak to Carter until I'd put Kerry down for the night and he'd returned from walking Liv Sanchez, the fourteen-year-old babysitter, to her home across the street.

We were in bed, and the lights were out.

"You should have told me," I said.

"You used to be a news junkie. I assumed you read about it in the *Tribune*, and since you hadn't mentioned it, I didn't bring it up."

This is too credible a counterattack.

His blood alcohol level had dropped, and he was thinking more clearly. He knew how to get me going and cause me to lose the focus of my argument.

His best defense was a good offense.

"You know I don't have time to read the damn newspaper." I began to talk louder. "I'm a 'mommy,' and all I have time for is taking care of our daughter!"

Which wasn't exactly the truth. For the past few weeks, I had chased a terrific story that I really wanted to write. Except for that, most days it seemed like being a mom was all I did.

He paused a few seconds. "You have a valid point, but I knew how upset you would be if I told you." He paused again. "And I didn't want to ruin a perfectly enjoyable evening with our friends."

"Now you know what I'm going to say before I say it? Couldn't you at least have had the common decency to tell me the facts and let me voice my own opinion?"

"But you would have reacted the same way."

"Maybe. Maybe not."

Carter took me into his arms. The faint aroma of the Tom Ford Black Orchid cologne I'd given him for his birthday drifted over me.

"Honey, please," he whispered. "It's too dangerous to work on another abortion clinic bombing story and risk getting blown up again."

There it is, the "D" word: dangerous.

My husband is consistent whenever we argue about this.

"Isn't your local column enough for you?" he continued.

I write a feature once a month in the *Lakeview Times.* It's total fluff and could be produced by a middle school writing student using simple declarative sentences.

"You know how I feel about that."

"At least it's writing."

"We've discussed this way too many times. I want to write front page stories again."

"You just did," he countered.

You have me there.

Since the Arlington bombing, I'd been in the penalty box for discredited investigative journalists. But last Thursday, an article I wrote about the story I'd chased was published above the fold on the front page of the *Chicago Tribune.*

To alert my former fellow reporters that I was back, I used the byline I'd written under for my entire professional writing career: Christina Edwards. I never considered using my husband's last name, even though all of our friends in Chicago now know me as Tina Thomas.

The problem for me was some content in last week's story – my reporting it as "industrial espionage"– was false, but I couldn't tell Carter the truth. He would go ballistic if I fessed up and he learned that to get the story I had inadvertently put myself and our daughter at risk.

I didn't say anything else. Instead, I kissed him and rolled over, praying I wouldn't toss and turn again as I replayed the events of last Wednesday over and over in my head, when Kerry and I had almost been killed.

Since then, I'd tried to cope with the emotional turmoil by daily journaling, which had previously helped me climb out of the abyss after being blown up five years ago in Arlington.

But now, writing down my thoughts no longer worked to relieve my anxiety. And my husband had only added to it by confessing that the bomber might be back.

That's where I have to begin.

7

I had another sleepless night as I relived what had happened to me last Wednesday, but Sunday morning, I wasn't too tired to run. The only time I'd ever missed doing it was while I recovered from the injuries I had suffered in Arlington. I'd even run daily in Afghanistan where I was embedded while writing a series of stories about the Marines. Insurgent gunfire and IEDs couldn't stop me.

The troops loved the stories I wrote about them and rewarded me with a Glock 19, which they taught me how to fire. I had it with me when I was blown up in Arlington, and it was destroyed.

But I had a replacement.

Last Wednesday, in our kitchen, the leader of the "industrial spies" tried to shoot me with his Glock 19.

We struggled.

He lost.

I won.

Now, as I began my run, I had his gun in my fanny pack, along with my cell phone, sunscreen, energy bar, and a bottle of water. Since the events of last Wednesday, including the "industrial spy" confrontation in my home and another at O'Hare, I carried the weapon because I had the eerie feeling someone was watching me.

I didn't have my ear buds in. I always listen to music when I run — but not today. I needed all my senses to alert me to any danger.

It was a typical hot and windy Chicago morning, but I still felt a shiver run down my spine.

Is the bomber watching me?

Or was it Jamie, the one remaining "industrial spy" who had not been arrested during the debacle at O'Hare? I was scared that he was still in the Chicago area and might want to get even with me for foiling their plot.

Unexpectedly, a voice called to me from across the street. "Hi, Tina."

It's my leprechaun!

I met David John once before, when I bumped into him while running.

I waved. "Hi, David."

After my story was published in the *Tribune* on Thursday, I debated whether to continue writing my monthly column in the *Lakeview Times*. But I promised my editor, Gayle Nystrom, I would consider submitting one.

Maybe David John is it.

With pale skin, red hair, and a well-trimmed red beard, David looked like a leprechaun. His large black glasses and New York Yankees baseball hat were the only items he wore today that didn't fit with his leprechaun-like persona. Running with him would be a way to get to know him and his backstory.

"Let's run together sometime," I suggested.

Normally, I would rather have a root canal than run with anyone, because I savor the solitude. But if I continued writing my local column, a guy who looked like a leprechaun might at least have an interesting story to tell.

"Great," he said. "I'll look for you about this time each morning."

"You're on." I waved as he continued running west.

As I watched him speed away, I was struck by a flashback, and it didn't do anything to calm my anxiety.

Dr. Mick Doyle.

Fourteen years ago, Doyle was the only other leprechaun-like person I'd ever had contact with and he'd threatened to kill me.

I sure hope David John is different.

I added research on him to my list of things I had to do.

But the bomber comes first.

8

On Monday morning, after I returned from my run and Carter left for work, Kerry and I went downstairs to our first-floor office. We played with the toy wooden blocks she received from Santa last Christmas. Ever the multitasker, I went online and opened the Sunday *Chicago Tribune* website.

I had to figure out if there was a connection between the Arlington blast and the recent Chicago-area one.

I scrolled down until I found the story about the most recent abortion clinic bombing. I read it while helping Kerry build and knock down block towers.

In Deerfield early Saturday morning, a bomb severely damaged a new women's abortion clinic. There was one victim, Dr. Colin D. Russell, the owner and head of the clinic.

Dr. Russell was called in to his private clinic for what proved to be a bogus emergency. The police theorize he was in his office in the clinic waiting for the supposedly bleeding post-op patient when the bomb was detonated. The explosion destroyed most of the building and killed the doctor.

Dr. Russell was thirty-nine years old. He leaves behind his wife, Sandra, and three children.

The investigation is ongoing, but at this time the police have no solid leads about the bomber.

I was furious Carter hadn't told me any of this, but I knew why: this was a planned killing. The doctor had been lured to the clinic and murdered. Carter knew once he told me this I would have a problem ignoring the story.

I put my fingers on the keyboard to begin my research on David John, but I stopped. I know my husband.

Maybe this isn't the only bombing story he didn't tell me about.

I typed "abortion clinic bombings in the past six months, Greater Chicago area" into the *Tribune's* search engine.

One story came up. It detailed how, in the early morning of July third, there had been an abortion clinic bombing in Hinsdale, a wealthy suburb community twenty miles west of Chicago. The bomb was made of C4 and had been placed in the men's bathroom. A laundryman had been seen going into the bathroom prior to the bombing.

Just like Arlington.

I checked the byline. Rody Janzen had covered the tragedy. No wonder they talked about the Deerfield bombing at the dinner party.

Wait a minute. July third?

Carter had been late coming home that evening for our date night. He said it was because he was editing a breaking story.

Now I knew which one it was.

We hadn't talked about it then because we left to catch a movie. My husband had kept the news of that bombing from me, probably hoping it was an isolated incident. But after the Deerfield bombing, he knew it wasn't.

I needed to visit the crime scene to get a visceral sense of what happened.

The Hinsdale clinic was out, since that bombing happened almost six weeks ago. But the damage at Deerfield was fresh, and I had to see it pronto.

9

"Kerry, I need to run an errand, so I'll leave you with Alicia for a little while," I said. "Let's try to use the potty before we go, okay?"

Kerry began screaming and pounding her tiny fists on the floor. "No, no, no, no, no!"

I hate the "terrible twos."

"How would you like some potty candy?"

She immediately stopped screeching. "I wuv potty candy!"

Our little girl has a problem pronouncing some of her words. I think it's cute. Carter's parents are both PhDs in English literature. They see no humor in Kerry murdering our language.

I've been a total failure at teaching her to use the toilet and have resorted to offering candy as a treat if she succeeds. It hasn't worked, but at least I have something to nibble on while I sit with her. And I usually give her a piece if she at least tries.

As I watched my daughter, I thought about the mess I'd been through last Wednesday and what could have happened to both of us.

It made me pause.

Was there any possible way going to the already bombed-out clinic building could be dangerous?

Better call Cas.

Kerry and I gave up on her using the toilet. We shared a piece of candy and walked upstairs to the kitchen. I called my friend Cassandra Olson. She is the feistiest of the Irregulars and would have my back if any problems did come up.

"I might have another story to work on, and I need your help," I said.

"Really?" Cas said.

"Yep. Once I saw my name on the front page, I realized how much I missed writing an in-depth article."

Even though the FBI made me change some of the facts.

"I can relate. I can't find a way to replace the adrenaline rush I got from working with a team to resuscitate dying patients and, later, the patients thanking us for saving them."

"Interesting you say that. It's like the feedback I used to get from readers who had their lives impacted by my stories. That made the hard work even more worthwhile."

"Does this mean I get to work on another story?"

"Only if you want to."

"Want to? I'm bored out of my mind teaching exercise classes to idiots who claim they do it to lose weight then eat a bag of Cheetos on the way home from class. When do you need me?"

"ASAP."

"Are you going to have Alicia watch Kerry?"

"I am."

"I'll call her and see if she can watch my kids too. If she can, I'll pick you up at her house."

"Great. Text me when you get close."

10

Eighteen minutes later, I stood with Kerry in Alicia Sanchez's driveway as Cas pulled in. Alicia is like family. She lives across the street from our home, and she, or one of her three daughters, is — thankfully — almost always available and willing to watch Kerry and my other friends' kids, even with little notice.

Cas hopped out of a silver Hummer H1, her version of a mommy van, and unloaded her kids: Luis, four, and Angelique, three.

Cas is six inches shorter than me. Her skin has an olive tone, and she's a buffed one hundred and five pounds with minimal body fat. She's a nurse who no longer works at her profession, choosing instead to raise her kids and teach a few exercise classes at XSport Fitness, our local workout facility.

We left our children with Alicia and climbed into the Hummer.

"Where are we going?" she asked.

"The abortion clinic in Deerfield that was bombed early Saturday morning," I said. "I need to see the site while it's still fresh."

I programmed Cas's Garmin. The trip to Deerfield took almost an hour. There was no yellow crime scene tape around the perimeter of the partially destroyed one-story women's clinic building.

"Looks like the cops are done with their investigation," I said.

"How do you know that?" Cas asked.

"The crime scene tape has been removed."

We climbed out of the Hummer and stared at the carcass of the building. Half of the roof was gone. There were chunks of wallboard, ripped draperies, broken medical instruments, and glass shards from shattered windows lying in the puddles of water remaining on the street from the firefighters' futile attempt to stop the blaze.

I pointed at the blown-out front door of the building. "According to the newspaper story, the bomber used C4."

"Wow. It caused a whole lot of damage."

"Criminals like the bomber love it because C4 is a stable explosive."

"You mean you can drop it and it won't blow up?"

"Yep. The bad guys mold it like clay into various shapes, attach a detonator to ignite it, and blast away. But they can also use chemical solvents to make it less viscous, almost like jelly."

"Why?"

"They can inject the reconstituted C4 into something like an empty toothpaste tube and carry it through airport security without it being discovered."

"Scary."

"Really scary."

I pulled out my cell phone from my backpack and typed a message to myself. Cas shrugged her shoulders and raised her eyebrows.

"A note to remind me to see if the DMDNB from the C4 residue here matches that from the bombings in Arlington and Hinsdale."

"Why?"

"All C4 isn't the same. Each batch has a fingerprint which can be matched to residue from other C4 bombs."

"So if there's a match..."

"It would be strong evidence that my guy is still alive and at it again."

11

"Let's do this," I said.

I slung my backpack over my shoulder. In it, I carried my cell phone and many other mommy and kid necessities. The Glock 19 handgun was on the top for easy access.

Cas had her backpack too. I counted on her having her self-defense weapons of a contact Taser and the Cas version of pepper spray: a can of Raid Wasp and Hornet aerosol.

We stepped through the remnants of the front door into a water-soaked hallway. I'd found the floor plans of the clinic online, so I knew the men's bathroom was located about fifteen feet further along what remained of the hallway. Three steps in, I sniffed and abruptly stopped.

Uh-oh.

Cas stared at me. "Are you okay?"

The stench of soot from the walls that had been fried in the blast, mixed with the irritating odor of the multiple medications and industrial strength cleaning products that had also been destroyed, flooded my olfactory center.

"The memory of the Arlington clinic odors has never left me," I said. "I was knocked out by the explosion, but for some reason, my brain recorded the smells, and each time I encounter them, it triggers extremely unpleasant memories of my injuries.

Carter calls them my 'dèjá-BOOM!' moments. My therapist said it's PTSD."

"You said your pelvis was broken and your bladder, liver, and diaphragm were ruptured, but I've forgotten the other injuries."

"Fractured ribs and a collapsed lung on my right side and a hematoma inside my head."

"It was an epidural bleed, right?"

"The ER doctor said I blew a pupil."

"That's a true neurosurgical emergency. Unless it's immediately treated, it'll be fatal."

"Tell me. Afterwards, I was gorked out for a few days, but I guess I don't have any residual neurological damage — although Carter might disagree with that."

We walked around the corner and found a gaping void in the wall.

I pointed at it. "According to what I read online, this was where the men's bathroom used to be."

"Ground zero."

"That's my bomber's signature."

"Meaning?"

"In the Arlington clinic, he hid the device in the men's bathroom. According to a story in the *Tribune*, the same M.O. was used in the July bombing in Hinsdale."

"Looks like someone's sending a message to you."

I touched the right side of my chest where a tube had been inserted after I was blown up. That scar and the longer linear one on my abdomen, plus the semicircular one on the right side of my head, were constant mementos of what had happened to me five years ago.

My stomach did a flip-flop. "It does, doesn't it?"

Something I don't want to worry about right now.

I began walking. She followed.

"The doctor's office should be further down this hallway," I said.

Sloshing through the water and debris, we turned another corner and discovered the office was completely gone, replaced by a gigantic hole in the side of the building. There was a hallway and then — nothing.

I turned to Cas. "We couldn't see this when we drove up because his office was in the back of the clinic."

"Do you think the bomber used two separate devices?"

"Looks like it. The bathroom bomb was placed there to start the fire, which destroyed most of the building. The second bomb in here was meant for only one thing."

"Which was?"

"To kill the doctor."

12

I shut my eyes and pictured the doctor's office. "I think the doctor sat at his desk waiting for the arrival of the 'emergency' patient he assumed was coming in. The phone rang. He answered. The bomber blew both bombs remotely, probably by using a cell phone."

"How did the caller get directly through to the doctor? Everywhere I worked as a nurse, all incoming calls went to an answering service first."

"I went online and checked on that. It's a new type of abortion clinic in the area where they not only advertise personal care but also a direct line to a doctor twenty-four hours a day."

"Dangerous."

"Only if a bomber calls."

"Was enough left of the doctor's body to be buried?"

The vision of his grieving widow and devastated children standing in front of what might have been an empty casket made me sick to my stomach.

Suddenly, I couldn't catch my breath.

"I have to get out of here."

Black dots flew across my line of sight. The harder I tried to breathe, the more difficult it was to move air in and out of my lungs.

I staggered into the hallway. The walls felt like they were collapsing on me.

I stumbled along the wet floor and wobbled outside into the windy, humid Chicago air. I bent over, dropped my backpack on the street, and gulped in fresh air.

Nausea overwhelmed me, and I barfed up the potty candy. I continued to retch until all that I had left were dry heaves and a yucky taste in my mouth.

Cas had followed me outside. "Another PTSD attack?"

I nodded. "Once I relax, it'll pass."

Shutting my eyes and breathing slowly usually worked, but in spite of the high heat index typical of Chicago in August, I shivered. Cas saw me do it.

"Is that part of your attacks?" she asked.

I continued to shake. "No, it's something new."

Opening my eyes, I took in another deep breath. "I have the feeling that someone is watching me," I continued.

This was the first time I'd told anyone this.

"When did it start?"

"Right after the story I wrote about what happened at O'Hare."

"You didn't have it after Arlington?"

"No, this is new."

I reached down to pick up my backpack and heard a rumbling noise behind me. Turning around, I saw a battered green pickup truck about two blocks away. It was moving down the street directly at us. Black smoke blew out of the exhaust.

The truck gained speed.

"Cas, run!" I screamed.

"What?"

"Get off the street!"

It's the bomber!

"Your spray and Taser aren't going to work!"

I yanked the Glock out of my backpack and chambered a round. The truck's windshield was filthy, but I could see that the driver wore a black hoody and sunglasses.

The truck was now a block away from us and picking up speed.

He's going to run us down!

I assumed a shooter's stance.

I'm going to end this right here!

Suddenly, the truck turned right onto the cross street in front of us and drove away.

I felt Cas's hands on my shoulders. "Are you okay?"

My fingers were white from squeezing the handle of the Glock. "It was the bomber! He was going to kill us!"

"Relax. It was just a guy in a crappy old truck — no more, no less."

I dropped the gun on the street and put my head in my hands. I began sobbing. "What's wrong with me?"

"Girl, I think we need to have a talk," she said, continuing to rub my shoulders. "Why don't we go sit in the Hummer?"

Cas picked up the handgun and my backpack and led me to her truck. I continued to sob.

She helped me up into the passenger seat and closed the door. Then, she climbed into the driver's side and fired up the engine. After turning the air-conditioner on full blast, she rotated the vents so they blew on my face.

"Is that the same gun you had last week?" she asked.

I stopped crying and wiped my nose with a Kleenex from my backpack. "It is."

"You never told me where you got it."

And I never will.

13

On Tuesday morning, I altered my usual route two blocks north of our home and turned left onto West Henderson Street. I needed to find out if Jamie was still in the Chicago area.

My goal was an antique-red brick home on the south side of the street where my friends Dr. Micah Mittelman and his wife, Dr. Hannah Eisenberg, live with their four children.

Their house is at least twenty percent larger than ours and has another feature we don't have: outside security cameras, a rarity in Lakeview.

I stopped in front of their home and jogged in place.

The cameras no longer rotated to cover the neighborhood.

Aren't Hannah and Micah concerned about Jamie?

Maybe they weren't worried because someone was protecting them. I surveyed the neighborhood looking for FBI agents guarding their home.

I didn't see any.

Not good.

I climbed up the front steps of Hannah and Micah's home and rang the doorbell.

Hannah opened the door. "Tina, I am glad to see you. We need to talk."

"Great, because that's why I'm here," I said.

She is about three inches shorter than my five eight and has closely-cut, gray-streaked hair. I first met her on July third, the fifth anniversary of my being blown up in Arlington.

Then, she was weak and needed assistance for many basic functions. She wore a shapeless summer dress, which draped over her deteriorating body. Today, she was decked out in a bright pink Lululemon yoga outfit complete with matching pink and white Nike cross-trainer shoes.

She effortlessly held open the door. "Please come in."

Doing a physical act like this shouldn't be difficult, but until recently, she could barely lift her arms. Thanks to her husband Micah's research and his subsequent embryonic stem cell treatment of her disease, multiple sclerosis, she was almost back to a normal life.

She ushered me into their great room. The sounds of a Bach piano concerto floated in from another room. Hannah noticed me listening.

"My son Jason should be studying for his Bar Mitzvah, but he prefers playing the piano."

"He's good."

"He inherited his father's motor skills."

Suddenly, there was a crash of drums, which drowned out the beautiful piano music. "Gerald, our eight-year-old, is fixated on playing his drums. I would have preferred that he take up the violin, but his father indulges the children and allowed him to choose percussion instead."

The banging continued, making conversation difficult. Hannah stood up. "I need to speak to the drummer. While I am up, would you like a cup of tea or a bottle of water?"

"No, thank you."

While she was gone, I scanned the room and admired the original oil paintings, especially the Renoir hanging on the wall facing me. The drumming stopped, and I could hear the piano again.

When she returned, we sat down on one of the couches. I couldn't resist running my fingers over the luxurious multicolored fabric.

Having truckloads of inherited money isn't all bad.

"Even though it is the weekend, Micah is not here," she began. "He is working at the lab."

"I totally understand. Kind of a weird past few days, right?"

"Oh my, you could say that for sure."

Hannah went to Harvard for undergraduate and medical school. While at Columbia for her pediatric residency, she traveled to Israel for a clinical rotation, where she met Micah. Her Ivy League-educated speech pattern had gradually changed to reflect his British schooling and her years with him.

There was no reason for me to make inane conversation.

"What is your version of what happened to you and your kids last Wednesday?" I asked.

"I thought you might want to discuss that."

"And you would be correct."

She paused before she spoke. "It began when Cas unexpectedly arrived at my home. She told me that Micah was in danger and we might be too. I did not know what else to do, so I followed her instructions and took my children with her to Molly's house."

"I'm responsible for that. I was worried about you and your kids, and I didn't have many choices."

Truthfully, the way things unfolded, I was scared out of my mind that one of the bad guys would go to Hannah's home and slaughter all of them. With no time to spare, having my friend Cas rush them to my other friend Molly's house was my only option.

"Later that afternoon, two FBI agents arrived there and then escorted us home," she said. "While my children resumed their normal activities, the agents told me about the events at O'Hare Airport."

"Which was what?"

"They said Micah had been confronted at O'Hare by an industrial spy who had attempted to steal the technology behind my husband's embryonic stem cell research," she continued. "One of the FBI's female agents and a Chicago detective thwarted the attack by shooting the spy."

That was the same FBI-edited story I'd written in my *Chicago Tribune* article. And I hated the FBI for forcing me to alter the content.

Her jaw muscles twitched. "The agents underestimated me. They thought I was a stupid female without a brain in my head." Her eyes flashed. "But they were wrong!"

14

I'd never seen this side of Hannah's personality. Previously, she seemed to be an emotional flat-liner, only displaying her consummate social skills when she had to.

But not now.

She's really pissed off.

"One month ago I might have believed the FBI agents, because I was so ill that I had difficulty taking care of my basic body functions, let alone using my cognitive abilities to evaluate what was going on in my daily life," Hannah said. "But after Micah started me on his treatment protocol, I began to feel ever so much better and realized something was drastically wrong in our lives."

"What did you do?"

"I began to investigate, and from what I discovered after sneaking into Micah's home computer, I was certain none of the events at O'Hare occurred the way the agents claimed they did."

"And?"

"I confronted Micah when he returned home from the airport. We sat down on this very couch, and I demanded that he tell me the truth."

"Including his part in it?" I asked.

"Especially that."

She spoke in a monotone voice as she related the facts that Micah had confessed to her. By the time she finished, I knew she was dialed in to the entire scenario and my part in it, the full truth of which I was not able to include in the story I wrote for the *Tribune* without landing in prison compliments of the FBI.

Before I could ask her about that, her eyelids narrowed. "My husband committed an unprofessional act. I am not sure I will ever forgive him for it."

What?!

She wasn't remotely concerned about what I'd done at O'Hare. Instead, she was mad at Micah, despite his having risked everything to push forward his research to keep her alive.

I didn't know what to say.

Her lips compressed into a thin line. "I can see by the shocked look on your face that you are surprised at what I said, yes?"

"I... Ah... Yeah, I guess you could say that," I stammered. "Your husband saved your life."

"He did, but at what cost?"

I ran my fingers through my hair. "I'm totally freaked out here. At our dinner party, Micah told me he would do anything for you and your children. He did what he felt he had to do. What am I missing?"

"Micah and I are physicians. We swore the Hippocratic Oath and also vowed *primum non nocere:* 'First, do no harm.' But he ignored it and chose to protect me and our family by risking the lives of thousands of people to accomplish that. In my view, that is unacceptable."

Whoa.

Last Wednesday, I had to decide whether to save Kerry or thousands of people departing in planes from O'Hare. I chose my daughter. Later that day, I'd done the same thing with Hannah and her kids. They'd come first. I never considered doing it any other way.

And I would do it again.

But I couldn't sleep because of what had happened at O'Hare and having been forced by the FBI to fudge a part of the content of the story afterward. I hoped Hannah might help me get past it.

But she isn't.

My mouth took over my scrambled brains.

"Let me get this straight. Micah did original research to find a cure for your multiple sclerosis."

"He did."

"And he was forced to do operations he didn't want to do to keep you and your kids alive."

She nodded. "But during the surgeries, he also chose to perform secondary procedures to harvest the patients' eggs to further his embryonic stem cell research."

"Come on, Hannah. That part of the operation didn't hurt any of those girls."

"That is *not* the point. He did not have the patients' consent to perform that procedure. In point of fact, he should have refused to perform any of the operations."

I thought about the abortion clinic bomber. "Some people, including several of my friends, think that when Micah sacrifices embryos in his lab, it is the moral equivalent to performing abortions."

Her eyes darkened. "That is ridiculous. The embryos my husband creates are for research. Nothing more."

I wanted to say those eggs could eventually develop into babies, but from the death glare she gave me, I decided there was nothing to be gained by debating this with her, especially since I still wasn't sure where I stood on the subject of abortion.

But there was something, as a mom, I needed to know.

"Those men would have killed you and your kids if Micah hadn't done what they wanted." I took in a deep breath. "Was that okay with you?"

"Israel is constantly at war. In any armed conflict there are always victims from collateral damage. The loss of a few people is acceptable to save thousands."

I flopped back against the couch. I'd never had a discussion like this before. I wanted to ask her if she really believed what she said, but from the intense look on her face she did.

I decided to return to the reason I was there. "What about the remaining bad guy, Jamie?"

"Who is Jamie?"

Uh-oh.

15

"Jamie is an American who is one of the so-called 'industrial spies' and was working in a store at O'Hare during the uproar there, but the FBI let him go," I said. "If he's still in this area, I need to know where he is. I thought maybe the FBI gave Micah that information."

Her eyebrows furrowed together. "My husband neglected to mention anyone else to me."

Not good.

"But Micah was involved with the bad guys. He has to know about Jamie."

Why wouldn't your husband tell you about him?

"Micah is a genius. He does not function on a level like normal people. That is the reason he followed their orders and did the operations even though he should not have. It was the easiest way to solve a problem that was keeping him from his work."

"You never knew there was a threat to you and your children?"

"As I said, I was too sick to realize that was an issue."

"And you only figured it out after Micah told you the truth?"

"Sadly, yes. I should have realized something was amiss when he mentioned the Hamlin Park Irregulars would save us, but then, I did not understand what he meant."

"The Hamlin Park Irregulars is Micah's code name for me and my group of mommy friends who you now know — Cas, Linda, and Molly. As with you, I met them at Hamlin Park."

"I know that now. On July third, I told him about meeting you at the park and that you mentioned doing a story about me for your local column. He chose the name after the dinner party with your friends at your home. He had been emotionally stressed, but I assumed it was about his research. I thought he might enjoy meeting all of you and hoped it would help relieve his tension."

"But his stress was not from his work."

"Obviously not. I did not know it then, but those men controlled our lives. After he learned that you were a reporter, he hoped you and your friends would uncover the plot and save us."

I knew it!

I'd felt an unseen force pushing me into the story about the men who had moved in across the street. It wasn't just my burning desire to write a story to resurrect my writing career. It was also Micah's hand on my back.

"I'm worried Jamie will want to get even with me for uncovering their plot, which resulted in the members of his group being either shot or arrested," I said.

She slipped into her methodical doctor mode. I'd seen it before at Hamlin Park the day we met.

"Let us assess this objectively." She spoke again in a monotone voice. "How would Jamie know what happened if he is now unable to speak with his associates who, as you just said, are either dead or have been arrested?"

"I guess he wouldn't."

"Even though he was inside a store at O'Hare, if he was working, he would not have witnessed your part in the events on the concourse. He would have to assume the female FBI agent was responsible for the shooting because that is what the security videos showed."

"But they were doctored."

"He would not know that."

"You're saying that I don't need to worry about him."

"I am. If Micah didn't mention Jamie to me, you should not be concerned."

Hope you're right.

16

Suddenly, Hannah's methodical doctor-face morphed into one of all-consuming terror.

What the heck?

She blinked several times, and then tears began cascading down her cheeks.

Dr. Hannah Eisenberg was the last person in the world I would ever expect to cry about anything. And now she was. The sterile doctor persona was gone. I didn't know what to do, so I waited.

She took in a breath, and her crying slowed down. "There is only one logical conclusion. If Jamie is still in this area, he will try and kill Micah, and possibly me and the children, in retribution."

"*What?*"

"Micah confessed to me that Jamie's associates threatened to torture and then murder me and our children if my husband told the authorities about their plans. Obviously, someone did."

I finished the thought for her. "The FBI foiled the plot. Jamie has to assume it was Micah who blew the whistle on them, and now you're afraid he'll go after Micah for payback."

She nodded again. "And they might not stop with him. These people have a scorched earth policy for their Jewish enemies."

"Jamie might try to kill all of you?"

"That is what they would do in Israel. I am afraid that will be the case here."

I took her hand in mine. "My friends and I are here for you."

The tears stopped. "Thank you, I appreciate that."

"What I mean is, we'll help you. I literally could not have survived last week if it weren't for the rest of the Hamlin Park Irregulars. I realize how important my female friends are to me, and now we can be that to you."

"I cannot ask you to risk your lives for us again."

"We're in this together. We're not superheroes, but we'll figure out a way to stop Jamie before he can hurt you and your kids."

Or any of us and our kids.

"What should we do?" she asked.

Darn good question.

"Can you hire people to help guard you and the kids?"

"I do not know anyone in Chicago. I would not know where to begin."

"I have a friend who is a detective on the Chicago PD. He should know security firms in this area. If it's okay with you, I'll call him."

"Please do."

"And cost won't be a problem?"

For the first time during our conversation, a smile appeared on her face. "That is one area that won't present a problem. Since my parents died and left me a large inheritance, money has never been an issue for me."

Like my friend and fellow Hamlin Park Irregular, Linda Misle, Hannah is a member of the lucky sperm club. Her parents left her oodles of Berkshire Hathaway stock. When we researched Hannah online after meeting her, it was worth four hundred forty million dollars.

"I'll call him on the way home, but what about Micah's lab?" I asked. "Does he have security there?"

"The only times I have been there were to be treated, and it never occurred to me to evaluate that."

"I'll drive by the lab this afternoon and check it out, but you might also have to set up a meeting there so I can get inside."

"I will arrange it immediately."

I stood up.

"I better get going and finish my run. I'll call or text you later."

"Please be careful."

She stood up and gave me a hug.

Once I was back outside, I stretched until my muscles loosened up. With the Chicago heat and humidity, it didn't take long. Sweat began pouring down my back. Glancing over my shoulder, I noticed the security cameras on the eves of their house were rotating again.

Hannah was taking this threat seriously.

But will Micah?

17

Later that morning, I left Kerry with Alicia while I drove to Micah's lab to assess his security. It took me forty minutes to get there.

The lab was a windowless, one-story gray cement building. A ten-foot-tall chain-link fence surrounded the lot, which was about the size of a typical Chicago city block. There were no signs to indicate what type of business was inside.

An empty guard shack stood next to a gate with a horizontal barrier bar blocking a single lane. The parking lot was full of cars and SUVs, but no one manned the gate. Apparently, the only way for the employees to drive in was by using a remote control device to raise and lower the barrier.

I scanned the premises for cameras or any other signs of security.

Nothing.

After parking my mommy van on the street, I grabbed my backpack and walked up to the guard shack. I peeked inside. It was empty. There wasn't even a chair for a guard to sit on, suggesting the small building wasn't being used.

I stopped.

Let's see if anyone comes.

After four minutes, no one did.

I ducked underneath the bar and walked into the parking lot. I stopped again and waited for security personnel to approach me and ask what the heck I was doing there.

But no one did.

This is stupid.

Walking across the parking lot, I approached the only door I saw. There was a loading dock next to it. The metal roller door was down. I walked up and grabbed the handle. I tugged on it, and it began to slide up.

Come on, guys. I'm breaking into your lab!

I rolled down the metal door and stepped up to the entrance. No keypad. I tried the doorknob. The door swung open.

This is getting worse by the second.

I stepped inside and discovered a small waiting room without any furniture. There was a closed door at the other end of the room.

Probably unlocked too.

Wanting to scream, I thought about how I could take out my Glock and start shooting and no one would notice.

Micah's a sitting duck.

18

I called Hannah on my way home from Micah's lab.

"I just went by your husband's lab," I said. "I gotta tell you, his security is basically nonexistent."

The line was silent a few seconds. "That is what I was afraid of. What do you suggest we do?"

"Maybe my friend on the Chicago Police Department can get you a discount for security in two locations." I paused. "But will Micah let us do this?"

The line was again silent. "I will discuss it with him when he comes home."

"Being married to a genius seems to be difficult."

"But I am alive because of him."

I disconnected and decided to drive by the apartment where Jamie last lived. It was a four-story, red brick building about thirty minutes from Micah's lab.

There was no parking lot for the apartment dwellers, which isn't unusual in Chicago given how expensive land is. Parking for rental units is rare, which means each apartment resident has to fight for a spot on the street.

I drove around until I found an empty parking place two blocks from the building. It took only eight minutes, a mini-record for Chicago.

Grabbing my backpack, I hopped out and walked to the building. The upper units had balconies. Each first-floor apartment had a patio surrounded by a five-foot cement wall with a lockable outside gate.

I didn't see any security cameras. I tried the front door into the vestibule. It was open. I stepped in and tried the second door into the building. It was locked.

I went back outside and wandered around, hoping someone would enter so I could go in right behind them through that second door.

It took another ten minutes.

A fit young woman opened the building's front door. I quickly followed her. She had long blond hair and was decked out in a blue yoga outfit.

She flashed her key fob over the security pad to open the inner door. I was right on her heels when she pushed the door open.

"Hi," I said from behind her. "Hot out there."

She turned to me. "You got that right."

Make some small talk.

"Have you been having any problems with your air conditioning?" I asked.

"You know, not really. Have you?"

"Yeah, every time I use my hair dryer and have the TV on, my system blows a fuse."

"Which floor are you on?"

Darn good question for which I had no answer.

Pick a number, Tina.

I noticed she wore a gold lady's Rolex watch.

She has money.

I crossed my fingers. "The first floor. It's all I could afford."

"I know, right? Their rents here are outrageous, but I don't have any electrical problems on the fourth floor."

"And let's hope you don't have any. See you around."

She stepped into the elevator and the doors swooshed shut. I walked to the end of the entrance hall and turned right. I diddled around until I heard the elevator move and then sped back to the vestibule. I counted twenty-two empty name plates on the building directory.

The young women who had been unsuspecting participants in last week's plot were gone. In the slot for apartment 111 was the printed name of Jamie Smith.

He's still living here!

19

Later on Tuesday afternoon, after I picked up Kerry at Alicia's and we had lunch, it was time for playgroup at the home of Molly and her husband, Greg Miller. They live on West Roscoe Street, three blocks north of our house.

Usually our playgroup meets at Hamlin Park where we all first met, but the heat index was over 100, and with Linda Misle being a pregnant mom soon to deliver, air-conditioning was the only way to go.

As usual, Molly's front door was unlocked, so Kerry and I walked in. We followed the noise to her family room. The rest of the playgroup was already there. Toys were scattered everywhere, and her two oldest sons ran around the room like tiny wild men. Molly didn't seem to care.

She is a slender blond with a fabulous figure. Four inches taller than I am, she was a world-traveling high-fashion model when she met Greg and gave up the bright lights of the runway and wild social life to marry him and deliver four sons now under the age of five.

"Hi, Tina," Molly said, waving at us as she wiped up a blob of blue finger paint one of her sons threw on the wall.

Linda sat with her legs up in a recliner. Her daughter, Sandra, was engrossed in doing a puzzle on the floor.

Linda is my height, and we look enough alike to be sisters except for her now near-term pregnancy. She is a graduate of the University of Chicago, with degrees in accounting, computer science, and law. She practiced law before she delivered her daughter, who is the same age as Kerry.

Linda doesn't enjoy exercise, but she loves using her math skills to do most of our computer research and, even though she's an attorney, occasionally illegal hacking.

"Have you received any feedback about your front page article, Tina?" Linda asked.

"Some of my old work friends texted me, but I haven't had any job offers," I said. "Not to worry, though, as I have a couple of stories in mind to pursue."

"That's a relief," Linda said. "We were worried your story would be a one-off, and we would have to go back to being bored out of our skulls with inane conversation."

"Whoa," Molly said. "We talk about lots of cool stuff."

"Like what?" Linda asked.

"You know: kids, clothes, hair stylists, nail girls, restaurants…"

Cas's jaw muscles twitched. "*Aburrido.*"

"Huh?" Molly said.

"I think she means 'boring,' " Linda said.

I held up my hands. "I need to say something. The reason I got into this was because I wanted to write a gripping, in-depth news story again."

"But it really was because you got dumped from your job in D.C., right?" Molly asked.

"Tina and I have discussed that," Linda said. "If I'd been her lawyer, we would have won a large settlement for the egregious act of her employer terminating her."

"Does that mean you wouldn't have been canned?" Molly asked.

"I was fired because I did something while chasing a story maybe I shouldn't have done. Against the FBI's orders, I ran into the Arlington abortion clinic to try and stop the bomber. I shot him, and he blew me up."

"And you damn near died," Cas said.

"What does this have to do with a future story?" Linda asked.

"My bomber might have survived those gunshot wounds and be here in the Chicago area."

20

My friends remained silent as I told them about the two bombings in the Chicago area.

"What do you want us to do?" Linda asked.

"Nothing," I said.

Molly shrugged her shoulders. "Huh?"

"We have a bigger problem," I said. "Do you guys remember Jamie?"

"How can any of us forget him?" Molly asked. "He's yummy."

"What does he have to do with the Arlington bomber?" Linda asked.

"Nothing," I said.

Her voice was hard. "Then why are we wasting time discussing him?" she asked.

It was time. Did I tell them everything about what had actually happened to me last Wednesday, or let the "industrial spy" story stand as fact?

If I told them the truth, and one of them couldn't keep her mouth shut and Carter found out, he would never trust me again. He would never let me near another story, even if it wasn't dangerous.

And I couldn't blame him, but my reporting career would be over. Plus, the FBI might toss me in jail if the true story came out.

"Industrial spies" it is.

"Jamie is one of the 'industrial spies,' " I began.

"No way!" Cas exclaimed. "According to your story, those guys worked for a big pharmaceutical company in Iran."

"Believe me, he worked with them, but the problem is the FBI let him go."

"Why would they do that?" Linda asked.

"They claimed they didn't have anything on him, and his record was clean, so they couldn't hold him."

"I think the feds plan to follow him," Cas said.

"Why?" I asked.

"To lead them to other industrial spies, and then they can find and arrest anyone else involved."

"That's a logical suggestion, but federal law enforcement agencies and local police departments do not have funds to follow one man for a low-level crime like industrial spying," Linda said.

"Then why did they let him go?" Cas asked.

"They want him to do their dirty work for them," Molly said.

21

Because Molly is street-smart, she sometimes has a different take on issues than the rest of us, and we've learned to listen to her.

"What are you talking about?" Cas asked, still smarting from Linda's rejection of her solution about why the FBI let Jamie go.

"Tina, you and Linda have been doing background research on Micah's financing for his lab, right?" Molly asked.

"Actually, Tina assigned me that task when we all began to investigate what kind of research Micah did in his lab," Linda said. "So far, over two hundred million dollars has been spent."

"But only — what — twenty-five million came from Hannah's trust fund?"

"Yes, the rest came from Sherman Krevolin, the billionaire in Dallas."

"And he's the best buddy of the president, right?"

"According to the press, he is," Linda said.

"But you think something is fishy with the money."

"It's possible the majority of the funding illegally came from someone in the federal government and was funneled to Micah through Krevolin."

"And you guys think it might be coming from the president because of his connection with Krevolin, right?"

"We do, but we can't prove it," I answered.

"Why not? You hacked into Micah's home computer. I thought all the hot poop was in there."

"There was a section we downloaded from Micah's computer that was encrypted," Linda said. "We think the proof of where his financing is coming from might be in there."

"Molly, where are you going with this?" Cas asked.

"Maybe some people on the president's staff, or in his political party, are worried that the story about the illegal funding might come out, and it would be really embarrassing to the president."

OMG! Like the Iran-Contra affair.

If the story of illegal funding involving hundreds of millions of dollars leaked out, it would be a political scandal that would discredit the president and ruin his party's chances in future elections.

People were killed to cover up the Iran-Contra affair. Did we have to worry about government agents protecting Jamie so he could permanently silence Micah for them?

22

Cas was still pissed off at Linda, and now she took it out on Molly.

"Molly, this is just plain stupid," Cas said. "That's something for a TV series or movie."

"But see, the farmers did stuff like this all the time," Molly said.

Molly worked for the CIA when she was a model. She's great at getting people to talk to her, and her outstanding physical assets are a useful distraction to any man under the age of dead. She calls the agricultural attachés "farmers." That they are actually CIA agents is of no concern to her.

Linda picked up on Molly's idea. "If Jamie killed Micah, there would be minimal publicity, and the illegal financing story would never surface."

"That's what I'm telling you guys," Molly said. "The feds will let Jamie do their dirty work."

"One problem with your supposition, Molly," Linda said. "We now know that Micah discovered the cure for multiple sclerosis using embryonic stem cell technology. If Jamie kills him, what happens to all of his research?"

"Nothing," Cas said, finally dialed in again with the discussion.

We waited.

"Most of the actual lab work is being done by lowly techs," she continued. "His work won't be lost because someone else in the lab will take up the slack."

Uh-oh!

I told them about the lack of security at Micah's lab.

"And for that reason, we have to focus on finding Jamie and stopping him," I concluded.

"I remind you that Jamie hasn't broken any laws," Linda said. "The FBI let him go. No police officer in Chicago will help us unless we can prove he has committed a crime."

"Then that's what we're going to do," I said.

"How?" Cas asked.

"Yesterday, I checked out Jamie's apartment building. It looks like he's still living there."

"And?" Linda asked.

"Maybe we'll have to figure out a way to give the police solid evidence that he's committed a crime."

"I'll pretend I didn't hear that," Linda the Lawyer said.

23

The Hamlin Park Irregulars had to do something to stop Hannah and her family from being slaughtered, but I also couldn't get the abortion clinic bomber story out of my head. I had to figure out what to do about all of this before I went cuckoo.

On Wednesday morning, I started my run, intending to go past Hannah's to make sure everything was okay there. It was a great plan, but my leprechaun got in the way. David John caught up with me two blocks before I got to Hannah's.

"Hi, Tina," he said. "Great morning for a run."

"You got that right," I said.

There wasn't much wind, and the humidity was low enough that I didn't feel like I was breathing through a soda straw.

We began running together and turned onto Hannah's street. I slowed down as we ran past her home. The cameras were on, scanning the neighborhood.

David watched me check out Hannah's house.

"Do you know them?" he asked.

"Them, who?"

"The people who live there."

We sped up. I wasn't sure how to handle his question. "Yeah, kind of. Why?"

"Since I moved here in June, I've run on all of the streets in Lakeview, and this is the only house with security cameras."

"That's an interesting observation. Why would you notice something like that?"

He glanced at me out of the corner of his eye. Sunlight flashed off of the lens of his black rimmed glasses as he turned his head. "No reason. Just thought it was strange."

Dude, are you lying to me?

With my paranoia sky-high from everything that had happened to me in the last week, and hearing about the recent abortion clinic bombings, I wanted to know more about David.

And I still needed a fluff story for the *Lakeview Times*. "How about having lunch with me tomorrow at the Wishbone?" I asked.

"Is it on Lincoln across the street from Dinkel's Bakery?"

Mentioning my favorite place made my stomach growl. "I guess you discovered our most famous neighborhood establishment."

"I went past it the first day I ran in this neighborhood and checked it out online when I got home. The rave reviews attracted my attention. I tried it, and now my wife, my daughter, and I are hooked on every item in the place."

Wife? Daughter? Need to check this out.

"Welcome to the club. So, how about lunch?"

"Great."

"Do you want my cell number in case you can't make it?"

We stopped and exchanged that information.

He put his phone away. "Done. See you then."

I had another day to research him. Maybe I could get Linda to help me.

24

Wednesday night, after I read two books to Kerry and failed again to coax her to use the toilet, I went down to the computer while Carter rocked her to sleep.

I was going to meet David John for lunch on Thursday, so I went down to our computer room to research him. I stared at his name on the screen.

Who are you, and why did you lie to me about your interest in Hannah's security cameras?

After an hour on LexisNexis, Intelius, and ADP, I had David John's life story in front of me. He went to grade school and high school in Twin Falls, Idaho, and had not participated in any extracurricular activities. He attended the University of Idaho and, after graduation, went on to receive a master's degree in computer science at Cal-Tech, where he, again, was not involved with any student organizations or activities.

After graduation, he took an entry-level software engineer position with the Hogan Company in San Jose, California, where he had been employed for the past ten years. Hogan had security contracts with a few large corporations and several government agencies.

Security?

Maybe that was why he lied to me about his interest in Hannah's security cameras.

But why?

I called my computer expert, Linda, and told her about David John.

"Send me what you have, and I'll do a little extra research," Linda said.

"Extra" meant hacking into computers that were supposed to be secure. I wasn't good at it. Linda was, and even though it was illegal, doing it didn't seem to bother her as an officer of the court system. At least it didn't as long as she wasn't caught doing it.

"Perfect," I said, as I emailed David's information to her.

"Does he have a wife?"

"He did mention one, and a daughter, but I haven't checked that out yet."

"I will."

Linda called me ten minutes later.

"That didn't take long," I said.

"I used the information you sent on David, and it was easy from there. His wife, Mary, attended the same grade school, high school, and university as her husband."

"Childhood friends and, later, sweethearts."

"That would be my guess. After graduation, she went to work as an accountant for the Santa Barbara-based J.P. Cooke and Sons, where she's still employed."

"What about the daughter?"

"Her name is Margaret. Her birth certificate indicates she was born in San Jose a little over three and a half years ago."

"Anything else?"

"In mid-June, the couple signed a month-to-month lease on an apartment five blocks north of your home. Both of their signatures are on the contract."

This was proof of Linda's ability to hack into bank and state government agency computers.

"David and Mary have money in the bank, great credit ratings, no outstanding debt, no list of criminal offenses, and no lawsuits or complaints against them," she continued.

"Looks like they're the perfect couple and model citizens," I said. "The Johns aren't the type of people I usually research."

"But there is one other thing. I couldn't find any real information about David's job with Hogan. That data is protected by a firewall."

"Meaning?"

"He probably had top secret security clearance. He might still have it."

"Thanks. Send me anything else you find."

"Done."

Top secret security clearance.

There was a little "reporter's ding" in my head, and I began to pull on my lower lip – my "tell" that something bothered me. Carter had been the first to notice me doing it at the *Post*. Gradually, all the other reporters began kidding me about doing the "Tina-tug" when I first began to sniff out a story.

Now I had something to talk to David about.

25

It was 11:55 a.m. on Thursday. Kerry was in her stroller. I pushed it inside the Wishbone, a restaurant in a brick building at the corner of North Lincoln and West School, across the street from Dinkel's.

The restaurant has a modernized southern comfort menu. As I pushed Kerry's stroller toward her special table, the aroma of spices and deep-fried foods from the chef's southern reconstructive style of cooking made my mouth water.

About Kerry's special table: it's a booth with a picture of a momma pig nursing her babies, which hangs on the wall above the table. I have no clue why she loves it so much, but when I call for a reservation, they know to give me that table.

And my daughter loves eating there, always demanding two pancakes and the original mac n' cheese. It's a weird combination but, truthfully, I've sampled it when her head is turned, and it's not too bad.

David John walked in at noon. A little girl held his hand as they entered. Like all moms, I evaluated how she was dressed.

She wore patent leather Mary Janes with sparkling white anklet socks. Her summer dress was checked green and white. Her blond hair was pulled back in precisely combed pigtails.

I glanced at my daughter. Her hair was tied in a sloppy ponytail with more than a few loose ends. She wore blue shorts, toddler Nike shoes, and a toddler San Diego Padres jersey, compliments of her Uncle Jimmy.

It was obvious David spent a considerable amount of time on grooming his daughter.

Me? Not so much.

I waved at him, and as he walked toward our table, his daughter spied the picture of the pig and her babies.

"Daddy, look at the picture!" she exclaimed.

He pulled out his cell phone and snapped a picture. "We have to show it to Mommy."

They arrived at the table. I turned to Kerry, who was busy with a coloring book. "Kerry, this is my friend David."

"Nice to meet you, Kerry," he said. "This is my daughter, Margaret."

Kerry is in her shy phase with strangers. She looked at Margaret and went back to her coloring. I didn't push her to respond.

"Margaret, this is my friend, Mrs. Thomas."

She held out her hand. "Pleased to meet you, Mrs. Thomas."

Pretty formal.

"It's Tina," I said.

We shook.

At least she didn't curtsy.

As David pulled out a chair for her, it was hard not to miss how big she was for a three-and-a-half-year-old girl.

Maybe Linda got Margaret's birthday wrong.

David took out an iPad and earphones from his backpack and set them in front of his daughter. He turned on the iPad. She put the earphones on and began playing a game.

He confirmed this was a well-practiced routine. "We don't know anyone here, and except for preschool, Margaret doesn't have anyone to play with, so she spends a lot of time on the computer."

I thought of the Hamlin Park Irregulars. "I might have an idea about that." I pointed at the menu in front of him. "I don't want to rush you, but let's order before Kerry melts down."

"What are her favorites?"

I told him what Kerry always had. "I usually have the herb-crusted tilapia, or sometimes the catfish, but everything is pretty good."

The waitress came to the table and greeted Kerry with her favorite drink: a small carton of chocolate milk.

"Kerry will have her regular order. I would like the tilapia."

"And for you, sir?"

"I'll have what she's having."

"The tilapia?"

"Oh, no. The pancakes and mac n' cheese. So will my daughter."

The waitress gave him thumbs up and walked to the kitchen.

26

Kerry and Margaret were busy, which gave us the chance for some adult talk.

"I used to be a reporter," I began. "The other day, I was curious when you commented about the security cameras on my friend's home. It's been bugging me, so I have to ask: why did you notice it?"

David lowered his head and stared at the table top. "I have to admit something here," he said. "I'm a computer guy, and I checked you out the first time we crossed paths."

I didn't want to tell him that I'd done the same thing with him and his family, but now I would have to be careful with my questions. He was a professional with security clearance, and I had to treat him as one.

"You already knew I was a reporter?"

He looked up and we made eye contact. "Do you mean knew you were or know you are?"

"You're referring to my *Lakeview Times* column, right?"

"Sort of."

"I don't consider that real reporting."

"But you just had a front page story in the *Tribune*. I always read the paper online, but it was so exciting, I actually bought a print copy of the newspaper to get a real sense of it."

"Did you have trouble finding a copy?"

"Funny you should ask that. I had to go to three different places before I found one I could buy."

"It's a new world out there, but let's get back to my question."

"Yeah, so before we moved here, I worked for the Hogan Company in San Jose, California. Hogan is a multifaceted security firm, and I was trained to notice things like that."

That corroborates my research.

"Do they have an office in Chicago?"

"They have offices all over the world."

"Do you keep in touch with them?"

"Sure. I still do some per case contract computer work for them at home." He paused. "Not to be nosey, but why are you so interested in my former employer? Are you doing a story on them?"

"Absolutely not. I have a friend who has a security problem. Actually, two security problems. One of them concerns that home you asked me about. And the other one is a medical lab."

"And?"

"And I need an expert to help her. Do you have time to talk to her?"

"I can talk to her, but that's all."

"I don't understand."

"I signed a non-compete agreement when I left the company. I can't do any independent consulting for any other company or work for myself in any area that involves security."

I had the feeling this was too easy.

Be creative, Tina.

"Do you still talk to the people you worked with?"

"All the time."

"Could you contact them about my friend's security problem?"

"Sure, but I have to tell you, Hogan is a big firm, and they charge a lot of money for their services."

"That's not a problem."

"Money is always a problem when it comes to security. Companies and individuals cheap out when it should be just the opposite."

"Don't worry about Hannah. One thing she has is money. She won't complain about spending whatever it takes to protect her family and husband."

"Good to know. I would like to meet Hannah before I call my former employers, but she has to understand that if they do a deal, I won't be directly involved."

I was putting a lot of trust in a man I'd just met, and that bothered me. But the Hogan Company had an international reputation, and since it would be doing the job, and not David, I began to relax. And I wasn't sure Tony would even take the time to help Hannah since the Chicago PD wasn't involved.

"Understood, and I might have an idea about helping Margaret meet some new friends."

I told him about the Hamlin Park Irregulars and invited him to bring Margaret and join us for our next playgroup get-together.

"Let me talk to Mary about it, but I am definitely interested. Thanks so much for inviting us."

27

Thursday, mid-afternoon, Cas and I were back in her Hummer. Molly babysat our kids. As she drove to Jamie's apartment building, we discussed what we were going to do.

"I checked the building directory when I was here on Tuesday," I began. "Jamie's name is there."

"You assume he's still living in the building."

"I do."

"What's our plan?"

"I'll unlock the back door to the apartment building so we can go in without anyone seeing us."

"And you'll do this with your lock-picker thing?"

"Yep."

A few years ago, I went online and bought an electric lock pick gun and torque wrench. They came in handy on stories I researched then, and recently, I'd used them again to investigate the "industrial spies." Using them was the only way we could break into the building and Jamie's apartment.

"After we enter through the back door, I'll walk to the vestibule and buzz his apartment. If he answers, we leave and come back another time."

"But if he doesn't answer, we assume he's not there and then what?"

"We go to his apartment. I'll open his lock. You stay in the hallway. If you see Jamie come in either entrance, you speed-dial me, and I'll leave through the patio."

I was positive I could either scale the five-foot wall or unlock the patio door to the street using my tools.

"What are you going to do in his apartment?" she asked.

"I'll make sure he still lives there, and if he does, I'll plant conclusive evidence that will link him to the 'industrial spies.' "

"Isn't that illegal?"

"Breaking into his apartment?"

"No… I mean yes, that, too, but hiding evidence. Will a judge allow that?"

"I won't tell anyone if you don't."

"What if something goes wrong?"

"Already thought of that and have a backup meeting us there."

She drove in silence for a few seconds. "You really want this, don't you?"

"Micah's a big boy and got himself into this mess. Hannah didn't. She and her kids are now my — or better, now our — responsibility. We have to protect them."

"Even if it means breaking the law."

"Even if."

28

Cas slowly drove by Jamie's apartment building.

"I don't see any security cameras," she said.

"Neither did I when I was here before. Let's find a parking place."

It took fifteen minutes, but we were lucky and found one across the street from our target building.

"Now what?" Cas asked.

"I'll text our backup," I said.

Detective Tony Infantino texted back that he was on his way.

"How much does Tony know about Jamie?" she asked.

"Pretty much everything. Tony was at O'Hare when it all went down. He bitched about the FBI releasing Jamie, but it didn't do any good. He said he would give anything to arrest Jamie to show up the feds."

"Tony doesn't like the FBI?"

"Don't know many cops that do."

We waited eleven more minutes. Someone drove up in a new white BMW 650i coupe and double-parked next to us. The windows were heavily tinted, making it impossible to see who was driving.

"Is that your cop friend Tony?" Cas asked.

"I think so. It's kind of hard to see the driver with those dark windows."

"How can a cop afford a ride like that?"

"Good question."

And one I would never ask Tony. He was a *mammoni*, an Italian son who lived at home with his mother. Maybe he'd saved enough money to buy the fancy ride by doing that.

Or maybe he had another source of additional income that might be off the books. Whatever it was, I didn't want to know. Tony was my only connection to the Chicago police force, and I didn't want to screw it up.

Fourteen years ago, after we met in Dr. Mick Doyle's penthouse on Lakeshore Drive, Tony and I had a steamy affair that lasted almost two years. I broke it off after I discovered he was cheating on me with several different women — and to take an investigative writing job with the *Post* in D.C.

The Beemer's driver window powered down. Tony has aged better than a great Italian Barolo red wine. His perpetually tanned face is wrinkle-free, and his black hair is devoid of even a single gray hair.

"Nice blue blazer," I remarked. "Is it new?"

This was what Tony expected me to ask. He has his clothes custom-tailored to display his overly-muscular body and cover up his gun, something he shows me each time I see him.

He made a production of slowly removing his designer sunglasses and then ogled Cas while he simultaneously spoke to me. "Italian silk. Needed it for all the interviews and such."

I remained silent, knowing what was coming next.

"Can't see it, can you?" he asked, still looking at Cas.

He was all about the cut of his clothes and his precious gun.

"No, Tony, I can't see it."

He opened his coat. "New Glock ruined the line of my coats, so bought a different shoulder rig for it. Had to get this gun after I blew away that perp at O'Hare. IA took my old one as part of the shooting investigation."

He'd become a local celebrity when he was involved in gunning down one of the "industrial spies" who I later reported was attempting to steal Micah's technology.

Which the FBI forced me to do.

He turned his attention to Cas. His ogle morphed into an all-out leer. "You the one who works out with Tina?"

I expected my feminist-friend Cas to be put off by Tony's hitting on her. But, of course, she wasn't. Tony has always had that effect on women.

Cas had her black hair in a ponytail, and she immediately began to smooth the strands back to make sure she didn't have any scraggly hairs out of place. "I am," she answered.

He smiled, flashing his overly bright teeth. "Might have to begin takin' some of your classes." He tightened his left bicep, causing it to bulge against the fabric of his blue blazer.

He said this without ever looking at me. Tony would tempt any woman with a pulse.

I broke in. "Tony, we need to get on with this."

He put his sunglasses on. "Whatever, sweets."

29

"What's the plan?" Tony asked.

"You park as close as you can," I said.

"No problem."

With the Chicago PD card on his dash, he could park his private car anywhere he wanted to.

"We go in," I continued. "If Jamie's there, we call it off and try again some other day."

"If he's not?"

"Cas will stand guard in the hall while I go into his apartment and look around. If I find evidence that links him to the bad guys at O'Hare, we'll come out. You wait until he comes home and then go in and arrest him."

"Might have a problem with probable cause."

"Meaning?"

"Can't just break the dude's door down. Gotta have a reason to do it."

"How about a woman screaming that she's being attacked?" Cas asked.

"Good by me. Who's the chick gonna do that?"

"Me."

"*What?!*" I asked.

"New plan," she said to me. "If Jamie's there, we knock on his door and go inside. You use your gun to persuade him to sit down and shut up. You give me the evidence, and I hide it. When that's done, I tear my clothes and start screaming for help. You text Tony and then you leave."

What Cas proposed was obviously illegal, but if we didn't catch Jamie, we might all be murdered. I crossed my fingers that Tony would buy into this.

"How do you keep the guy from actually attacking you while you wait for Tony?" I asked.

"I spray him with Raid."

"Raid?" he asked.

"Works better than pepper spray," she said.

"Good to know," he said.

"Then what?" I asked.

"Tony happens to be walking in the neighborhood. He hears the screams and runs inside. He sees my torn clothes and maybe a scratch or two on my arms. He arrests Jamie, cuffs him, searches the apartment, and finds the evidence." She paused. "Just what is the evidence anyway?"

"Trash that has C4 residue on it."

"Where did you get it?" she asked.

"I stole a bag of garbage from the 'industrial spies' trash cans in the alley across the street from our home. I gave some of the trash to Tony. The Chicago PD lab found C4 on them. The trash I have with me is from the same bag."

"Got it," she said.

"Sweets, why are you in his apartment in the first place?" Tony asked Cas.

"Jamie took a lot of my classes," she said. "He invites me over to hang out. I do it, but he makes advances. I resist. He won't take no for an answer. I resist some more. He attacks me. I fight back. You save me."

"Not sure if I'm comfortable with any of this. Too many moving parts. Kinda pushing the edge of breaking a few laws here."

"Please, Tony," I said. "We really need to get this guy before he gets us."

He tapped his fingers on the steering wheel.

"Question," he said. "What if the dude isn't there?"

"I'll hide the evidence and come up with a new plan," I said.

30

I opened the Hummer passenger door and stepped out. Cas jumped out of her side. We shouldered our backpacks and walked toward the back of the building.

Tony parked his BMW and climbed out of his car. As we neared the back corner, I saw him slowly begin to walk past the front of the apartment building so he could hear Cas if she began screaming.

Digging into my backpack, I pulled out the electric lock pick gun and torque wrench. "Shield me while I open the lock."

"Done," Cas said.

She stood with her back to me, blocking the view of anyone who might approach from the alley. I inserted the device into the door lock and turned it on. It bucked in my hand and stopped. I inserted and twisted the torque wrench. The lock clicked open.

I put my equipment away, and we stepped into the first-floor hallway. The ceiling was low, and the brown, patterned carpet was cheap but new. I heard the thumping from a stereo in one of the upper-floor apartments. The pungent odors of several different types of cooking hung in the air.

Cas sniffed. "Another reason I could never live in an apartment building again. I hate the stink of curry, and," she sniffed again, "it smells like some of these people are bathing in it."

"I'm going to the vestibule to buzz Jamie's apartment. If he answers, I'll let Tony know we're going in."

"And if Jamie's not there?"

"I go into his apartment alone. If it looks like he's still living there, I plant the evidence and we leave."

She bounced up and down on her toes. "I'm ready. Let's do this."

Cas waited for me in the hallway. I ran to the vestibule and buzzed Jamie's apartment. He didn't answer. I jabbed the button several more times. Still no answer.

I rejoined Cas. We walked down the hallway to apartment 111. Cas knocked on the door. No one answered. She knocked again. Nothing. She turned to me and shrugged her shoulders.

I reached into my backpack and pulled out my tools. The lock was part of the doorknob. "This won't be a challenge."

I slipped on latex gloves. It took me fifteen seconds to unlock it. I put the equipment into the backpack. I grabbed the Glock and popped the clip. I reinserted it and chambered a round.

Cas removed her contact Taser and can of Raid wasp spray from her backpack. I placed my backpack outside the door.

"You wait out here and make sure he doesn't surprise me if he unexpectedly comes home," I said.

She scanned the hallway. "I'll stand over there where I can see both entrances. If he comes in one of them, I'll call and then go out the other one."

My pulse thudded in my ears. Holding the Glock in my right hand, I opened Jamie's door.

31

I ran through the apartment. It was empty. I took out my cell phone and texted Cas.

Me: *not here.*

Cas: *k.*

I stepped into the hallway and grabbed my backpack. I pulled it inside and shut the door. There was a security latch in addition to the door lock. I secured the latch to give me time to run to the patio if Jamie came home and Cas somehow missed seeing him.

Slipping my cell phone in my back pocket, I kept the Glock in my other hand. I placed the backpack next to the door.

I sniffed as I stepped forward into the living room. Stale cigarette smoke.

Jamie smokes?

It was hard to believe since he appeared to be a fitness freak.

I started in the living room. It was larger than the typical overpriced Chicago rental units. The walls and carpet were off-white. There was a two-cushion light blue couch and a dark blue stuffed arm chair grouped around a low glass-top table. On the table was a TV remote for a fifty-inch HD TV on the far wall.

I searched under the cushions but didn't find anything. Ditto beneath the couch and chair. There were no pictures on the walls or personal items of any kind anywhere.

I needed documentation of everything I saw in his apartment, so I slid the gun into the back waistband of my pants and pulled out my cell phone. I took pictures and then videoed the entire room.

Moving to my right, I went into the bedroom. The walls and carpet matched what I'd seen in the living room. The bed was made. A brown wood, three-drawer nightstand stood next to the bed. There was a lamp on it but no clock or anything in the drawers.

On the adjacent wall was a chest of drawers. It matched the nightstand. I checked the four drawers, but other than neatly arranged underwear, workout gear, and socks, I didn't find anything suspicious.

The closet was full of a man's clothes hanging in an orderly fashion. Patting down the clothes didn't reveal anything. Once again, I took out my phone and snapped both individual photos and a video of the room and the closet.

I went into the bathroom. I didn't find anything other than the usual men's toiletries. I didn't see any moisture in the sink or bathtub. The bar of soap in the shower looked dry. I repeated the process of taking pictures and video.

No man is this clean and tidy.

I walked back out into the living room and then into the kitchen. His kitchen drawers were pristine. I searched the cabinets.

The cereal boxes were arranged according to height. I took more pictures.

I put the phone back in my pocket. I was getting a weird vibe, like he'd moved out but purposefully left his stuff behind.

But why?

Maybe he anticipated me coming there and wanted to make sure I stayed long enough to look around.

A disturbing possibility.

I opened the refrigerator door. It was empty except for the top shelf. Sitting on it were what appeared to be two baggies full of a clear jelly. There was a cell phone behind them. Wires ran from the cell phone to the baggies.

Bombs!

32

Déjà freaking boom!

Grabbing the first baggy, I threw it as hard as I could against the far wall adjacent to his bedroom. The contents splattered over the wallpaper.

The cell phone lit up as I turned and grabbed the other one. I tossed it in the same direction with the same result.

I sprinted toward the front door and fumbled with the security latch. The phone rang from inside the refrigerator.

Hurry up!

I flipped the latch back, ripped the door open, and dove into the hall. Cas saw what was going on and began to sprint toward me. I waved my arms to stop her.

"Get out!" I screamed. "Bomb!"

A barely audible third ring of the phone was followed by the loud thump of an explosion from inside the refrigerator.

I jumped up. Cas hadn't moved.

"Go!"

"But…"

"I'll be right behind you."

But I need evidence.

I rushed back through the still-open apartment door. The main room was beginning to fill up with acrid black smoke.

Through the haze, I saw that the refrigerator door had been blown off its hinges.

Running to the far wall, I scraped off some of the jelly-like substance that dripped down the wallpaper. I closed my hand around a blob of it and ran back out the apartment door.

I was almost to the back door when I realized I'd forgotten my backpack. I ran back to the open apartment door. Smoke billowed into my face. I couldn't see anything. Still holding onto the blob, I got down on my hands and knees. I felt around and finally found my backpack.

People yelled at me as I ran down the hallway. I ignored them and sprinted into alley.

Cas waited for me in the hazy late morning sunlight. With my free hand, I texted Tony to leave. I didn't want him to have to explain why he was here.

Before I could call the fire department, sirens began blaring in the distance. It sounded like they were still a couple of blocks away.

"We need to split right now!" I yelled.

Cas took off on a dead sprint toward her truck. I did too.

We hopped into the Hummer.

"Okay, what just happened?" she asked.

I told her.

"Why the heck did you go back inside?" she asked when I finished.

"For this." My left hand shook as I held up the blob. "It's a sample of the C4 from the bombs."

Reaching in my backpack, I grabbed one of the lunch sacks I always carried for emergencies. I wiped the C4 into it.

"Like I told you before, C4 has a signature," I continued. "With this," I held up the sack, "I can prove Jamie was part of the 'industrial spy' group the FBI caught at O'Hare."

33

The cops arrived before the firemen. A police car with its lights flashing and siren blaring screeched to a halt. The driver double-parked in front of the apartment building. The siren stopped. Two officers jumped out and ran inside. The black and white's lights still flashed.

Thank God Tony left.

We watched them enter. I took out my cell phone and took several more pictures.

"How did Jamie know you were in the apartment?" Cas asked while I did this.

"I think he had cameras and maybe even microphones hidden in his apartment. That's how he knew I was there."

"Did you take pictures in his apartment?"

"I did."

"Why don't we check them out?"

I ran the video of the main rooms first. Cas watched over my shoulder.

It took five minutes. "There it is," Cas said.

"Where?"

"Look at the black bolt in the middle of the kitchen light fixture. It's moving."

I enlarged the picture. She was right. The "bolt" that held the fixture to the ceiling moved when I opened one of the kitchen cabinets.

Uh-oh.

My stomach began to churn. "He left his name on the building's directory to lure me to his apartment."

"But if he could see you, why didn't he blow you up as soon as you walked into his apartment?"

A chill ran down my spine. "He was sending me a 'gotcha' message before he killed me."

Two people ran out the front door of the apartment building. Three more followed.

"He left his clothes to make it look like he still lived there so I would take my time searching the place and eventually find the bombs."

"So he could blow you up while you stood directly in front of the refrigerator."

"Yep. He watches me open the door of the refrigerator. He dials his phone and blows me up. He wants me to know it's him just before he kills me."

"But you survive."

"I do, but I have to admit that his plan was ingenious. He murders me, and that puts the rest of you on notice he can do the same thing to any of the Irregulars whenever he wants to."

"His plan wasn't that good. He didn't anticipate that you would throw the bombs at the wall and escape before he exploded the detonator."

Black smoke began to float out of the building's front door. More people exited the building.

"How far away do the monitors have to be to receive the videos?" she asked.

"I don't know for sure."

"Do you think he's still in the apartment building watching the video monitors from another unit?"

"It's possible he's still inside or in another building close by." I scanned the neighborhood. "Or sitting out here in a car monitoring the video feed on a laptop."

A fire truck screeched to a halt in front of the apartment building. Firefighters in full gear rushed into the building. Thicker black smoke billowed out of the front door.

Suddenly, flames shot out of several windows on the third and fourth floors. "It looks like the entire apartment building is on fire," she said.

I pictured the bombs. "Uh-oh."

"Uh-oh, what?"

"He blows me up. What does he not want to leave behind?"

"I don't know."

"Any evidence of the C4, because that would connect him to the 'industrial spies.' "

"But you scraped some off the wall, didn't you?"

I patted my backpack. "I did. Now we've got him."

34

Two more fire trucks rumbled to a halt in front of the building. Three firemen appeared on the roof. They chopped holes over the apartments that were on fire below them. Other firemen assisted people out the front door. I could see more residents standing behind the building.

"I'm only a nurse, and I don't know much about stuff like this, but how the heck did a fire spread from apartment 111 to the upper floors so quickly?" Cas asked.

My question too.

Windows blew out on other floors, followed by thick smoke and flames. More people from other homes and apartments in the neighborhood wandered outside to see what was going on. Even with the Hummer's windows rolled up, the acrid smoke seeped inside the vehicle and irritated our eyes and noses.

The only person who didn't seem interested was a lady with long blond hair and big sunglasses driving a white Prius. She pulled out from a parking spot four cars in front of the Hummer and drove away without a second look at the disaster.

"Like I said, Jamie isn't a rookie at stuff like this," I said. "Notice how the fire seems to be skipping units." I pointed to the one of the apartments on the fourth floor. "Twenty-two girls were part of the 'industrial spies' plot. They lived in that building. They're gone, and their apartments are empty."

"Maybe he had their door keys."

"If he did, he could have put incendiary devices in those units and rigged them to explode after he blew me up. A fire is a terrific way to destroy evidence."

I pictured standing in front of the open door of the refrigerator and discovering the bombs. "I threw the bombs against the wall and dove out the front door. The detonator went off behind me. Did you smell anything in the hallway?"

"Smoke."

And then it hit me. "Smoke followed by a whiff of what you smell when an appliance shorts out."

"Like ozone."

"Exactly. Maybe he also had his cell phone attached to a detonator for the wiring of the refrigerator to make it look like an electrical fire too."

"I bet the fires in the other units will also appear to be electrical."

"The fire department's arson team will do an investigation but they're understaffed. Once they think it's an electrical fire, they'll stop looking for another cause and never find the C4 residue."

Cas pointed to the people standing on the street and behind the building. The fire raged out of control. "These poor people are going to lose everything. I hope the owner has good insurance."

Owner?

"That might be a problem. I learned that, through a shell corporation, one of the 'industrial spies' owned this apartment building and the surgery center where Micah did the operations. I would be surprised if the owner had any more than the basic coverage."

"Then these poor people won't receive anything, and in addition, some of them could have been incinerated as collateral damage."

"Jamie didn't care what happened as long as he accomplished his goal of killing me."

Cas pulled out and drove two blocks before she suddenly stopped. "Oh, my God! You think he's burning down the apartment to destroy the evidence of the C4 he used?"

"I do."

"You went back into his apartment to grab samples of the C4 so you'll have proof that he is one of the bad guys."

"So what?"

"We're assuming he watched you walk into his apartment."

"And?"

"And unless the explosion from the refrigerator screwed up his camera feed, he saw you return and grab the C4 sample."

35

Late Thursday night, Carter walked into our bedroom. I was in bed with Kerry. She was asleep in my arms.

After what had happened with Jamie attempting to blow me up in his apartment, I didn't want to leave her alone.

"How was your day, honey?" he asked.

How do I answer that one?

"My day was, you know, my day," I whispered, trying to not awaken Kerry.

He stared at me, apparently not sure why I'd responded like that. I was not going to tell him what had happened with Jamie.

Need some distraction here.

"Want me to warm something up for you?" I asked. "You must be starved."

"No, thanks," he whispered back. "Would you like for me to put Kerry to bed?"

"Sure. She might like to have you rock her."

I knew he needed some "daddy" time with his little girl. We had a rocking chair in her room for that specific purpose.

He smiled as he reached down and picked her up. She stirred in his arms. He began to sway with her.

He stopped in the doorway. "Good-night, Mommy," he whispered for Kerry.

Twenty minutes later, he came back into our bedroom.

"Our little one is finally asleep," he said.

"Are you sure you don't want something to eat?"

"I ordered Gino's pizza in for everyone at the office so they could keep working, and I ate with them. With a reduced staff, it's ridiculously difficult to cover any breaking story."

He referred to the last round of job cuts at the *Tribune*. The newspaper business that we both love is gradually dying. But I want to keep writing great stories to slow down the death of the industry.

"By the way, you should hire someone to assist you around the house," he continued. "You'll need free time to help us with the investigation of the bombings."

I sat up. "Help you? I thought you were against me working on the abortion clinic bombing story."

"I am, but we really need you on this."

His flip-flop on this made no sense to me.

Unless he needs access to my mole.

My involvement with the clinic bombing story began five years ago when I was an investigative reporter for the *Post* in D.C. I received an email from a dissident member of the Psalmists, a staunch anti-abortion group.

The person saw me do a short segment talking head on CNBC where I profiled the clinic bombings. My utter disgust for this form of protest pleased the member, who then contacted me by email and indicated he or she would become a mole for me inside the group. Six weeks later, the mole emailed me the details of the bomber's plan to blow up the Arlington abortion clinic.

"My help, or my mole's?"

"Actually, the mole's," he confessed. "If that person still exists, maybe this time we can trap the bomber and finish the story."

"You really don't want me to actively work on this, do you?"

"I wouldn't ask you to do this if I considered for one second it might be dangerous."

"That was a clever answer. You're carefully avoiding the central issue. Do you, or do you not, want me to work on this story?"

"I need your help, and yes, I would like you to work on this story."

I kissed him goodnight. "I'll think about it."

36

It was early Friday afternoon. I pushed Kerry to Hamlin Park. The lake effect was having its way with Chicago again. The temperature was sixty-two degrees, and with the wind howling, it was at least ten degrees cooler than that.

My cell phone rang when we were one block away.

"Tina, it's Gayle Nystrom."

Ah, man.

Gayle is the editor of the *Lakeview Times*, our free, weekly, neighborhood newspaper. I was supposed to submit my monthly article today for publication on Friday the twenty-fifth of August.

But it isn't gonna happen.

I'd been just a little too busy to research and write one.

"Hi, Gayle," I said. "I know I'm supposed to have my article in today, but I've been a little busy."

"I totally understand, and I applaud you for your recent article in the *Chicago Tribune*. As I told you before, it was terrific. But I gave you the opportunity to write again, and I hope you remember that."

"I do have an idea for next month, and I'm working on it."

That was kind of true.

Sort of.

"Wonderful. Let's keep in touch. I'll need to know before next month's deadline in order to save the space."

I disconnected and kept walking. The Irregulars frequently have playgroup at Hamlin Park. The park has almost eight acres, with four baseball/softball diamonds, lacrosse and soccer fields, a free swimming pool, and a fully equipped playground. There is also a field house with a fitness center, two gyms, an assembly hall with a stage, and meeting rooms.

It's where I first met Linda and, later on, Cas and Molly. These adult conversations stimulated me to write again and, thanks to Gayle Nystrom, my column in the *Lakeview Times* was born. I was grateful she provided that opportunity when no one else would hire me. But I considered it a temporary situation until I could resurrect my career with a breaking front-page story.

Yesterday, on the way home from Jamie's burning apartment building, Cas and I decided we needed to alert Molly and Linda about what Jamie intended to do to me. As I pushed Kerry into the park, my senses were once again assaulted by the feeling that someone was watching me.

Jamie?

Bomber?

Or both?

Once we reached Hamlin Park, we played with our kids on the equipment. As we did, I told Molly and Linda what happened.

"Jamie really tried to blow you up?" Molly asked after I finished the story.

"He did," I said. "But I recovered a sample of the C4 from his apartment wall. It has to be from the same batch of C4 the 'industrial spies' used, so we have him cold."

"Except for one tiny problem," Linda said. "It's called chain of custody. How do the police or the FBI know where you obtained the C4? For all the feds know, you could be one of the perpetrators."

"Are you telling us we have evidence to prove Jamie is a bad guy but we can't legally use it?" Cas asked.

"I most certainly am," Linda said. "Plus, the evidence was acquired during the crime of breaking and entering."

"But he might be after all of us," Molly said.

"Since he attempted to blow up Tina, and I could've been in the apartment with her, I think that's a reasonable assumption," Cas said.

"How come this wasn't in the news?" Linda asked.

"I looked for it online and in this morning's *Tribune*," Cas said. "I found a small story about an apartment fire. It said it was caused by short-circuits in the wiring of the refrigerators in several units."

"Which means the fire inspectors won't find any C4 residue because they won't do a thorough search through the rubble," I said. "At least I have some of the C4 from his apartment."

"And I respectfully remind you that it is evidence you cannot use," Linda said.

"Guys, all we need to do is catch Jamie and plant Tina's C4 on him," Molly said. "When the cops search him and find the C4, they'll run it in the lab and arrest him for being one of the spy guys."

"A sound plan, although it breaks several laws," Linda said. "And speaking of that… Tina, do you know how many laws you've broken so far?"

"TNTC," I said.

Linda shrugged her shoulders.

"Too numerous to count, but we might as well break a few more if it'll put him behind bars and keep all of us safe. Molly, how do we go about planting the C4 on him?"

"Gosh, I don't have a clue," she said. "The farmers always did that stuff."

"Where's a good farmer when we need one?" Linda joked.

"You can be such a bitch sometimes," Cas said.

"For many female lawyers, that would be a compliment. And I hate to say it, but I no longer have any time for this. When I leave here, I'm going to see my doctor and then visit the new hospital I selected where I will have my baby."

"Which one is it?" Molly asked.

"The MidAmerica Hospital," Linda said.

"It's no surprise that I usually disagree with you about most subjects, but you are right about this one: that hospital is the fanciest one in the state," Cas said.

"And how would you know about that?" I asked.

"I worked there before I stopped to have my kids," she said.

37

Saturday morning, I ran with David. At about the three-mile mark, we turned toward Fellger Park, another green space in our neighborhood.

"I think I might need Hogan's help with a bomber story I'm working on, but I don't have any money to pay them," I said.

"Bomber story?" David asked. "Maybe I can provide some free advice. Tell me more."

I did.

"My goodness," he said. "When I read about you online, it didn't mention how serious your injuries were. I sure can't tell it from how you look now."

"I was lucky."

"Maybe you should have bought a lottery ticket after you got out of the hospital."

"Funny you say that. My brother told me the same thing."

We turned right and continued to run.

"Bottom line: I'm terrified the guy who blew me up might be back to finish the job."

"Job?"

"To kill me. He missed the first time. If he knows I live here, he might want to finish what he started."

David didn't respond. We ran another mile.

"I think you're wrong," he said.

"About what?"

"I've been trained in threat assessments. You said you were blown up over five years ago, right?"

"Yep, on the morning of July third."

"Where has the bomber been since then?"

"Good question. Initially, I thought he might have died from the gunshot wounds."

"Gunshot wounds? That wasn't in the newspaper story that was in the *Post* immediately after the bombing."

"The FBI held that information back, and because it's still an open investigation, they won't release it until the case is closed."

I didn't want to admit to David that I was the one who fired the shots. He might not understand why I would do something like that.

"That's why I need your help," I continued. "I need to know if he's back."

"But what if he is? Why are you now afraid?"

"Because if he traveled all the way from D.C. to Chicago, I'm afraid he's here to kill me."

"I disagree. He's had five years to, as you say, 'finish what he started.' Why hasn't he done it already?"

"I got married and moved to Chicago. I hoped that if he was alive, he'd lost track of me."

"That's pretty naïve. I didn't have any problems finding every detail about your life. I admit I'm pretty good with a computer, but it wasn't that hard. It wouldn't be for the bomber either."

"Then why hasn't he tried to kill me?"

"Was he trying to kill you the first time?"

Huh?

"That's a good question. I don't know."

"From the online reports I read, the FBI maintained the bomber might not have detonated the bomb when he did if you hadn't gone into the building and confronted him."

"The FBI did tell me to stay out of the clinic, and I didn't."

"Why?"

"You're not a reporter so it's hard for you to understand, but I was consumed with chasing the story."

"Why do you think this bomber is in the area?"

"To blow up abortion clinics?"

"He can do that anywhere. Why in the Chicago area?"

"I don't know."

"Do you think it's because you live here?"

"I do."

"But I don't think he's here to kill you."

"Why?"

"Maybe he's trying to entice you to write about why he's doing these bombings and to raise awareness about abortion."

"That's what my husband has always maintained."

"If my threat assessment is right, the furthest thing from the bomber's mind is to kill you. He wants you alive now more than ever, especially since you're writing major stories again."

"I hope you're right. But I need help to figure out if it's even the same bomber."

38

"Can you hack into someone's security footage?" I asked.

David elevated his eyebrows. "I, ah... You can't tell anyone this, okay?"

"No problem," I said.

"As I told you during lunch on Thursday, I had something to do with security at the Hogan Company, but it was a little more than that. We had several government contracts, and I worked with the NSA to prevent computer hacks from outside sources."

"Does that mean you can do this for me?"

"I'll try. But I need access to a computer."

"We're close to my home. Let's go there."

Carter was upstairs giving Kerry a bath when we walked in.

"Honey, I have to do a little work on my computer," I yelled up from the foot of the stairs.

"Take your time," Carter yelled back down. "We just started playing in the tub."

I would introduce David to Carter when we finished. As we walked down to the office, I told David what I needed from the security footage of the two clinic bombings. He sat down at my computer and put on latex gloves.

What's up with this?

He noticed me staring at him.

"The gloves, right?" he asked.

"Well, yeah."

"I have a little phobia about germs. Computer keyboards are filthy."

I wanted to assure him that mine wasn't, but before I could, he turned back to the computer and went to work.

Guess we're done talking about germs.

His gloved fingers flew over the keyboard faster than Linda's. He no longer seemed to realize I still stood next to him.

With nothing else to do, I went upstairs and joined Carter and Kerry. Fifteen minutes later, I walked back down to the computer room. Carter stayed upstairs to dress Kerry and dry her hair.

David looked up at me. "Okay, I have it cued up to the moment a laundryman walks into the Hinsdale Clinic at 9 a.m. on July third."

We watched the footage. The rack of clean coats the laundryman pushed inside partially shielded his face from the camera.

"Let me speed it up," he said. "He's inside for eighteen minutes before he leaves."

When the laundryman departed, he pushed a hamper piled full of wrinkled clothes. I could see that he had a sparse black beard and scraggly, shoulder-length black hair.

"It could be him," I said. "But the elevated position of the security camera makes it difficult to tell."

"Let's look at the other one."

The video sequence from the Deerfield bombing was more helpful. The recording at 4:22 p.m. showed Dr. Russell walking out of the clinic and driving off. So did several employees. The laundryman entered as they exited. He held open the door for two nurses. This time he carried a laundry bag full of something, probably the bomb materials.

He was inside thirty-one minutes, the time it took for him to plant the two bombs. After he left, a security guard walked out and locked the door. It was 5 p.m.

David fast-forwarded the video to 2:12 a.m. the next morning. The doctor drove up and entered the clinic. Eleven minutes later, there was a blinding flash of light and the screen went black.

The doctor had been killed.

It's my bomber.

I heard my husband clumping around in the kitchen.

"Come upstairs," I said. "I want you to meet Carter."

39

Carter poured cereal into a bowl for Kerry as we walked into the kitchen. I glanced at Kerry and Carter and saw them through David's eyes.

Kerry inherited Carter's sandy hair and blue eyes, and thanks to his six feet two DNA, she's at the top of the height chart. All of her short girlfriends in high school and college are going to hate her super-long legs. If she inherits any of my athletic skills, we might not have to pay for her college tuition.

"David John, this is my husband, Carter Thomas," I said.

Carter's mouth dropped open. "You're Lyndell's leprechaun!"

I felt my face flush.

You busted me out!

"Guilty," David said. "Everyone says that about me."

"Sorry about that," Carter said. "I was rude."

"No problem."

They shook hands.

"One question," David said. "Who's Lyndell?"

"Lyndell Newens was our next door neighbor," I said. "She sat in her chair and watched the ebb and flow of the neighborhood through her front window. She saw you run past and thought you looked like a leprechaun. She suggested you might make a good story for my monthly column."

Carter set the bowl of cereal down in front of Kerry. She promptly shoved it off her high chair onto the floor. "I want hot dogs for bwekfast, Daddy!"

I really hate the terrible twos.

Before either Carter or I could react, David stepped forward.

"Kerry, hi!" he said. "How would you like to see a trick?"

Kerry sat speechless, with her spoon in her hand.

He picked up a slice of banana from her plate with his left hand. He transferred it to his right hand and held it in front of her face.

"Blow on my hand, Kerry," he instructed her.

Her mouth was open. She didn't move.

"Like you do with a birthday candle," he continued.

She took in a deep breath and blew on his hand. He opened it and the banana piece was gone. He reached up with his left hand and pulled the banana out of her right ear. She clapped her hands and bounced up and down in her high chair.

What the heck?

"How did you do that?" I asked.

"I was just going to ask the same thing," Carter said.

David ignored us. "Kerry, if you eat your breakfast, I'll do another trick for you."

"David, you don't have to do this," I said.

"I love to do it. Margaret and I play the same game each morning, but I will need more food."

Carter cut up the rest of the banana and reloaded her cereal bowl. Before I could move, David efficiently cleaned up the mess on the floor.

"Kerry's food tastes fluctuate on a daily basis," I said. "For the past week, it's been hot dogs, apple slices smeared with peanut butter, and grapes."

"But not for breakfast," Carter said. "She usually eats fruit, healthy cereal, milk, and juice."

"And an occasional Dinkel's donut, but she always sits with Ralph and Elmo," I said.

I referred to her pink baby blanket and her favorite toy, a twelve-inch, plush red Elmo who always "eats" the same thing she does. Ralph, the blanket, usually just "watches."

"Carter, David and I talked about the recent bombings. He has an interesting take on it. Why don't you two talk about it while I do something on the computer downstairs?"

40

I went down to the office. A few weeks ago, unbeknownst to me, Jamie broke into our home and installed a keystroke logger on my computer. This allowed the "industrial spies" to keep track of everything I did while I pieced together the story about who they were and what they were up to.

Linda discovered it, and we originally thought the FBI had installed it using a system called Magic Lantern. We left it in place to keep the feds from discovering we were on to them.

It seemed like a great idea, but right before the events at O'Hare, I learned Jamie was the one who had put it in. After the events at O'Hare, Linda removed it, so my computer was no longer compromised. Now I could begin working on the bomber story.

The files from my Arlington debacle were archived in my hard drive under the slug line: *Psalmist*. Scanning the material, I pulled out what I considered to be the relevant information and transferred it to a new file: *Chicago bomber*.

I hadn't heard from the mole since I was blown up, but to begin this story, I needed to contact that person. The mole's email address was on the screen in front of me.

Taking a deep breath, I began typing:

He's in the Chicago area. He has blown up two abortion clinics and murdered a doctor. Are you willing to help me catch him?

I shut down the computer and went back to the kitchen.

"Did you have a nice talk?" I asked.

"We did," Carter responded. "You're right. David has an interesting view of the bomber story."

"It's what you and the FBI have always maintained," I said. "I shouldn't have gone into the clinic in the first place."

"But I also said that I wasn't there, and you made a split-second decision," Carter said. "It wasn't my story. I honestly don't know what I would have done."

"Carter, you wouldn't have done that in a million years. When I was jumping out of planes in Afghanistan chasing stories, you sat in front of a computer writing two Pulitzer Prize-winning stories."

David's face blanched. "You jumped out of an airplane?"

"Planes. Helicopters. Shot handguns and rifles. Blew up some IEDs. My approach to a story is a little different than Carter's."

"Gosh, I never would have guessed that about you," David said.

Thank God I hadn't admitted to him that I shot the bomber in Arlington. He might not know what to think about me.

I turned to my husband. "Honey, I want to work on the bomber story but only from afar and with one of your reporters."

For the second time that morning, his mouth fell open. "Are you sure about this?"

"If David is right, there's no risk to me or you or Kerry. If the bomber really wants me to write his story, I'll do it. And I won't do anything risky because I don't have to. I'll be an observer and collector of facts. I'll work with your reporter. Nothing more, nothing less."

"No more going into clinics?"

I thought about my recent visit to the Deerfield clinic. "Not as long as there is any obvious risk."

Carter lifted Kerry out of her high chair. She ran off to the family room.

He held out his hand to David. "We have you to thank for this."

They shook again. "I'm not sure exactly what I did, but I'm glad it's going to work out."

"And I'll find a reporter to help you," Carter said to me.

"Great. I've already started to work on the story," I said, and winked at Carter. I wanted him to know I'd emailed my mole.

I wouldn't tell David about the mole, because I never reveal my sources to outsiders unless it's absolutely necessary.

Plus, the mole was my only leverage to stay in the story, and I didn't want anyone screwing up that relationship.

41

On Monday, I ran with David. My phone dinged with a text. When I saw who sent it, I stopped to read it. David stopped with me.

Hannah: *Need immediate help with our security problems.*

Me: *Might have solution with me. Can I bring him to you?*

Hannah: *Great! Hurry!*

"Remember my friend with the security issues?" I asked David.

"Sure, and I said I would be glad to help but I can't do it as an independent contractor," he reminded me.

We started running again. "Turn left at the next corner. You're going to get your chance."

I noticed David checking the security cameras as I rang Hannah's doorbell. They were moving. He nodded to himself.

Hannah greeted us at her front door.

"This is David John," I said to her. "He used to work for the Hogan Company in San Jose, California. It's a security corporation. He still has contacts there."

She held out her hand. "I am Dr. Hannah Eisenberg." They shook. Her grip looked firm. Micah's treatment of her multiple sclerosis was still working.

"Please come in," she said.

We sat in the living room. I watched as David assessed the opulent furnishings. Someone in another room played a Donkey Kong game. It was a sound from my youth. I'd previously seen it in their family room and wanted to play it then but was too busy helping Linda hack into Micah's computer.

"Tina, the reason I texted you is my concern about the protection of Micah's lab," Hannah said. "He still does not have any."

"You're kidding. Why not?"

"He feels it is too expensive, and he does not need it."

David raised his eyebrows and gave me the "I told you so" look.

"Your husband is right about the cost," David said. "Good security is very expensive."

"Mr. John, trust me when I say that price is of no concern. I will pay for everything."

"I didn't mean to suggest that you couldn't afford it. I just wanted you to know he has a valid complaint."

Hannah turned to me. "How much does Mr. John know about any of this?"

"Actually, nothing."

"I did read Tina's article in the *Tribune*, if that helps any."

Hannah stared at him and then at me but remained silent.

"Okay, here's the deal, David," I began, sticking to the story the FBI forced me to write. "Micah invented a process to cure multiple sclerosis. 'Industrial spies' from Iran attempted to steal it.

The FBI arrested them but let one man go. His name is Jamie Smith."

David had a puzzled look on his face. "Do you mean the danger here is that Jamie Smith might try and steal the process?"

How much do I tell him?

The only things I knew about David were from my online research and talking with him the short time we'd known each other. But I was terrified of what Jamie might do to me, my family, and my friends. And even more worried for Micah, Hannah, and their family.

What else can I do?

The police wouldn't help us. Neither would the FBI, especially since they were the ones who had let him go free. I had to trust David with everything.

He's my only option.

I took in a deep breath and said a silent prayer that I was going to do the right thing.

"Actually, it's way more than that," I said. "Hannah, you don't know this yet, but I went to Jamie's apartment building Thursday. While I was there, he tried to kill me."

Hannah assessed this new information without any obvious emotion. David was a different story. His face turned white, and for a second, I thought he might pass out.

Hannah noticed. "Mr. John, is something wrong?"

He swallowed before he spoke. "I... Ah... I've never been a field operative. I don't do well at all in stressful situations. It was one reason I didn't mind taking a break from Hogan. I'm really good with a computer and assessing data, but not so good otherwise."

"Don't worry about that, David," I said. "Right now, all you need to do is arrange to set up tight security here and at Micah's lab."

I wanted to add, "and help us neutralize Jamie," but I didn't want to confuse him.

The color returned to his face. "Dr. Eisenberg, if it's not too much trouble, would you show me your home? I need to assess the risks here first in order to give my contacts at the Hogan Company the necessary information to keep you and your family safe."

"Certainly, and after we are finished, I would like you to do the same thing at my husband's laboratory." She paused. "Before we do that, there is one other element to this story. Your expertise with computers might be the solution there too."

42

"Tina, as you know, since the confrontation at O'Hare, I have been working to unravel the layers of what happened," Hannah began. She turned to David. "Mr. John, I was totally uninformed about what was happening to me and my children, but as I have learned more, new and startling revelations keep arising."

David and I kept quiet. Donkey Kong played in the background.

"I have, and continue to have, grave concerns about the medical issues associated with," she glanced at me, "the 'industrial spies' in this situation. But this is no longer my concern. The financing of my husband's entire project is."

Ah, man, this is trouble.

"I thought money wasn't an issue for you," David said.

"It isn't," she said. "My trust fund easily contributed twenty-five million dollars to begin work on the lab here in Chicago."

"Wow," David said. "That's a lot of money."

Hannah dismissed that amount with a wave of her hand. "Mr. John, to date, well over two hundred million dollars have been spent."

David gulped. "How much?"

Another wave of her hand. "The amount is not important. Where the money is coming from is."

"And where is that?" he asked.

"Without his knowledge, I accessed my husband's home computer. I coupled that information with the facts as I know them from my own trust accounts. Most of the money for his lab did not come from me."

"Who provided it?" he asked.

"Sherman Krevolin, a billionaire in Dallas," she said. "But there is an encrypted section in my husband's hard drive. I want to know what is in there to learn if it explains why Krevolin is giving large sums of money to my husband."

David didn't say anything.

"I could hire another computer expert to do this, but it would take too long to find a competent one," she said. "Tina has recommended you, and I trust her judgment."

And I hope you're right.

"I would like you to download that information from my husband's office computer and see if you can break the code on that section," she continued.

"You really want to know about his financing?" he asked.

"I must know," she said. "If this process is illegal, I must stop it!"

This is worse than I thought.

43

"Hannah, Linda and I have been working on this," I said. "We think Krevolin is a conduit to illegally funnel money from our government to Micah's lab."

Hannah's lips compressed into a thin line. "I knew it! Micah presented a paper in Boston on his embryonic stem cell research and his preliminary results on the treatment of MS. At that time, my condition was worsening, and shortly after his talk, a representative of the U.S. government visited our home in Israel. The next thing I knew, Micah needed twenty-five million dollars to start his clinic, I provided it, and we moved to Chicago."

"Linda and I think someone high up in the government is behind Micah's financing."

"How high up?" David asked.

"High enough that they're afraid if the story of this illegal financing comes out it could severely damage the president's political party for the next several elections," I said.

"My former company has security contracts with the government," he said. "You have no idea how big a mess this information would be if it came out."

I remembered the Iran-Contra affair and what Molly said. "Big enough to kill someone to keep it quiet?" I asked.

"Without question," he said.

"How would the government handle a situation like this?" Hannah asked.

"They would hire an asset to do their wet work and eliminate the person or persons who could tell the world about the illegal financing."

"My husband would be one of them," Hannah said.

"Obviously there are several people involved, but he's the one who received the funds and would know the whole story," he said.

"The feds let Jamie go, even though he was one of the industrial spies," I reminded him.

"Then Jamie knows someone alerted the FBI about his group," he said. "If he assumes that person is Micah, he might want to kill Micah, and even you and your children, because of that."

"Is it possible that someone in the government purposely let him go to do this 'wet' work for them?" she asked.

"It would be a win-win for them," he said. "There would be no record of the government doing this, and their problem with the illegal financing issue would be solved."

"What should I do?" Hannah asked.

"Protect yourself and your kids here and Micah at his lab," he said. "It's the only thing you can do."

I kept quiet. They came to the same conclusion the Hamlin Park Irregulars did.

Jamie had reason to kill everyone involved.

44

Three hours later, David and I stood in front of Micah's lab. The people from Hogan's Chicago office arrived at Hannah's as we ran back to my house to grab my mommy van.

Nothing had changed at the lab since my last visit. I parked on the street. We climbed out and stood on the driveway to the lab.

"Oh, my," David said. "This is not good, not good at all."

"Exactly what I was thinking."

We walked to the empty guard stand, ducked under the gate, and moved into the parking lot.

"Where are the security guards?" he asked.

"There aren't any."

His eyebrows shot up. "None at all?"

"Zip. Nada."

"According to your article, his scientific technology is worth millions of dollars. How is it possible there is no security?"

"Micah is a genius. He doesn't concern himself with things like that."

"Then we'll have to do it for him. Show me where to go."

We walked through the unlocked front door and into the small waiting room. No one greeted us. I opened the second door, and we entered a long, windowless hallway. The cement floors and walls were painted white. The acoustic ceiling tiles were also white. The fluorescent lighting was almost too bright.

There were no internal security cameras. People in white lab coats bustled around in the hall, going in and out of doors. The cloying smell of heavy-duty cleaning solvents irritated my nose.

Fight it.

I couldn't let the smells trigger a PTSD attack.

Relax.

I stopped and shut my eyes, placing my hand on the wall for support. I took several deep breaths before I could follow David, who was already fifteen feet in front of me.

Increasing my pace, I caught up with him. He stopped one of the workers and asked where to find Micah. She pointed at a door to our left.

We knocked. Micah told us to come in.

45

We entered a high-ceilinged office the size of a four-car garage. Thick light-blue carpet was laid wall-to-wall. Lush pastel fabrics covered two club chairs. They were grouped around a distressed leather couch. Low voltage lighting illuminated early twentieth century works of art hanging on the walls.

The subtle scent in the room came from freshly-cut summer flowers arranged in four matching Lalique crystal vases standing on polished mahogany end tables. I also detected a faint aroma of lemon-scented furniture polish.

Pictures of Hannah and their four kids were prominently displayed. Behind Micah's modern chrome and glass desk, and next to an American flag on a pole, was a picture on the wall of a smiling Micah and the guy who worked in the Oval Office. He smiled too.

"Welcome," Micah said. He stepped out from behind the desk and shook our hands. "Hannah called and told me you were coming. We have much to discuss and not much time, so please find a place to sit."

Micah is about Molly's height, and his light brown skin tone complements his black eyes and hair. He has a soft bass voice with the trace of a British accent. He wore a heavily starched, long white lab coat. His crisp white shirt looked like it was custom-made, and he wore a Hermès patterned tie. It was hard to see his slacks because of the length of his lab coat, but his polished black loafers appeared to be Italian leather.

David picked a club chair. I sat on the couch and checked around for security cameras. So did David. We didn't see any.

"David, since you are new to this, I will give you a PowerPoint presentation summarizing my work here," Micah said, as he sat down behind his desk and turned to his computer.

He hit a button on his desk, and a white screen rolled down on the far wall. "Speaking to both of you will give me a chance to polish a speech I am going to deliver at the United Center on September 11th. Feel free to break in at any time with questions. I need that feedback."

46

I remembered the phone call from Gayle Nystrom reminding me to write a story for my column.

"I'm sure what you're about to tell us would make a terrific story for my local column," I said. "Are you open to giving me an exclusive interview about this?"

"I think the announcement about my embryonic stem cell technology might make a better story, especially since the president is going to introduce me. He will be here for a 9/11 speech earlier in the day, and this was the best time for him to do this for me."

The president? Here?

My heart began to pound.

This is what I really want: another front page opportunity.

And working on it wouldn't be risky.

"In fact, I suggested to the president's people that you write the story for the *Tribune*," he continued.

I could tell by the distressed look on his face there was a problem. "Is there a 'but' coming here?" I asked.

"Unfortunately, there is. The FBI has specifically requested that you not be allowed to have anything to do with the story."

Dang it.

I was still paying the price for ignoring the FBI's orders not to enter the clinic in Arlington and my recent encounter at O'Hare.

"May I at least go to your speech?"

He smiled. "Most certainly. I do not want you to miss it. I will arrange for a special priority pass to be delivered to your home for you and for the rest of your friends. Hannah actually suggested it."

"That would be terrific."

There's something you're not telling me.

"I do have some influence, and I requested that Carter be selected as the reporter to have an exclusive interview with me and the president," he continued. "That way, you can keep the story in the family."

Wow!

"My hubby will be thrilled. Thank you for thinking of him."

Micah bowed his head to me. "It is the least I can do for what you did for me and my family involving that business at O'Hare."

47

Micah turned to David. "For my speech, I will need to provide some of my personal background information. Please bear with me because Tina has already heard it."

Walking out from behind his desk, Micah moved closer to the screen. He had a remote control in his left hand to change his PowerPoint slides. I pictured him addressing several thousand people. He cleared his throat and then stared at the wall behind us as he began to speak.

"I began my career as an OB-GYN specialist, but my interest gravitated to *in vitro* fertilization."

He clicked the remote control to move through images of his lab at the Assuta Medical Center in Tel Aviv and another one at Northwestern. He used a laser pointer to drive home the content of his speech. A third photo of a laboratory that I hadn't seen before appeared on the screen. It had to be the one we were in.

"I can now reveal to you that I have perfected a technique using embryonic stem cells to effectively treat, and possibly cure, multiple sclerosis. David, according to what Hannah texted me before you arrived, you know that 'industrial spies' attempted to steal the technique from me, but thanks to a female FBI agent and Detective Infantino, they failed."

David nodded but didn't respond.

"I was going to begin Phase I trials, but because of the dramatic success I have had with a few courageous patients, the FDA has fast-tracked my technique, and on September 12th, we will begin treating patients from all over the world."

I raised my hand. "Why wait until then? Why not start today?"

"In order to move this quickly, my lab requires a massive infusion of funds. As I said before, the President of the United States is going to join me on the 11th to announce his full support for embryonic stem cell research, in general, and my technique, in particular."

Here we go.

"But the president is against that, or at least I thought he was," David said.

"Yes, about that. The tiresome debate about when life begins is unimportant compared to the diseases physicians can treat — and cure — using fresh embryonic stem cells. The president now agrees with this concept and has authorized the necessary funds."

"My grandmother in Idaho has Parkinson's, and it's killing her," David said. "All the medicines she takes have terrible side effects and don't help all that much. Can embryonic stem cells help her?"

"I am sorry she has such a devastating illness, and you are correct about the present medications available to her. The side effects are almost worse than the disease, which brings up a pertinent point: doctors rarely cure their patients."

48

An ominous silence engulfed the room.

"Obviously, that statement grabbed your attention," Micah said. "I will add it to my speech."

"If you do, you'll need to clarify what you mean," I said. "I don't think David and I understand what you're saying. At least, I don't."

David nodded, indicating he agreed with me.

"An operation to take out your tonsils or gall bladder will cure you of that disease process. But David, what about your grandmother with Parkinson's, or a child with type 1 diabetes? Their physicians can treat and control their symptoms but not cure them. It is extremely frustrating for all involved. With more funding, I will expand our lab's focus to include degenerative diseases like Parkinson's or traumatic injuries of the spinal cord. Physicians will finally be able to successfully cure these problems."

"Can you explain to me how you do this embryonic stem cell technology?" David asked.

"Gladly," he said. "Fresh embryonic stem cells are the source for the originating cells from which all tissues in the body develop during the earliest days of gestation. I use somatic cell nuclear transfer, SCNT for short, to turn these cells into rejection-free transplant tissues."

"My wife, Mary, had IVF with our daughter, Margaret," David said. "Is your technique the same as creating IVF embryos?"

"Actually, far different. I have invented a laboratory procedure to create a cloned embryo with a donor somatic nucleus that matches each individual patient."

"But aren't U.S. scientists already using existing cell lines for this research?" David asked.

"They are, indeed, but in this country these lines are being used at a very limited rate. And those cells are not fresh and healthy and do not provide the essential tissue for my needs."

"But I've read the embryos are living organisms," David said. "If you're cloning embryos in a Petri dish with SCNT technology, aren't you killing the embryos when you harvest those cells?"

Micah glared at David. "You said you have a daughter, do you not, David?"

"Yes."

"Do you consider a five-day-old embryo in the blastocyst stage and your daughter to be equivalent?"

"Personally, I'm not sure about that, but there are many who believe that an embryo, from the moment of conception, has the same moral status as my child."

"So, in their view, the early embryo is a person."

"It's my understanding that they feel creating and then killing embryos to obtain embryonic stem cells is wrong, even if it can save lives."

Micah glanced at David and then at me. "Both of you are parents. If you had to choose between saving your children from dying of a lethal disease, or sacrificing cloned human embryos to harvest embryonic stem cells to find a cure to save them, which one would you choose?"

David and I looked at each other but didn't speak.

"In my judgment, the early embryo is simply a cluster of human cells lacking any moral status, and given its promising potential, embryonic stem cell and cloning research is an imperative for all physicians."

Micah paused and then continued. "IVF is laboratory support for human reproduction. My procedure is not intended to evolve into a human being. The embryos I create from SCNT are no more than a tissue culture."

"Then this is exactly why you need security here," David said.

49

"I agree with David," I said.

"I have no idea why," Micah said.

I told him about my being blown up in an abortion clinic bombing five years ago and the recent bombings in Chicago. He sat down as he listened to me speak.

When I finished, he stood up and then sat on the edge of his desk. "I can see the logic in your argument, but the general public does not know about my specific discovery and will not until September 11th. And you did not mention the theoretical connection of my process with abortion in your article in the *Tribune*."

"I omitted it because of this controversy," I said.

"I now understand that, but after the 11th, the government can take care of the expense of protecting this lab."

"But you might not live long enough to get that protection," David said.

"I do not understand what you mean."

"Do you remember Jamie?" I asked.

"Hannah said you mentioned this man. All I remember about him is that he was one of the 'industrial spies.' As far as I am concerned, all this discussion and worry keeps me from focusing on my work, and I do not have any time for this."

Hannah was right. A genius is different. Micah's only interest was in his research.

"On Thursday, Jamie set a trap for me in his apartment," I said. "His plan was to blow up two small C4 bombs to kill me. Fortunately, he failed."

"I have no idea what this has to do with my security here at the lab."

"Did the 'industrial spies' threaten to kill Hannah and your children if you went to the FBI?" I asked.

He hung his head. "They did."

"The FBI arrested all of them, but then they let Jamie go," I said. "Who does Jamie think told the FBI about their plans?"

He didn't respond.

"The only conclusion Jamie can reach is that you told the FBI about their plot," I continued.

I didn't want to suggest that Jamie might think I, or any of the Hamlin Park Irregulars, might have done it instead of Micah.

He nodded. "I can see that, yes."

"There is one other thing," I said. "It's about your financing."

A blood vessel popped up in the middle of his forehead and began to throb. "The financing of this laboratory is no concern of yours!"

"But it might be to the rival political party of the President of the United States," David said.

For the first time, Micah's professional persona cracked. He was shaken and couldn't speak. Clearly, he thought no one would discover the government illegally funded his work.

"I know people at a company who can provide total security to you and your family, both here and at your home," David said. "No one will have the skill set or resources to get to any of you."

Micah smacked his head. "But the expense! *Oy!*"

"Hannah has already committed to paying for it," I said.

"In fact, a Hogan team is working at your home as we speak," David said.

Micah sighed. "When can you begin here?"

"Right now," David said. "Even though I no longer work for Hogan, I can speed up the process with them if I can access your computer to begin the online hookup to their computers. It will take me about thirty minutes. Maybe you can take Tina for a tour while I get started."

Finally, Micah smiled. "I will be happy to do that."

David put on latex gloves and sat down at Micah's computer. He winked at me. He would download everything from Micah's hard drive too.

Micah ushered me into the hallway to begin my tour.

50

Forty minutes later, David and I were back in my mommy van heading for home. Another Hogan team was on its way to Micah's lab.

"That was pretty slick how you accessed Micah's office computer without him realizing what you were really doing."

"I downloaded everything from his hard drive," David said. "Is it okay if I share this with your friend Linda?"

"That's a great idea," I said. "Why don't we drop by her place? You can meet her and talk about it."

"I hate to drop in unannounced."

"Unannounced visits are what the Irregulars are all about, but I'll text her and tell her we're coming."

While I contacted Linda, David scanned his emails on his phone.

When he was done, he looked over at me. "What did you make of the lab? I never got to see all of it."

"It's a big operation. There are lots of lab employees."

"How many?"

"At least fifty."

"And no security. Amazing."

I parked in Linda's driveway. Her home is about the size of ours, but that's where the similarities end. The interior is professionally decorated — paid for by her parents, who are in the Big Leagues of the rich people in Chicago.

This was the reason the Irregulars always entered her home through the lower-level door. Linda doesn't like little kids running crazy in her fabulously decorated upper levels. As a playgroup, then, we were relegated to the first level, which actually wasn't bad. Her parents had purchased every conceivable toy for their only grandchild.

And Howard, Linda's husband? A lawyer and a great guy, who is the beneficiary of Mr. and Mrs. Shrier's largesse. And he's smart enough not to let it bother his ego.

We walked into Linda's computer room. Her nanny was upstairs playing with Sandra. I always shiver when I go from the outside heat into this frigid room, which is never more than sixty-two degrees.

As always, the air smelled artificial, and there was the ever-present low hum from the servers. Three computer screens sat on her desk. On the far wall were six more wall-mounted units.

I introduced David to Linda.

"David, the first time I came in here I felt like I was on the flight deck of the Starship *Enterprise*," I said.

"It's a great setup," David said.

Wonder if the one you have at home is better?

Obviously, Linda was curious about the same thing. "What kind of equipment do you have?" she asked.

For the next ten minutes, I listened to them compare their computers. What can I say? It was boring, but they're computer nerds, and it's what they're passionate about.

But, kids, enough is enough.

I clapped my hands. "Okay, let's get on with this," I said.

David straightened up. "Sorry about that." He handed the flash drive to Linda. "This is what I downloaded from Micah's hard drive."

Linda plugged it into the computer.

"Tina said you have the download from Micah's home computer, and there was an encrypted section in it," he said.

"I still haven't been able to crack it," she said. "My thought was that he might have the same material on his office computer, but it might not be encrypted there."

"I agree. It would be cumbersome to work with encrypted files on a daily basis."

She pushed a flash drive across the table to him. "This is everything from Micah's computer."

"I'll download it as soon as I get home." He snapped his fingers. "Could you burn a copy of that flash drive from Micah's office computer for me?"

"I'll do it straightaway," she said.

I quietly departed.

They won't miss me.

But we were on our way to understanding exactly what was going on with Micah and the President of the United States.

51

Tuesday morning, after David and I completed our six-mile run, he went home to work on his computer. I cleaned up the kitchen while Kerry took her morning nap.

There was a knock on our front door. When I opened it, Detective Tony Infantino was standing on our front porch. "Your husband gone?"

"Carter left about an hour ago," I said.

"Where's the kid?"

"You're safe. She's sleeping."

The inherent messiness of little kids freaks Tony out. Raising them would interfere with his testosterone-filled life of working out, catching bad guys, and having sex, not necessarily in that order.

"Good 'cause we gotta talk."

I stepped back. He walked into the kitchen. The scent of Bleu by Chanel drifted over me. He sat down at the table in the breakfast nook. While I made coffee, he munched on a glazed donut from Dinkel's.

Once his black coffee was poured, I joined him with a donut and a cup of herbal tea.

"Rumor going around about you screwin' up the arrest of a perp during the abortion clinic bombing in D.C.," he said.

"Did the FBI tell you that?"

"Yeah, and sweets, they don't like you very much. They don't want you anywhere near these recent bombings."

"I get that, but why is a Chicago PD homicide detective working cases in Hinsdale and Deerfield?"

"Not directly involved with those two. Caught the one last night because it's on our turf."

Last night!

"What happened?"

"This time your bomber guy popped an abortion doctor."

"Popped?"

"You know, shot — like in the head. Doc was dead before he hit the street."

What!?

"Why are you so sure it's my bomber?"

"Like Deerfield, perp called the doc's direct line saying his girlfriend was bleeding after having some kinda abortion surgery. Doc got outta his car at the clinic. Shooter nailed him. It's a homicide. Gotta get on this and need your help."

"Give me fifteen minutes."

"Give me another cup of coffee and two more donuts."

"Done."

52

Liv Sanchez came over to babysit Kerry. I rode with Tony in his BMW to the women's clinic in Lincoln Park. It was located near the corner of West Roslyn and North Clark Street.

Antique brick apartment buildings lined both sides of the street. Businesses and restaurants occupied the first floors of most of the buildings. A yellow crime scene tape surrounded a silver ML 550 Mercedes SUV. We walked toward the vehicle, but Tony stopped me at the tape.

"Can't let you any closer," he said. "Active crime scene. Authorized personnel only."

"Got it. I'm close enough to see what happened."

The driver's side door stood open. Dried blood, bone fragments, and human tissue were smeared on the roof, window, and doorframe. There were irregular blood spatters on the street beneath the door and on the front seat and steering wheel.

The faint odor of tarnished copper still drifted up from the dried blood. The smell clashed with the aroma of BBQ and pizza cooking in the neighborhood's restaurants.

About thirty yards further down and across the street was more crime scene tape. It blocked the front entrance to an apartment building with green shutters on the first-floor windows.

I nudged Tony. "What's going on over there?"

"Our guys think that's where the shot came from." He pointed at the Mercedes. "The vic, Dr. Rod Kestel, parks here and gets out of his SUV. Before he can close the door, his cell phone rings. He answers, giving the shooter time to line up the shot. *Bang*, one to the doc's head."

"Why was the shooter so far away?"

"Thinkin' he needed the practice sighting in his rifle."

"Practicing to shoot someone?" I asked. "I've never heard of that before."

"You don't know much about sniper rifles, do you?"

"No, I've never fired one."

"Sniper has to take into account the distance, the elevation, the wind direction, temperature, and humidity and then adjust his scope before he pulls the trigger. Hard to do all that on a flat shooting range in controlled conditions. Needed to work with the rifle and scope in the field, so to speak."

"So he can shoot other doctors?"

"You said it, not me, sweets."

"But my bomber doesn't use a gun."

"Yeah, about that. Was also a C4 bomb in the men's bathroom. Had a remote control detonator."

"If he planned to shoot the doctor, why bother with that?"

"Shooter gives himself two options. If the doc parks so the shooter doesn't have a clear shot, he waits for the doc to enter the building and then blows him up."

"But why didn't he detonate the device as long as he was here? That's his M.O."

"Bomb guys think he tried to, but he made a mistake. Men's bathroom is located next to the room where the x-ray machine is. Room is lead-lined. Bomb was placed in a trash can next to the lead-lined wall. They think he didn't count on that and had the wrong type of remote control to deal with the shielding effect of the lead."

"Bet he won't make that mistake again."

"Agree. CSI guys also think he used a special-made sniper rifle."

"I'm not following."

He motioned for me to follow him to the other side of the SUV. We still stood outside of the crime scene tape. Sitting on the ground about ten feet from the car was a white card with a yellow "1" on it.

"Bullet hit the doc in the head and blew through his skull. Our guys found the slug right here." He pointed at the card. "Bullet looks handmade. Fired by a homemade rifle."

"Homemade?"

"Preliminary report on the rifling of the bullet suggested it. Doesn't match any guns they have in the database."

"Why would he use something like that?"

"Hard telling because sniper rifles are easy to buy."

"Sounds like he's had special training."

"Your guy knows a lot about C4 bombs and sniper rifles. SEALS, special forces, black ops guys have training like that."

"It's nice to know that our tax dollars are being so well spent to train killers."

53

We walked across the street to the apartment building. Several people were leaving through the front door. They took off paper booties and latex gloves and threw them in a trash can.

"Got anything, Steve?" Tony said to a well-fed man who came out last.

"Nope," Steve said. "The suspect has to be a pro. I haven't seen a crime scene this clean for a long time, but he did leave one item."

He handed Tony a sealed clear plastic evidence bag containing a cell phone. "A burner phone. Only two numbers have been called. The second one is to the victim's phone."

"And the first?" Tony asked.

"To the doc who got blown up in Deerfield. Your suspect wanted someone to know who did this."

My stomach felt queasy.

I know who that someone is.

The CSI team departed.

"Can I get in there?" I asked.

"Fresh case. Don't want to contaminate the scene and piss off the D.A., but I'll tell you what's in there."

He took out his small spiral notebook.

"Apartment 3E. One-bedroom unit with an efficiency kitchen," he began. "Room spotless. Smelled like recent use of cleaning products. Brown couch and dark green chair in living room. A table and kitchen chair in dinette. Other kitchen chair positioned in front of an open window which faced the street."

I pictured the scene as he spoke.

"Smelled gunpowder next to the window. Best guess is shooter sat on the chair waiting for the doc. SUV pulls up. Doc gets out. Shooter calls him on the cell. Doc stops moving and answers. Shooter fires."

"Who rented the room?" I asked.

He flipped a page in his notebook. "Rented a couple of days ago through an Internet broker. Credit card used was stolen."

"Did the neighbors see anything?"

He flipped two more pages in his book. "Talked to everyone in the building. Shooter is either tall and skinny or short and fat, with blond — or no — hair, and he's Caucasian or Hispanic."

"Narrows it down."

"Like always, but we'll interview them all at least once more. Maybe someone'll remember something we can use."

"Until then?"

"FBI says you gotta mole feeding you inside info on these bombings."

"I might have one."

"Need him."

"Or her."

"Whatever."

54

Tony drove me home from the scene of the shooting. I'd noticed security cameras attached to the clinic building, but he hadn't mentioned them.

"Is there anything you forgot to tell me about the shooting?" I asked.

Tony glanced at me out of the corner of his eye. "Don't think so."

"What about the security videos?"

"You didn't give me everything you knew about what went down at O'Hare."

He was right. I'd held back some important facts about that story, but he had done the same thing to me then, and now he was doing it again.

"Okay, I admit I did, but if I'm going to be of any value on this investigation, I have to know everything."

He hesitated.

"Need to know, right?" I asked.

"You got it, sweets."

"Well, I need to know."

"Security video shows the doc driving up and getting out of his SUV. Stands up and then answers his phone. Waits with the phone to his ear. Gets shot in the head. Bada bing, bada boom.

Neighbors must've heard the shot because someone calls 911. Next thing the video shows are the cops arriving on the scene."

I knew Tony and something wasn't right.

"But there's more."

"Not there."

"Where?"

"Here."

I stared at him.

"Wasn't gonna say anything, but a car has been following us since we left the crime scene at the apartment building," he continued.

His face was expressionless. He was telling me the truth. The surge of adrenaline that rushed through my system made my head begin to pound.

"Please tell me you're kidding," I said.

"Would love to but can't. Bomber guy of yours is not the usual nutcase we deal with. He's a pro and left the cell phone in the room to prove it. Means he's toying with us. Could be watching to see what we're gonna do next."

"But is that even realistic?"

"Realistic?"

"How often do criminals follow cops? It doesn't seem likely."

"You're right. Wouldn't make sense for him to follow me."

I thought about that statement a few seconds. "You think he's tailing me?"

"Pretty obvious he knows you're part of this. According to what the FBI told me, he saw you five years ago, so he knows what you look like. Could be he's following you to get a feel for what you're up to, maybe to have an idea about what you know and, through you, what we know too."

Or is it Jamie?

55

"Maybe it's not my bomber in that car," I said.

"You think it's Jamie instead?" Tony asked.

"It could be."

"What's he got to do with the bomber?"

"Nothing."

He shrugged his shoulders. "I missing somethin' here?"

"I didn't tell you, but after Jamie tried to blow me up, I went back into his burning apartment and grabbed a blob of C4 residue off the wall. I'm afraid he saw me do it."

"If he did, you gotta problem 'cause it'll match the C4 used by his buddies, and he knows we can nail him with that."

"What about the chain of evidence problem?"

"Gotta' work on it. There are ways around evidence problems."

Something's not right here.

"I really appreciate you doing this, but why risk getting in trouble?"

"Dude pisses me off because I coulda' been in there too. Asshole coulda' blown me up!"

There it is. It's always about him.

"When you drop me at home, I'll give you some of the C4 residue from Jamie's," I said.

"Done."

He kept looking in his rearview mirror as he drove.

"Car following us has a sticker that looks like it might be a rental, but can't make the front license plate. Mud or somethin' on it."

I twisted around in my seat. "Which car is it?"

"Black Ford compact three cars behind us."

I continued to stare out the back window. "Prove it to me."

"Thought you might say that."

Abruptly, he turned right at the next corner and stepped on the gas. My chest and shoulder tugged against the seatbelt. He went two blocks and turned left. The black Ford followed. I saw that a female drove the car. She had long blond hair and big sunglasses, which covered the upper part of her face.

He made another left turn, but the Ford continued on. The driver stared straight ahead, seemingly ignoring us.

"Looks to me like your bomber has a helper," he said.

She also looked like the woman I saw drive away from the fire at Jamie's apartment, but that woman drove a white Prius.

"Did you see a female sitting in a white Prius at Jamie's apartment building before you left?" I asked.

He double-parked in front of my house and took out his spiral notebook. He thumbed through a few pages. "White Prius, blond, sunglasses, couldn't see her body."

"Plates?"

"Dirty, just like that Ford's. Couldn't make them."

"Your thoughts?"

"Maybe the bomber likes to dress in drag."

"Not funny."

He snapped his fingers. "Got it. It's Jamie."

"You think he dresses in women's clothes?"

"You asked me what I thought. That's my answer."

I ran inside and retrieved part of the C4 residue from Jamie's to give to Tony. With his help, we might have a way to stop the man who wanted to kill all of us.

56

Wednesday afternoon, Linda texted me. She wanted to meet and discuss what she and David had found out from the download from Micah's office computer. It was raining again, so we decided to meet at Dinkel's.

I texted Cas and Molly. Linda texted David.

A fresh donut would brighten everyone's day in this miserable weather.

Dinkel's Bakery is located on North Lincoln, about two blocks from our home. It opened in 1922, and according to the elderly locals who frequent it, the taste of the yummy baked goods hasn't changed much over the years.

I'm in love with the contents of the glass cases in the main room. They're filled with all types of fresh baked goods, including chocolate and vanilla cupcakes slathered with multiple flavors of frosting and multiple varieties of their famous donuts.

The new addition is a full bay-sized eating area off to the right side, accessed through a doorway next to one of the glass pastry cases. This room has become a meeting place for the Irregulars when, like today, the weather turns sour and we don't want to stay in our homes.

Everyone was there, including the kids. Linda did the honors of introducing David to the rest of the Irregulars. Since none of them had met Margaret, David took care of that introduction.

David seemed to have picked up on how he'd previously overdressed his daughter. This time she looked like a normal kid wearing red shorts, a white T-shirt, and sandals.

Margaret gravitated to Molly's two older sons, and they began playing a game on her computer.

I took Kerry out of her stroller, and we sat down. She sat on my lap, and we shared a glazed donut.

"David, if you don't mind, let me give our report on what we learned from Micah's office computer," Linda said.

"Go right ahead," David said.

"To prove what we discovered, we had to hack into several federal computers," she began. "But we found the major source of Micah's funding."

We waited.

"As we suspected, the President of the United States is behind it."

The only noise in the room came from our kids jabbering and playing.

"There were only two patients in Micah's MS treatment trial: Hannah and one of the president's daughters," Linda continued. "He illegally provided almost all of the funding to save his daughter and, secondarily, Hannah."

"I guess the Big Guy doesn't mind breaking the law to save his kid," Molly said.

I thought of the recent events at my home and O'Hare where I confronted that same issue. I agreed with the president. I would do anything to save my daughter too.

"How did you figure it out?" Cas asked.

"Using the information from Micah's lab computer, David broke the encryption code Tina and I had previously downloaded from Micah's home computer," Linda said.

"Once I had that, I was able to uncover the real reason Micah didn't elaborate the details on his financing to Tina and me," David said.

"You're certain that all of Micah's funding has been obtained from the president?" I asked.

"Yes, except for Hannah's original money from her trust," Linda responded.

"The president isn't stupid," David added. "He knew he would have to break the law to shift the funds to Micah's lab, so he used Sherman Krevolin to do it for him."

"And since Krevolin is one of his biggest supporters, no one would ever question the real source of the funds," Linda said.

"This brings us back to Jamie," David said. "Hannah and her kids at home, and Micah and his lab, are now being covered by around-the-clock security teams."

"Jamie can't get to them?" Cas asked.

"He can still try," David said. "But he'll really have to work at it to get close to them."

57

"On September 11th, the president is coming to Chicago to announce his full support for embryonic stem cell research," I said.

"Then why would Jamie even bother going after Micah?" Molly asked. "Once the Big Guy announces his full support of what Micah is doing, the news'll be out, and no one will care about all this funding business."

"But a motivated reporter could eventually uncover the same financial information Linda and I did," David said.

"One reason reporters might not do it right away is because they'll be covering why the president is unexpectedly supporting embryonic stem cell research when he's always been against it," I said.

"Plus, there's the possibility that Micah has discovered the cure for MS, and he'll probably win the Nobel Prize for medicine," Cas said. "Those will be the stories of the year, but everyone will miss the most important one."

"Which is?" Molly asked.

"Micah is illegally cloning embryos and then killing them to harvest their stem cells," Cas said. "In my opinion, he's performing abortions in his lab."

"David and I suggested this to him, and that was one of the reasons he let David help place security in his lab," I said.

I munched on a second donut and put a coloring book in front of Kerry. I considered what we had just discussed.

"Guys, I have to tell you that, as an investigative reporter, I lived for stories like Micah and his illegal financing," I continued. "What if one of my former colleagues wonders why one of the president's daughters is suddenly better? I would chase that down, and if you two could discover this, a competent reporter could too."

"And to answer your question, Molly, that's one of the two reasons to worry about Jamie," Linda said.

"With a little nudge from someone in the president's party, Jamie might still make a run at silencing Micah to prevent that story from coming out before the president's September 11th speech covers it up," David said.

"Linda, you mentioned this is one of the reasons to worry about Jamie," Molly said. "What's the other one?"

"If Jamie can't get to Micah, he might settle on another target for what happened to his group at O'Hare,"

I felt like puking up my two donuts. "Me."

"Not just you, but all of the Hamlin Park Irregulars," David said. "He already tried to kill you, Tina. It's not much of a stretch to assume that he might try it again."

"And if we and our kids are around Tina and Kerry, we might be collateral damage," Linda said.

"What do we do?" Cas asked.

"No brainer, guys," Molly said. "Catch him."

58

"How would you suggest we accomplish that?" Linda asked. "We don't know where he lives now that he burned down his apartment."

"As a starter, we could show his picture around in the other exercise clubs in this area," Cas suggested. "It seems logical to me that he'll keep working out, and that's where we'll find him."

"Good suggestion, but we don't have a picture of him," I said.

"Wrongo," Molly said. "As you guys probably noticed, Jamie talked to me in the exercise classes all the time. He digs hanging with a hot chick while he works out."

"And how does this help us?" David asked.

"Start with the picture," Molly said. "He's really proud of his body. You know where I'm going with this?"

"Don't tell me he sent you some pictures," Cas said. "I can't stand it!"

"You don't have to look at them if you don't want to."

"Give me your phone," Cas demanded.

Molly opened it up and showed Cas what was on the screen.

"Oh, my God!" Cas yelped.

"Kind of what I thought too," Molly said. "The dude is really a stud."

"Let me see," I said.

Cas handed me Molly's phone. There were multiple pictures of Jamie. In most of them, he had some clothes on. In several, he did not. "I have to agree that he's a stud, but hung might be a better word."

I handed the phone to Linda. She didn't blink as she stared at the screen.

"Is she still breathing?" Molly said to Cas.

"I'm not sure, but if she isn't, I understand why."

All David did was blush. "Ladies, I don't understand how this is going to help us."

"I have to agree with you, David," I said. "Jamie might try to kill all of us. We need to do something right now."

"Okay then, here's our plan," Molly said. "First, as Cas said, he's gonna keep working out, so we check all the fitness places in this area."

"I'll do that," Cas said.

"And what about all those women you say he likes?" David asked.

"I'll handle that," Molly said. "I know which websites he's always on."

"One small question," Linda said. "What do we do when we find him?"

"I've got an idea about that," Molly said. "Let me handle it."

59

It was late Thursday night, and Carter was upstairs putting Kerry to bed. I went down to the laundry room to run a load of laundry. As I turned the knob to start the cycle, my computer dinged.

I ran into the office. On the screen was a message from my mole:

I lost track of him after Arlington.

I assumed he might have died as a result of the injuries he suffered from either the explosion or the gunshot wound after you shot him.

Or both.

Are you sure it's him?

I replied:

In Hinsdale, Deerfield, and a new attack on the North Side of Chicago, the C4 bomb was hidden in the men's bathroom, as it was in Arlington. I think he may be using this technique to alert the authorities and the national press that he is back, but he has added to it. In the Deerfield attack, he lured a doctor to the building before he detonated the bomb. The doctor was killed in the blast.

On the North Side, he shot and killed a doctor with a sniper rifle. A bomb had also been placed in the bathroom there, but the bomb squad thought it couldn't be remotely detonated because the lead shielding in the adjacent room blocked the signal.

The response was immediate:

Clearly, he is back and seems to be accelerating his attacks.

I will do anything to stop this monster.

I will begin an active search to find and stop him before he strikes again.

If I cannot, I will at least try and discover his next target for you.

I ran upstairs. Carter rocked Kerry in her room. "Houston, we have lift off. My mole just contacted me."

"Outstanding," he said.

I took in a deep breath. "Have you selected a reporter to help me?"

"I did. It's Brittany Simon. I recently moved her from the police desk to be a feature reporter."

"Is she a rookie?"

"She is relatively new, but she's tenacious and works extremely hard."

"Like I did when I first started."

You just described me as a cub reporter, my dear.

He didn't say anything.

"Do you expect me to be her mentor?"

"That would certainly help."

"Is she cute?" I continued.

"I never noticed."

Which means she is.

"I told you I would do this story your way, and I will. Give me her text and I'll set up a meeting as soon as I can."

I went back to the office and called Tony. "I need something from you."

He waited.

"Carter picked a young reporter to work with me on the bomber story. If you want me to continue to help you, she's going to be part of the package."

"Looker?"

"I haven't met her yet, but Carter didn't deny that she was cute."

"He picked you, so he's got great taste. I'm in."

"Is that simply a compliment, or are you hitting on me again?"

"For you to figure out, sweets."

He'll never change.

60

On Friday afternoon, I sat in Dinkel's dining room. Kerry was at Cas's. Brittany Simon, the reporter Carter had assigned to the clinic bombing story, was next to me with her *Tribune* work laptop on the table in front of her. Carter had one exactly like it.

Brittany has long, straight blond-streaked hair, way too cute dimples, flawless tanned skin, and an athlete's body. Her short white skirt prominently displayed her muscular legs.

Tony sat next to her. His testosterone level had risen so high it was bubbling out of his ears. I had shown him the copy of the email I had received from the mole confirming a commitment to help us.

So far, Tony hadn't said anything. Since most of his brain cells were located south of his belt, he was clearly not concentrating on police business.

He wore a beige linen suit, a patterned, green silk shirt with matching tie, and tasseled light brown loafers with no socks.

"New threads?" I asked him.

He nodded. "Got this on sale at Ralph Lauren. Purple label. Forty percent off. Couldn't pass it up."

"Did they tailor it for you?"

"No way, sweets. My guy always fixes my clothes."

I didn't mention his gun, and when he didn't ask me why, I knew he wasn't interested in anything but Brittany's legs.

"Tony," I said.

"Huh?"

I pointed at the email. "What do you think?"

"Amazing."

The mole, you dope! Not Brittany.

"Tony, focus," I said. "We need to get to work on this."

"Okay, what I need from you," Tony said, as he tossed the printout of the email on the table, "is something concrete I can take to the captain to convince him this mole of yours is the real deal. This crap coulda come from anyone."

"If the FBI lab discovers that the C4 residue from Hinsdale, Deerfield, and the North Side bombing match, that should be enough to convince your boss to take this seriously," Brittany said.

She's all over this story.

I wondered how long she'd been working on it.

Tony didn't respond. The blank look on his face proved he was not fully invested in this.

"How about asking them to compare the C4 residue from Arlington with the three Chicago area bombings?" I asked. "That should be more than enough."

"Yeah, okay." He took out his small, spiral cop notebook and wrote it down. "Don't expect the FBI lab guys to bust their humps to get the results to us any time soon."

The FBI lab is notorious for taking a long time sending results to local law enforcement agencies.

I knew a way to speed up the process. "Tell them this might involve Dr. Micah Mittelman."

"You mentioned him in the O'Hare story," Brittany said. "But I haven't seen his name associated with the bombings."

"Good pickup," I said. "There's a new element to this story."

61

I told Brittany and Tony about Micah and the therapeutic cloning in his lab. Brittany recorded what I said on her cell phone.

Tony took out his cell phone and logged on to his Facebook account while I talked. I should have been pissed, but I wasn't. Science wasn't in his wheelhouse, and I didn't want to take the time to explain SCNT to him.

I finished.

Brittany immediately understood.

Tony did not.

She tapped her finger on her laptop. "Tina, what do you think the abortion clinic bomber's been doing the past five years?"

"I've wondered the same thing," I said. "I shot him as he detonated the bomb, so he was obviously injured in the Arlington explosion. The FBI assumed that either the bullets or the blast, or both, might have put him out of commission."

"And your mole wrote you the same thing."

"Yep."

"But it didn't happen."

"Obviously. But it takes money to live, so where has he been getting it?" I asked.

"Robbing banks would be the perfect way to stay financially solvent," she said.

"Don't think so," Tony said. "Dude is keeping his head down working at a nondescript job."

"Maybe he has some anti-abortion supporters with money providing funds to him," she said.

"I'll research it," I said, adding that to the notes I was making to transfer to my computer file.

"Tony, in case you're wrong, why not have the FBI compare this C4 with any other bombings in the U.S. for the past five years?" she asked. "This might give us some clues as to where he's been and what he's been doing before he arrived in this area."

He wrote it down in his little book, but he didn't seem too happy about it.

Brittany observed this. She leaned over and put her fingertips lightly on his upper arm. It looked like she had a fresh manicure. My short nails could use one, but being a mommy, I didn't have time — and it wouldn't last anyway.

"It would help a lot if you would do this for me," she said.

He glanced down at her hand. "Okay, I'll handle it. You both stay out of my way. That way, the boss won't complain."

"No way," I said. "If we're going to help you, we want an exclusive on everything you have."

"Ain't happenin'." He put his notebook in the inside jacket pocket of his suit coat.

"Maybe we can have a drink somewhere tonight and discuss this further," she said to him.

"Was thinking the same thing," he said.

My cell phone pinged.

It was a text from Molly: *Found Jamie. Need you and Tony.*

I texted Molly back: *OMG! You found Jamie? Where?*

Molly: *His new place.*

Me: *Tony with me. Where R U?*

Molly: *With Jamie.*

Me: *Address?*

Molly texted it to me.

62

I'd walked to Dinkel's, so I rode shotgun with Tony in his detective car, a brown Ford Crown Vic. It took us fifteen minutes to speed to Jamie's new apartment. It was located in Wrigleyville.

At the front door, Tony checked his gun to make sure he had a bullet in the chamber. I took mine out of my backpack and did too. He noticed but didn't say anything. The front door of the building was locked.

I texted Molly.

Me: *Here. Which apartment?*

Molly: *401. Buzzing front door 4 u.*

The buzzer sounded. We opened the door and rushed into the hallway.

Tony punched the elevator button. I couldn't wait. I shouldered my backpack and ran up the stairs.

"What the...?!" he yelled at my back, as I opened the stairway door and began my sprint up the stairs.

The elevator dinged on the first floor as I reached the second floor. I continued to sprint to the fourth floor.

When I reached it, I took out my gun. The elevator door slid open and Tony stepped out. He took out his gun and looked at me. I shrugged my shoulders.

We walked quietly to 401. I held my Glock in both hands. Tony raised his arm, preparing to knock, but before he could, the door flew open.

"Hi guys," Molly said.

Tony's mouth fell open. Mine did too.

"Molly?" I gasped.

"I know, right? Sorry about the way I'm dressed, but these are some of the clothes the farmers bought for me when I worked for them."

"Farmers had a skimpy budget," Tony observed.

He was right. Think black silk push-up bra, matching thong, black fishnet hose, and six-inch-heeled, knee-high black boots. Oh, and thick eye makeup, fake eyelashes, and a heavy dose of expensive perfume. Her blond hair was covered by a black wig.

"Where is he?" I asked.

"Where else?" She jerked her thumb toward a closed door. "The bedroom."

Tony stepped toward the door with his gun in front of him.

"No need for that," she said. "He's tied up."

Jamie was so muscular it was hard to picture her restraining him without a fight.

"He wanted me to," she continued.

Tony looked over his shoulder at her when she said that. "Oh, baby," he whispered to himself.

He moved toward the bedroom. I followed.

"Ah, Tony, you might want to wait out here for a minute or two," Molly said. "I need to talk to Tina in there first."

63

We walked into the bedroom. Jamie was on the bed, spread-eagle on his back. Each of his wrists was handcuffed to a bed post. Each ankle was cuffed to the foot of the bed. He had a ball-like gag in his mouth. A white sheet covered his body.

I noticed a short black whip on a chair close to the bed. The plug from an orange extension cord dangled out from under the sheet.

The aroma of incense burning on a table by the bed irritated my nose. Enya sang from a matched set of Bose speakers on each side of the bed.

Jamie began squirming when he saw us come in. Molly picked up another extension cord that was stuck in a wall outlet. She held the far end of the cord in one hand and picked up the opposite end — from the bed — in her other. She brought them close together.

"Now, Jamie, remember I told you to settle down or there will be consequences," Molly said, as she acted like she was going to plug the two cords together. She spoke with a distinct southern accent.

That's new.

Jamie's eyebrows shot up, and he stopped moving.

I put my gun in my backpack.

"How did you find him?" I asked.

"Yesterday, I went on one of his favorite porn websites. We connected, and today, I came over."

She continued to speak with the southern belle accent.

I whispered in her ear so Jamie couldn't hear me. "How did he not know it was you? He sat next to you each time you were in spinning class together."

She whispered back to me. "Yeah, about that. No guy really looks at my face for obvious," she glanced down toward her massive boobs, "reasons. In fact, none of them even know what color my eyes are."

Count me in that group. I stared into her eyes. They were brown.

She noticed. "They're actually blue." She continued to whisper. "I'm wearing brown contacts. And with the black wig and heavy face and eye makeup, there was no way he knew it was me." She turned to Jamie and spoke up with her southern belle accent. "Right, sweetie?"

He strained against the cuffs. She brought the cords close together. He stopped moving.

"But anyway, I know what guys like, so I suggested we play a couple of games," she continued with her accent.

"That's how you were able to handcuff him?" I asked.

"That and do a couple of other things."

Not sure I want to know what those are.

"You didn't...?" I asked.

"The big ugly?" she responded.

"Well, yeah."

"Never came up. He was so excited about what I told him I was going to do to him that he never got around to going for it."

"What's with the extension cords?"

"Insurance," she said. "At first, he was super excited about what I was going to do. But then he got a little out of control, so I changed the game around a little."

She jiggled the ends of the cord. Jamie's eyes widened.

"You settled right on down, didn't you, big boy?"

I wasn't sure exactly what she'd done, but it worked. Jamie didn't move a muscle.

"When I did this for the farmers, we used to record what the bad guy confessed to us after I had them controlled."

"Great idea," I said.

"Yeah, but Linda always brings up this legal crap, and she says whatever we do is illegal. What do we do about that?"

She was right. How could we get Jamie to confess to anything with him handcuffed to a bed and some kind of "insurance" device attached to him under the sheets?

64

"I did think of one solution," Molly continued. "That's why I wanted to talk to you without Tony hearing it, just in case it's illegal too."

"Tell me," I said.

"Jamie and I talked about why the FBI let him go at O'Hare. At first, he fibbed about it, but," she twirled the cords in her hands, "he realized that was a mistake, and he told me the truth."

"Which was just as you suggested: he was going to do wet work for the feds."

"You got it, and that might be the solution to our problem. He's afraid that if he's busted by the Chicago cops, the feds might think he'll roll over on them about what they hired him to do."

"Hired?"

"Jamie doesn't work for free."

I turned to him. "That right?"

He nodded.

"Let me get this straight," I said to him. "If Tony arrests you, you'll try to beat the rap with the cops by confessing that the feds hired you to kill Micah."

He nodded.

"And if the cops release you, the feds will hunt you down to keep you from testifying against them and confessing to the plot to kill Micah."

He nodded again.

"Looks to me like you'll be safer in jail. At least you'll be alive."

He stared at me and then slowly nodded.

"Before we call Tony in, we might want to take off his handcuffs and remove the other stuff," Molly said. "We don't want it to look like we forced him to confess."

I took out my Glock from my backpack and pointed it at Jamie. Molly reached under the sheets and tugged on something. Jamie squirmed and then relaxed. Molly unlocked the cuffs.

Jamie sat up and pulled out his mouth gag. He stared at me. "Do I know you?"

"You should. You tried to blow me up."

He turned to Molly. "Then who the fuck are you?"

Molly pulled off her black wig and shook out her blond hair. His eyes widened as he watched her.

"Like Tina just said, you should know me too." Her accent was gone.

"But…" he stammered.

Molly tossed his clothes to him. "Get dressed, darlin'."

He stood up and did as he was told.

I opened the door and beckoned for Tony to join us in the room. I told him Jamie wanted to confess to burning down his apartment building.

"Not trying to blow you up too?" Tony asked.

"I don't want to testify in his trial and be associated with him in any way."

"Hubby might not like that?" Tony asked.

"Something like that," I said.

"You good with this?" Tony asked Jamie.

"Yeah," Jamie grumbled.

I pushed the record button on my phone. Tony recited his name, badge number, time, and date. He then read Jamie his rights.

"Do you understand your rights?" Tony asked.

"Yeah, I do," Jamie said.

"Do you want a lawyer?" Tony asked.

"No."

We had one crime we could pin on him: arson. Tony asked him about it. Jamie told him details only he would know about how he burned down the building.

We had him.

I stopped the recording. Tony cuffed Jamie and led him into the main room.

"Liv is babysitting. She needs to leave in an hour, so I have to change and get home," Molly said.

I stepped into the living room. Molly closed the bedroom door. Eight minutes later, she walked out with a large Louis Vuitton tote slung over her shoulder. She wore white sweat pants, a red tank top, and flip-flops. She had removed her makeup, eyelashes, and brown contacts. Her blond hair was now in a ponytail.

Jamie lunged at Molly and me. "Fuck both of you!"

Tony grabbed his arm and shoved him toward the door. "Button it, slick."

I remembered that line from fourteen years ago when he helped arrest Dr. Mick Doyle, the "Fat Doctor."

I wondered how many times he'd used it during that interval.

"Send me the video," Tony said.

"I will. Do you think you can make this stick?"

Tony prodded Jamie in the back. "Any comment on that?"

"I'm guilty. I want a speedy trial, and I want to go to jail."

"Wish catching bad guys was always this easy," Tony said.

Tony pushed Jamie through the door and left.

"What can I say, Molly?" I asked. "You saved my life, maybe all of our lives." I gave her a hug.

"The only way we could protect ourselves and our kids was to get him arrested," she said. "I know how men think, so I did what I do best. It was actually pretty easy."

"You got that right."

We walked into the hallway.

"Can you give me a ride home?" I asked. "Tony brought me here."

"Sure."

Do I want to know what was going on under the sheet?

We stepped onto the elevator. "There is one thing," I began.

Molly blushed as she anticipated my question. "It's probably best you don't ask."

"It was that bad?"

"Let's just say, it's really effective. I've never seen it fail."

"But…"

"All I can tell you is that I'll need a new curling iron."

She was right.

That was all I needed to know.

Part 3

65

We had a fun family Saturday at the shore on Lake Michigan and a quiet Sunday at home. On Monday, there was a thunderstorm in the area, so that afternoon, we nixed Hamlin Park and, instead, sat in the main level of Cas's family room.

Her home has the same three-story above-the-ground style as ours, but there is one distinct difference: the décor is basic. Her husband, Joe, wasn't into expensive decorating.

All the kids, including Margaret, played in the same room with the moms and David while we discussed Jamie. David brought treats for all of us: a shrimp and hearts of palm salad with homemade dressing for the adults and mini-cheese Frenchie's and hamburger sliders for the kids.

After I finished the saga about Jamie, we thanked Molly for her role in ensuring our safety. With Jamie headed to prison, I now had the other potential danger to deal with. If I was going to be able to finally focus exclusively on the bomber story, I would need the Irregulars help.

It was time to tell them about my mole.

I did and included Brittany's upcoming role in the discussion. "I'm still concerned the bomber may be here to get even with me, but I'm really worried his next target will be Micah's lab, their home, or both," I said.

"Why?" Cas asked.

"Because of the abortion-issue conflicts with his embryonic stem cell lab techniques," I said.

"Exactly what I've been arguing about all along," Cas said. "He's doing abortions when he harvests the embryonic stem cells."

"What do we do next?" Molly asked.

"That's why we're here," Linda said. "I'm on — to use Tina's baseball term — the disabled list until I have the baby, but at least I might be able to contribute something mentally."

"Are you having more problems?" I asked.

"Other than my blood pressure going up and spilling proteins in my urine, I'm in perfect shape."

"Preeclampsia?" Cas asked.

"That and I'm having some strong contractions."

"Don't be surprised if your doctor puts you on bed rest," Cas said.

"He actually threatened to put me in the hospital."

"Wow, I had no idea you were having so many problems," Molly said. "Anything we can do to help you with Sandra?"

"Luckily, my nanny can stay with us full time until this mess is over."

David walked into the room after cleaning up in the kitchen. "I've been in Micah's lab and their home a couple of times. With the amount of security at each site it seems highly unlikely that the bomber will be able to do anything to Micah or his family."

"Then why are you worried, Tina?" Molly asked.

"I still feel like someone is following me."

"Do you think it's the bomber guy?" Molly asked.

"I do. Tony thought he saw a blond woman in a car behind us when he drove me home from the crime scene at the abortion clinic where the doctor was shot and killed."

"And we both saw a woman drive away from Jamie's apartment building after it was blown up," Cas said.

"When did this feeling begin?" Linda asked.

"Right after I wrote the 'industrial spy' story."

"But could it have been the bomber?" David asked.

"If it is, we have to do something," Cas said. "If the bomber and these helpers are following Tina, Micah, and Hannah, they could be following us too."

66

"What do we do?" I asked.

"It's easy," Molly said.

We turned to her.

"It is?" David asked.

"Sure, we do what the farmers taught me."

"It's not about what you did with Jamie, is it?" I asked.

"Oh, no, this is way different."

We waited.

"We follow the followers."

"I don't get it," Cas said.

"I don't either," I added.

"It's one of the techniques my company used too," David said. "Tina doesn't know for sure if she's being stalked, but there's one way to find out. We take turns following her when she goes out. If anyone is shadowing her, we can take pictures of them so we'll know who they are."

"Okay, say we prove there are people tailing her, then what?" Cas asked.

"I never was a field operative," David said. "I guess we call the police."

"And they'll do what?" Linda asked. "Arrest them? What crime have they committed? Sorry, but this isn't going to work."

"Guys, it's pretty simple," Molly said. "I did work in the field with the farmers."

"What did you do?" I asked.

"We followed the bad guys to their base of operations."

She picked up her cell phone and began going through her emails.

"Molly, what did you do when you discovered their hideout?" David asked.

"Gosh, I don't know. The farmers took care of that."

67

Monday night, Linda's blood pressure skyrocketed and she was hospitalized. Tuesday morning, I walked into the MidAmerica Hospital on Chicago's Gold Coast. I paused to center myself before I walked into Linda's room. I didn't want to embarrass myself by having a PTSD attack brought on by the hospital smells.

"You feeling okay?" I asked.

"Pardon my language, but I FUCKING hate bedrest!" Linda bitched.

"But this room is unbelievable," I said, glancing around.

I felt like I was in a suite at Chicago's Peninsula Hotel. The walls were covered with muted light violet wallpaper. There was a sleek tan art deco couch and matching chairs. A large flat screen HD TV popped up out of a bird's-eye walnut chest.

Linda had been in the room less than one day, but already, there were flowers from family members. There was also a three-foot-tall arrangement that would have been suitable in the finest restaurants in Chicago.

I pointed at it. "Is that from Howard?"

"No, he's too cheap to spend money on flowers. It's from the hospital. They want me to feel like I'm at home."

"Only if you live in a funeral parlor."

"The flower arrangement is a little much."

"But somehow it goes with the room. Everything in here is a little excessive."

Cas and Molly walked in, followed by a male lab technician. His skin was white with a sprinkling of freckles. He was completely bald.

He wrapped a blue rubber tourniquet around Linda's right arm. We stepped away from her bed while he did his vampire thing.

She grimaced and rotated away from us when the man took the needle and syringe off his tray. Her hospital gown fell open in the back, and a multicolored tattoo of a disturbing prehistoric creature peeked out at us. I saw part of its head and one claw clutching a banner with small, hard-to-read letters.

She began to whimper as the lab tech jabbed her twice with the needle before he found a vein.

Linda with a head-banger tattoo? She obviously hated having her blood drawn. There was no way she would have her delicate skin repeatedly poked by some stranger.

But she had.

First, I watched as Molly used her dominatrix skills to capture Jamie, and now, I spot Linda with a large tattoo.

How much do I know about my friends?

When the tech had enough blood, he removed the needle and applied a Band-Aid to her arm.

"The results should be back in the morning," he said.

"Speed it up, buster," Linda said. "I'm already tired of this place."

I'm glad I'm not her doctor.

68

Cas and I stepped back up to Linda's bed. Molly wandered around Linda's room touching the fabric of the chairs and the wall coverings.

"Your room smells so amazing. The aroma reminds me of sandalwood. I even catch a hint of jasmine."

"Probably all these flowers," Linda said.

I noticed Cas staring through the window at the nurse's station.

A group of young doctors stood behind an older one. He appeared to be lecturing to them.

"An old friend?" I asked Cas.

"Hardly," she said. "That's the famous Dr. J. Randall Fertig. He doesn't have any friends."

"The breast cancer doctor?" Linda asked.

"And how would you know that and I don't, Linda?" I asked.

"Howard's mother is one of his patients. She thinks Fertig is the greatest thing since heated toilet seats."

"What's the big deal about him?" Molly asked.

"All of his breast cancer patients survive," Cas answered.

"Unless he's God, that's statistically impossible," I said.

"Trust me," Cas said. "All surgeons think they're God. Fertig knows he is."

I studied Fertig through the window of Linda's room.

"He's wearing a starched white scrub suit under his form-fitting long white coat," I said. "All the doctors with him have on wrinkled green scrubs and white coats that don't fit."

"Notice anything else?" Cas asked.

Fertig was short and slender. His totally black hair was shoulder length and scraggly. He wore cowboy boots and sunglasses.

"He's wearing cowboy boots," I said.

"Is it to make him look taller?" Linda asked.

Cas laughed. "You got it. He uses a step stool in the OR and won't allow a scrub nurse who is taller than he is to assist him."

"The sunglasses are Prada," Molly remarked.

"He wouldn't wear anything cheap, but that's something new."

"You said he thinks he's God," Linda said.

"Maybe he thinks he's Bono too," Molly added.

"If he had a beard, he'd be a Jesus look-alike but with sunglasses," I said.

"The last time I saw him, he had a scruffy beard."

"Maybe he got tired of the Jesus comparison and shaved it off," Molly suggested.

"He would never tire of a comment like that."

"I'm assuming you don't like him," Linda said.

"He's the most egocentric, misogynistic, pompous asshole I've ever met," Cas replied. "All the nurses hate him."

There might be a story here, but with the abortion clinic bomber and Micah, I already had more to do than I could handle.

But maybe in the future?

69

For the rest of the Irregulars, at least we had a plan. Each time I ventured out, I would call one of them, except Linda. They would follow me and see if there was someone tailing me. If someone was, we would figure out a way to track the watcher to his, or her, lair.

Tuesday afternoon, I was tired of waiting. I wanted to catch the bomber. I called Molly and asked her to babysit for Kerry. She was okay with it, so I took my daughter to her home.

My next call was to Cas. I was certain she was better prepared to protect me if anything happened. My destination was the scene of the latest abortion clinic doctor's shooting. It made sense to me that any hint I was working on the story would interest the bomber and encourage him, or his helpers, to follow me.

Cas was a block away when I saw her in my rearview mirror. I waited until I pulled out onto Belmont before I called her and put her on my van's Bluetooth.

"Can you hear me?" I asked.

"I can, and I can see you," she said.

Glancing into my rearview mirror, I saw her swing in one car behind me. "I think you're too close."

"I don't want to lose you."

"I understand, but if there's only one car between us, there won't be room for the bomber to follow me."

"Sorry, I've never done this before, and I don't want to make a mistake."

Cas's OCD tendency might ruin our plan.

This is going to take a little work.

"Relax," I said. "Take a deep breath."

Stoplights were now our enemy. Twice, I went through an intersection as the light changed and Cas got stuck at the red light. Each time, I slowed down enough for her to catch up, but now I was concerned that if a person were following me, he or she would realize something was fishy.

A more pressing problem was the angry people jammed up behind me who might kill me before the bomber did. Their blaring horns became so loud I had to turn up the radio.

"In two blocks I'm going to turn right," I said.

"Say again," she said. "There's a lot of honking, and I can't hear you."

"Right!" I yelled. "Turn right in two blocks!"

70

I parked my van in front of the closed abortion clinic building. I got out, shouldered my backpack, and walked to area on the street where the doctor had been shot. The crime scene tape was gone.

I put my cell on speakerphone but held it in my hand at my side so it wouldn't appear that I was talking to anyone. The doctor's car was gone, having been removed by the CSI for further tests. I took off my backpack and squatted down so I would be closer to the phone in my hand. I pretended I was examining his dried blood spatter on the street.

"Cas, can you hear me?" I asked.

Silence.

"Cas," I said louder, trying to talk without my lips moving. "Can you hear me?"

Silence.

"Cas," I said "Where are you?"

"Would you *please* stop bugging me?" she asked. "I can't concentrate."

"Concentrate? Concentrate on what?"

"Parking. You took the only parking spot."

I stood up and glanced around. There wasn't an available parking place on either side of the street.

"I'll hang around until you find a place," I said.

Silence.

"I said..."

"I heard you. This is maddening."

Multitasking is my specialty. Since I didn't have anything else to do while I waited for Cas to find a temporary home for her car, I walked to the sniper's apartment building across the street.

"I'm going into the apartment building where the sniper hid," I said softly, trying not to move my mouth and hoping the speakerphone would pick up what I said. "It's the building across the street with green shutters on the first-floor windows."

"What did you say?" she asked. "You sound funny."

"What?"

"You sound like you have a mouth full of marbles or something."

"It isn't easy to talk without moving your lips."

"Why are you doing that?"

"Forget it, okay?" I said, picking up my backpack.

"Why are you going into that building?"

"I want to check out the sniper's apartment."

"Didn't you already do that?"

"No. It was a crime scene, and I couldn't go in."

"Why go in now?"

"I have an idea."

"In case something happens, which apartment?" she asked.

"3E," I said. "And relax. Nothing's going to happen."

I said that with more conviction than I felt.

Glad I have my Glock.

71

The yellow crime scene tape that had been positioned across the front door of the apartment building had been removed to allow the residents to enter again. The front door was unlocked, so I walked in like I lived there and went up the thinly carpeted stairs to the third floor. The hallway smelled moldy.

The door to 3E was locked, the entry still blocked by crime scene tape. I put on latex gloves and took out the lock pick gun and torque wrench from my backpack. I did the same thing I'd done at Jamie's apartment, but this time it took less than fifteen seconds.

I shoved my gear back in my backpack and took out my Glock. I checked the clip, made sure I had a round in the barrel, and then put the gun back into the backpack.

Next, I confronted the crime scene tape. The simplest solution is usually the easiest, so I ripped the tape off, hoping the neighbors would think the apartment manager had decided to show the space to a potential new renter.

I jammed the wad of tape into my backpack and checked both ends of the hall before I opened the door. The unit was as Tony had described it. One chair was still positioned by the window facing the street. I looked out and spotted the place where the doctor's SUV had been parked.

It was an easy shot.

I turned around. The bathroom was my target. I'd used a swabbing technique weeks before, when I found DNA from one of the "industrial spies" on the edge of a sink. Once I was in the bathroom, I checked the edges of the sink.

Yes!

I saw something glistening on the porcelain. Pulling a few pieces of toilet paper off the roll, I swabbed the area and put the paper into a baggy, one of the staples of my mommy backpack. I swabbed the toilet too.

Standing up, I put the baggy back into the side pocket of my backpack.

My cell phone rang. "She's... She's... Here!" Cas screamed. "Tina, she's coming into the building! Run!"

72

A car alarm went off outside the building. There was a rapid clump of footsteps on the stairs coming up from the first floor. Adrenaline surged through my system.

The window!

I ran to the window the sniper had used when he shot the doctor. I opened it. It was a three-story drop to the street and no fire escape.

The car alarm continued to blast away. The footsteps moved to the second floor landing.

My Glock!

I hadn't planned for this confrontation, but so be it. I took a deep breath to center myself. The footsteps grew louder.

I crouched behind the stuffed chair for the minimal cover it would afford me. Reaching into my backpack for the Glock, all I could feel was a tangled mass of crime scene tape.

I tried to yank out the twisted blob of tape with both hands, but my hands began to sweat, and the latex gloves got squishy and loose. The more I struggled, the harder it was to grip anything.

This can't be happening!

The footsteps stopped in front of the apartment door just as I felt the handle of the Glock. I ripped off the latex gloves and pulled the gun free from the backpack.

The doorknob turned. The Glock was in my hand.

The door lock clicked open. I had one bullet in the chamber. I was ready.

The door flew open. I assumed a shooter's stance behind the stuffed chair.

Aim for center mass.

"I have a gun, and I will shoot," I said.

Cas darted into the room, a can of wasp spray held high in her right hand.

"Where is she?!" she yelled, wildly waving the can around.

She saw my gun pointed at her chest. She backed up, raising her hands. "Tina, don't shoot! It's me!"

I lowered the gun and dropped to my knees. I'd almost shot one of the Hamlin Park Irregulars.

73

"What happened?" I asked, as Cas and I walked down the stairs to street level.

My hands were still shaking.

"Just as you walked into the apartment building, I found a place to park," Cas said. "Out of the corner of my eye, I saw a woman walk past me. She crossed the street and went toward the apartment building with the green shutters. At first, I assumed she lived there, but then I saw her reach into her purse and pull out a gun."

We stepped outside. I began to lose feeling in my legs and had to hold onto the wall of the building to keep from collapsing. "A gun?"

"Big boxy one, kind of like yours."

"Probably a Glock."

"Whatever... I saw her turn to the front door of the apartment building you were in. She did something to the top of the gun before she opened the front door. That's when I called you and started running across the street toward her."

The car alarm was still blaring away. Cas took out her car keys and punched the alarm button to shut it off.

"I also did that. I read that a car alarm noise will attract bystanders and might also scare off an intruder. I always keep my car keys on top of my bedside table in case someone breaks into our home. It's my first line of defense."

"I think you do pretty well with that wasp spray and your Taser."

"Thank you, but you can't have too much help in a crisis situation."

"I think I'll sit down a minute here," I said.

I slid to the sidewalk, picturing the woman chambering a round so she could shoot me.

Cas took a water bottle out of her purse and handed it to me. I tried to drink some, but my stomach was a little queasy, and I couldn't do it. She took the bottle out of my trembling hands and poured some water on the back of my neck and then held the bottle to my forehead as everything went black.

74

It took a couple of minutes before my vision cleared and the ringing in my ears subsided.

"I can't believe I did that," I said.

"A vaso-vagal response from being scared," Cas said.

"The thought of getting shot does that to me." I waved my hand for her to continue with her story. "Then what happened?"

"The woman must have heard me coming up behind her, or maybe it was the sound of the car alarm. Whatever it was, she saw me and ran into the building. I took out my can of wasp spray and Taser and followed her in the front door. She was gone. I assumed she was in the apartment trying to shoot you."

"Instead, I almost shot you. Did you consider calling 911?"

A glazed look appeared in her eyes. "It was all happening so fast, I guess I didn't think about it. Stupid me. I just reacted. Sorry."

"The cops probably wouldn't have gotten here in time anyway, but it would have been nice to have them as a backup."

"But you had a gun."

"There is that."

"We need better planning next time."

I held up my hand. "If Carter finds out what just happened, he'll kill me, even if the shooter doesn't." I took in a deep breath. "This is way too risky."

"But we almost had her."

"Or she almost had me. All we proved so far is that we're not superheroes." I stood up and brushed the street dirt off the seat of my shorts. "What did she look like?"

"Short, slender, medium-length brown hair. Gray warm-up with long sleeves. Large brown purse. Big sunglasses."

My legs felt weak again. "Not a blond?"

"No, I'm positive this woman had dark brown hair with a flip curl."

My stomach began to churn. "The other woman I saw was a blond. I guess this means the bomber has at least two helpers."

As I walked out to my van, I called Tony. "I have some new DNA samples from the shooter's apartment."

The line was silent.

"Tony?"

His voice was hard. "How did you get them?"

"You don't need to know."

"If you contaminated a crime scene, we won't be able to use any of it as evidence."

I pictured the crime scene tape I'd ripped down and stashed in my purse. "All I need it for is further proof the bomber is my guy from Arlington."

"Don't do this again."

"I won't. Will you pick it up, or do you want me to drop it off at your mother's house?"

I thought I heard him grinding his teeth. "I'll be at your joint in an hour. Do *not* go to her house."

I knew this was the way to save me a trip to deliver the samples to him.

"There was an unaccounted blood spatter in the hallway in Arlington. The FBI agents on the scene assume it came from the bomber. Have their lab compare that DNA to these swabs."

"At least it's not freaking C4."

"Gosh, I hadn't considered that. Better have them check for that too."

He groaned and disconnected.

75

Linda was discharged from the hospital Wednesday morning. She didn't admit it, but I suspected she left before she was supposed to.

But that's our girl. She pretty much does what she wants to. God bless her husband, Howard, for putting up with that. On the other hand, she controls the purse strings, so he knows his place in their batting lineup.

And having a full-time nanny helps.

David joined me two miles into my morning run.

"You won't believe what happened yesterday," I said, when he came up beside me.

"I already know," David said.

I stopped and faced him. "Know what?"

He stopped too. "A dark-haired lady tried to shoot you."

"Did you talk to Cas?"

"No, I was there."

"No way. I didn't see you."

"You didn't see me for the same reason you didn't see the woman following you. She used a GPS tracker she'd stuck to your van."

My stomach dropped to my toes. "How did you find that out?"

"It's been bothering me that the bomber might be following any of us. He would have to have a lot of people helping him to do that. Unless he had tracking devices on all of our cars or pinged our cell phones."

"He can do that?"

"Anyone can. That's how I knew where you were, but unless he has your cell phone numbers, he has to use tracking devices."

"Just like I did on the 'industrial spy' story."

"What?"

"I didn't know about the cell phone technique, but I had access to tracking devices so I used them. Looks like he did too."

"You're right. I went over my car and found one under the back fender. Yesterday, I came by and checked your van. You have one too. So do the rest of the girls."

"This guy is worse than the FBI. Tell me the rest of it."

"When you drove off yesterday, I pinged your cell phone and followed you from a safe distance."

"And you saw the woman."

He nodded. "She drove three cars in front of me. You were already out of your car by the time we arrived. She parked two blocks away and walked to the apartment building. I found a spot to park close to her."

"And you followed."

"Not exactly. I used binoculars to watch her. I saw her pull out a gun and enter the apartment building. Before I could react, I saw Cas take out her equipment and follow the woman into the building. I also saw and then heard Cas set off her car alarm."

"That was really smart, but she should have called 911. You should have too."

"I started to, but I saw the woman run out of the back of the building before I could. I had to hurry up and finish what I was doing."

"Doing?"

"I stood next to the car she drove and put a tracking device on it. It's old fashioned, but I didn't have access to her cell phone number. I escaped before she saw me."

"That's brilliant."

"We still have to catch them."

"We sure do. Where did she go?"

"Follow me."

We ran down Belmont and then went right on Paulina and stopped about twenty feet from the corner. Our home was on the other end of the block.

I stared at him and shrugged.

"Don't be too obvious, but they're right here," he said.

"Right here, where?"

"In this apartment building."

I almost threw up.

The bomber lives across the alley directly behind our house.

76

I clenched my hands into fists. "If it wasn't the middle of the morning, I would go in there right now and finish this, especially after what happened yesterday."

"I can understand why you're angry, but they're probably not here," David said.

"And how would you know this?"

"Before I started my run this morning, I checked their GPS and the car wasn't here."

"Do you think they found your tracking device?"

"No, I think they switched cars."

I glanced up at the four-story apartment building. "If we're going to discuss this, we might want to find a safer location to stand than right here."

We walked toward our house. I counted the steps from the front door of the apartment building to our front gate.

The bad guys are thirty-three yards from our home.

"When I hid the GPS device, I took down the license plate number too," he said. "I checked it on my computer. It's a rental car."

"You think they're changing rental cars at regular intervals."

"I do, and that takes deep financial resources. They must have a lot of money at their disposal."

I did a hamstring stretch. "I'm not sure what we should do next."

"The police won't act until we have some proof."

"You sound like Linda, but you're right. We need to convince Tony that the bomber is in there," I nodded toward the apartment building, "and then set a trap to catch him."

"You have to break in and get the evidence we need."

"No way, David. It's too risky."

"It's the only way you're going to catch the man who tried to kill you," he stared at me, "and then finish writing your story."

77

Wednesday afternoon, I pushed Kerry in her stroller to Whole Foods. I had my shopping list for the meal Carter was going to prepare for dinner. He wanted to do a frisée salad with pears, goat cheese, and salted pecans, followed by Italian braised spareribs with rigatoni.

I didn't want the Irregulars to have to leave their families for a simple trip to the store, so I hadn't called any of them to follow me. And I was reasonably certain the bomber, or one of his helpers, wouldn't attack Kerry and me when lots of people were around us out in the open. He hadn't done it in the past, and I was pretty sure he wouldn't do it now.

But I did touch the outline of the Glock in my backpack for reassurance that I could defend myself if the bomber, or one of his helpers, showed up.

After purchasing the ingredients I needed for dinner, I wandered down to Dinkel's. Esther Guadeloupe Escobar, one of the managers, stood behind the glass display counter. She's from Costa Rica, short, and always happy, but who wouldn't be, working in an establishment like this? But she enjoys her job a little too much, resulting in her weight being way past two hundred pounds, which isn't healthy, especially since she's so short she can barely see over the top of the pastry cases.

"Do you have any pies, Esther?" I asked. "I need dessert for tonight."

The pies would be my only contribution to the meal.

"Sure do," she said, in heavily accented English. "Apple and cherry."

"I'll take one of each. Do you mind if I use the back door? I need to run an errand."

"Sure, no problem. You know where it is."

"I'll be back in about fifteen minutes to pick up the pies."

My plan was to sneak out the back door and return to the apartment building behind our home. I needed to find the bomber's hiding place. If he, or a helper, watched me from the front of Dinkel's, I didn't want them to see me leave.

Having Kerry with me was a major plus, especially if the apartment manager was a female. No one would ever guess that a mommy with her daughter was up to anything suspicious.

I exited from the back of Dinkel's and pushed Kerry in her stroller to the front door of the apartment building. The door was locked, so I rang the buzzer that said "Manager."

A lady in her mid-forties opened the door.

"Hi, I'm Tina," I said. "This is my daughter, Kerry."

"I'm Annie Foley, the building manager."

"We live in the neighborhood, and we need an apartment for my parents who want to move here from Omaha. Do you have any available?"

"Gosh, I'm so sorry. I rented the last unit in June."

"Do you think you might have any coming up?"

"I haven't heard any of the renters mention moving."

"Could you check your list, you know, sort of refresh your memory? Maybe something will pop out at you." I gave her my best pleading look. "Please."

She let me in and walked to the first apartment on our right. I took Kerry out of the stroller and followed.

Annie left the apartment door open and went to her computer-free desk. Picking up a ledger, she thumbed through it and shook her head. "Sorry, I don't see any vacancies coming up."

"How about if I give you my phone number and then you can call me if anything changes?"

"Sure, be happy to."

She picked up a pad and pen. Stepping into the room, I looked around and then gave her my phone number.

"I couldn't help but notice that you don't have a computer," I said.

She pointed to her ledger. "I will never use a computer, as long as I live. That's all my three kids do. Facebook this, blog that, Twitter in between. I'm sick of it. I don't think they've ever seen a newspaper, let alone read one."

"I can relate. My husband works for the *Chicago Tribune*. The circulation continues to decline, and there doesn't seem to be an end to it."

"My point exactly."

"Pardon me for asking, but this is an awfully small room. I hope all the apartments aren't this tiny."

She laughed. "Oh no, our units are quite nice. This is the manager's office. I live in Lincoln Park with my kids."

I need one more piece of information.

"Then you're not here at night?"

"No. In fact, you caught me just as I was about to leave. I try to get home by five so I can cook dinner for them. Teenagers need at least one healthy meal a day."

"Don't you have a night manager in case someone needs help or something?"

"Mr. Kavich, our owner, thinks it's too expensive. If there's a problem, the tenants call me at home, and I come back and take care of it."

"Reassuring to know."

"For them, but a pain in the you-know-what for me."

"Thanks again, Annie. Please call me if anything changes."

As I walked out with Kerry in my arms, I scouted the door locks. The one on the door to her office would not be much of a problem. Neither would the one on the front door. I put Kerry into her stroller and pushed her back to Dinkel's to pick up our pies.

Annie would never know I was going to return, after Carter went to sleep, to find out who the new renter was.

78

Late Wednesday night, I sat in our family room. The Glock sat in my lap. Carter was conked out, thanks to the full bottle of Fourth Estate Pinot he'd consumed along with the Italian braised spareribs and rigatoni.

The last time I'd done something like this, I'd forgotten to disconnect the old baby monitor and Kerry's whimpers had awakened him. This time, I shut off his cell phone so he wouldn't hear the Nanit. I kept my cell phone app on to monitor her movements in case there was a problem.

I stared out the back windows. All the apartment units facing me were dark. If it came to having to use my gun, I felt confident in my skills. I had spent many hours with Tony at the gun range. He hated that I was a better shot than he was, but I'd never told him that Jimmy and I had grown up hunting ducks, geese, and pheasants with my dad in Nebraska.

And I was a better shot than Dad and Jimmy.

The simplest thing would be to call Tony and let him handle this, but I was positive he would laugh at my suggestion that the bomber lived behind me.

And I hate to have any man laugh at me.

My plan was to find out who had moved into the building in June. My next move would be to knock on that apartment door, with my right hand on the Glock. If the tenant was a man who looked like the bomber, or one of the female helpers, I would hold him, or her, at gunpoint and then speed-dial Tony. If the person didn't look like any of them, I would come up with some ridiculous excuse for being there and go home.

Walking away from our house, I watched to see if I was being followed. After two blocks, I was certain no one was there and backtracked to the apartment building.

I arrived at the same time a cop car pulled in and parked in the lot of the Walgreen's diagonally across Belmont from the building.

Better go home.

I turned to do that, but over my shoulder, I watched as both officers got out of their car and walked into the pharmacy.

Do it while they're in there.

I whipped around, ran to the front door of the building, and jammed the lock pick gun into the lock. I kept peeking around for the cops as I applied the torque wrench. When I pulled on the doorknob to open the door, I found myself face-to-face with a wide-eyed elderly man who stood in the hallway holding the leash of a growling Pekinese.

Damn!

79

"Hi," I said, my heart rate accelerating to a near lethal rate.

"Who are you, and what are you doing here?" the man asked.

"Who am I? I'll tell you who I am."

Gotta come up with something fast.

Linda!

"I'm the knocked up ex-wife of the worthless dickhead who's been hiding from me since June," I said. "I followed him here, and this time, he isn't going to get away from me. That's why there are two cops over there at Walgreen's." I jerked my thumb toward the black and white in the parking lot. "Once I make sure it's him, those cops are gonna throw his sorry ass in jail." I stepped forward. "That's who I am."

Sounds good to me.

He held up his hands. "I don't want to know anything about this. Mildred has to do her business. Please, let me by."

I stepped aside, theatrically waving my arms. "Gladly. I have work to do here, and you better not try and stop me."

He ran out the door and moved quickly in the opposite direction of the still-empty police car. I inserted the pick gun into the manager's lock and was in her office within seconds.

Picking up her ledger, I ran my finger down the page and found that a man named James Edwards had moved into 3C in June.

My brother's name!

The renter in 3C used it to taunt me.

It has to be the bomber.

I locked Annie's door and ran up to the third floor. Standing in front of the door to 3C, I held the Glock next to my leg and knocked.

No response.

I knocked again, harder this time.

Still no answer.

I considered knocking again, but I was afraid I would wake up the neighbors. After putting on latex gloves, I took out my lock pick gun and torque wrench. I held the Glock in my left armpit.

The lock was cheap and easy to open. I put the devices back in my backpack and put it on the floor. I grabbed the Glock in my right hand and slowly turned the knob with my left.

Pushing the door open, I stepped inside. The only light in the darkened apartment came from the uncovered windows opposite the front door.

I listened, but all I heard was the thumping of my pulse in my ears and the low-level hum of machines. There was a red glow coming from two video cameras, which were on and pointed toward the back windows of our home. They were positioned far enough away from the glass that they couldn't be seen from the outside.

On a large table next to them were ten glowing computer screens filled with multiple camera views of my home, my life.

The place looked like the command center for an FBI stakeout. The room had the same electronic smell as Linda's home computer room. The only other odors came from cleaning products.

I pulled out a small penlight and scanned the room. It was a combination living room/dining room. To my left was an efficiency kitchen and to my right, a bedroom. No one was there.

Stepping back into the hallway, I pulled my backpack into the apartment and shut the door. I flipped on the room lights and snapped pictures with my cell phone. I went into the bedroom and took more pictures. The closet was empty. So was the chest of drawers. The bathroom was devoid of any toiletries.

I moved into the small kitchen and found nothing, not even a cracker. The bomber used this location, but didn't live here.

My mental break-in time clock continued to warn me to hurry, but I took the time to take a video with my cell phone. I relocked the door and left, this time using the elevator.

When the front door creaked open, the elderly man stood in front of me once more. He backed up, holding his arms up in a defense posture. The pissy little dog began growling again.

"Oh, hi," I said. "I had the nicest chat with my ex. I love him so much. You'll be happy to know he'll be moving out and back in with me before the baby is born. I've never been happier."

I stepped off the elevator and walked out the front door before he could respond.

80

Thursday morning, While Kerry was upstairs taking her nap, I invited David over to show him the pictures of what I'd discovered in the apartment behind our home.

He walked into our entry hall. "I want you to see something," I said. "Follow me."

We went into the family room. My plan was to show him the way the apartment faced our back windows to give him a sense of what he was going to see on my cell phone pictures.

We didn't get very far.

"Oh, my," he said.

"It's okay, David," I said, as I gently pushed him away from the chaos of glistening DVDs and paper jackets covering the hardwood floor. "Kerry's found a new form of self-expression."

For the past six weeks, she'd been yanking DVDs out of their jackets and flinging them haphazardly around the room. I attributed this behavior to a gene she inherited from her Uncle Jimmy, who seemed to have several loose screws in his head even though he graduated Phi Beta Kappa from Stanford. Being a pitcher for the San Diego Padres might have had something to do with it too.

Disorder of any type seemed to be out of David's comfort zone.

Not a big surprise.

He began scurrying around the room picking up DVDs in one hand and empty paper jackets in the other.

"David, stop." I grabbed the DVDs and jackets out of his hands. "I have to show you something."

His eyes blinked several times behind his big glasses. "It's just that... Clutter like this... It's really hard for me to concentrate when I'm around chaos. Please, let me clean it up."

"I need to show you something first, but I think we should do it in the kitchen."

He visibly relaxed when he turned his back to the mess on the floor. I put the discs and jackets on the dining room table. I would deal with those later.

To distract David from the disorder in the family room, we stepped out on the front porch. I handed him my cell phone. He scrolled through the pictures of the apartment. As he watched the screen, sweat appeared on his upper lip.

And it's not from the DVDs on the floor.

"Amazing," he said. "Unbelievable."

"Oh, it's believable, especially after you watch the video."

I flipped it up on the screen. He watched it three times before he said anything.

"Something doesn't make sense," he said. "There are two cameras, but ten screens. Why not have only two screens?"

"That's what I couldn't figure out until I drove by Molly's house this morning and found it."

"It?"

"A video camera hidden in the tree in front of her house." I took my cell phone from his hands and flashed another picture on the screen. "Here, check it out."

He stared at the picture. "We had these units at Hogan. They're expensive." He paused. "Let me scroll though those original pictures again."

He did and then ran the video. "There." He pointed at the video. "The screen on the top left. It's Molly's house."

"That's how I figured it out."

"Let me watch the video one more time."

When he finished, he looked up at me.

"The camera shots rotate on a timed basis," he said. "Like the security systems in large buildings."

"Why do it like that?"

"To send recorded information to another set of computers. That way, they don't have to be close to you, or even in the same city, to see what's happening."

"And they know where our cars go by using the GPS trackers."

"They do."

"Why not sit in that apartment and watch the house?"

"This setup allows them to work regular jobs and still monitor what we do by checking the recordings when they get home."

"That's a little scary. He, or his helpers, might be going to work in the daytime like everyone else. The only time they physically have to be on site is when they want to kill a doctor or blow up a building."

He handed my phone back to me. "The bomber has our lives on his screens. Like it or not, we're all part of this, and the sooner we catch him, the safer we'll all be."

Hard to argue with that.

David began to fidget.

The DVDs.

"Would you like to help me clean up the DVDs in the family room?" I asked.

His face brightened. "I would, but do you mind if I do it alone?"

"You have your own way to do it, right?"

"Kind of."

"Let's go back inside. I'll wake up Kerry. Have fun."

Without another word, he opened the front door and ran into the family room. He was so upset, I noticed he didn't put on his latex gloves to protect himself from the germs covering the DVD covers.

81

Thursday afternoon, The Irregulars met at Linda's home since she was now on bed rest. Her nanny watched all of our kids play while I told the moms about the bomber spying on us from the apartment building I could see out my back window.

David was in the kitchen preparing snacks. He already knew what I was going to say.

"We have to assume that he pretty much knows what we're doing in our daily lives," I concluded.

"Can he see in our windows?" Molly asked.

David walked into the playroom. "Tina is the only one who has physically seen his setup, so I haven't had a chance to assess the resolution of the cameras. He might be able to zoom in enough to see activity in some of our rooms."

Linda lounged in a recliner. "But I'm sure he won't. He's too busy bombing clinics and killing doctors."

"I have a question," Cas said. "The bomber has two stationary cameras aimed at the back of your house, right?"

"He does," I said.

"Why does he need to live this close to you?" she asked. "If he can put portable cameras outside of all of our homes and not be close to them, why didn't he do the same thing at your house?"

Uh-oh!

"They might have audio in my home," I said.

"How do you know that?" Cas asked.

"The 'industrial spies' had to be close to Micah's home because of the short range of the audio reception so they could listen to everything Micah and Hannah said."

"Does this mean you have listening devices in your home too?" David asked.

"I did have."

"When did you find them?" he asked.

"After Linda found a keystroke logger on my computer, I assumed the feds had also planted electronic listening devices all over my home, so I checked for them."

"How?" he asked.

"I have an electronic scanning machine I purchased when I was working on a story in Afghanistan. I found the bugs, but I was wrong about who planted them."

"It wasn't the feds?" Linda asked.

"No, it was Jamie. He broke into our home and planted them. At the same time, he put the keystroke logger on my computer. It was the one you discovered and later removed."

"Did you check your house for listening devices after the events at O'Hare?" David asked.

"I did. When I returned from the airport, I swept the house and found the devices were not functioning. I assumed the bugs had been removed by the FBI and were no longer a problem."

"What if the FBI didn't remove the listening devices but only turned them off after they caught the industrial spies?" he asked.

"Why would they do that?" Molly asked.

"It would have taken the feds a long time to find all devices, since they didn't know exactly where they were placed," he said. "Not removing them could simply have been a matter of expediency."

"Or maybe they kept them in place in case they needed to activate them again to listen in on what is being said in my house," I said. "They're aware I'm writing investigative stories again and might want to be dialed in on what I know."

"Could the bomber have seen Jamie install the bugs and he knows they were never removed?" Linda asked.

A very disturbing question.

82

"If you're right, how could the bomber get into my house to turn on the listening devices?" I asked.

"He could do it from his computer, especially since it's clear he's techno-savvy," Linda said. "David, did you check his electricity bill?"

"I did," he said. "You and I know how much power it takes to run the setup he has. After Tina showed me the bomber's videos, I hacked into the city records and checked his electric use ever since he moved into that apartment in June. Initially, it was normal for a single man, and then, in July, it went up substantially."

"When he activated the computers and cameras," Linda said.

"And the electrical use remained at that level until August sixth, and then it escalated even more."

"Which was a few days after I initially discovered my home was bugged, and I later assumed the devices were shut off by the feds," I said.

"I think when you check again you'll find that the listening devices are back on," he said.

Damn!

"I can't believe this," I said. "He's been watching and listening to my entire life."

"I'm glad we discussed this on your front porch yesterday," David said. "If we hadn't, he would have heard every word we said."

I let out a deep breath. "That's the first lucky thing that's happened to me."

"At least your computer is clean," Linda said. "Or at least it was when I last checked it."

"You think the bomber is going to do something soon, maybe to Micah, right?" David asked.

"Or to me, or the rest of you."

"I think you're wrong about that," he said.

"Unless you're the bomber, I don't see how you can be so sure of that."

"According to you, the bomber's ultimate goal is to gain widespread publicity for his cause."

"I'm sure of it."

"And he's accelerating his attacks to entice you to tell his anti-abortion story, especially since your recent article shows you are writing this kind of story again — and in a big city paper that can be accessed by potentially millions of readers."

"I think he is."

"If you're right, he'll keep attacking until you write his story," he said.

"Then that's the solution," Molly said.

"Solution?" Linda asked.

"We set a trap and catch him," Molly said.

83

David came home with Kerry and me to see if he was right about the listening devices. Margaret walked next to her daddy.

We entered the kitchen. I put Kerry in her booster chair and gave her apple juice in her sippy cup. David put Margaret's iPad and earphones on the kitchen table. She climbed up on one of the chairs and logged on.

I didn't have to worry about entertaining her.

"You're having trouble with your dishwasher again, right?" David asked.

After our discussion, I was so rattled about what we might find that I wasn't tracking with what he was saying. "I have?"

He arched an eyebrow and pointed at his ears.

"Right, right, I have," I said. "Here, let me show you."

I walked over to my kitchen junk drawer, opened it, and pulled out my electronic scanning device. I switched it on. The red light began blinking. Kerry watched me.

Here we go again.

There was at least one listening device active in the kitchen.

I opened the dishwasher and rattled the dirty dishes around. David made a circuit of the room and pointed to several locations where the red light stopped blinking and remained on.

That's where the bugs are.

"Turn it on," he said, as he walked into the family room.

"Sure, but stand back in case it begins leaking," I said to his back.

While he was gone, I put soap in the machine and turned it on. It filled with water. I stopped the cycle by opening the door and then restarted it.

"See, that's what's been happening," I said to the machine and listening devices. "It goes on and then off. Drives me crazy."

I repeated the sequence several more times until David reappeared.

"I see what you mean," he said. "Let me check it out."

He opened the door and rattled the racks. "Does Carter have any plumbing tools?"

"Carter? My husband, Carter?"

Carter graduated from the University of Chicago. They don't "do" any kind of tools there. The only one he used on a regular basis was his fingernail clipper.

"Oh, you know what?" I said, picking up Kerry. "He has them downstairs. Follow me and I'll show you."

He helped his daughter down and carried her iPad and earphones to the lower level.

84

When we bought the house, the room we now use as a wine room was intended to be a storm shelter. Carter had lovingly converted it to a full wine storage facility with wooden racks to the ceiling.

He'd purchased two vintage White Sox bleacher seats from the now-demolished Comiskey Park. They were positioned next to a used French oak wine barrel topped with a never-used candle stuck in an empty Bordeaux bottle. He'd even added speakers that hooked up to his iPod dock.

The plan was for us to sit in the wine room listening to romantic classic music – which was his choice, not mine – savoring a glass of wine from one of his favorite vintages. The concept was fabulous, but the first night, after ten minutes of freezing my ass off in the fifty-four-degree temperature, I went back into the warmth of the computer room, which was adjacent to the wine room.

And there was no way a true Cubs fan was going to plop her butt down in a seat that had been in Comiskey Park.

I put Kerry on the floor with her blocks. David put Margaret on the chair in front of my computer. She began playing on her iPad. David and I walked into the wine cellar. I activated the detector. The light turned green, indicating there were no functional listening devices.

"A few weeks ago, when I checked the wine cellar, it was clean, and it looks like it still is," I said.

"If your cell phone works in here, you have a location from which you can make calls undetected by the bomber."

"One way to find out is to call Carter from in here and tell him what's going on."

I pulled my cell phone out of my shorts and dialed my husband. He would be furious when he found out what was going on, but he would also understand the realities of the situation. We could catch the bomber, have a fabulous story, and finally be safe. No more worrying about the "D" word.

The phone rang, and Carter's secretary picked up.

"Hi, Moura. Is Carter around? I have something to tell him."

Carter picked up right away. "Is Kerry okay? Are you safe?"

"We're perfect," I said. "I was just getting ready to carry our sweet daughter up for her nap."

"Then what do you want?" His voice hardened. He didn't like to chit-chat at work.

"We now have unique control of this story."

The line was silent a few seconds. "That's an interesting choice of words. What exactly does that mean?"

"The bomber has bugged our home with listening devices."

The prolonged silence was ominous.

"Carter?"

"Yes?"

You don't sound happy.

"The bomber doesn't know that we've discovered his bugs, and we can now set a trap for him."

"That is intriguing, but how are you talking to me now without him hearing you?"

I told him about the device-free wine room.

"We can talk more about it tonight in here," I said.

"Fabulous!" he exclaimed, a little too excited about the prospect of spending time with me in his favorite room.

85

Thursday evening, after Kerry was down for the night, Carter and I sat in the wine cellar on the used seats from Comiskey Park. I opened our Nanit app on my cell phone so we could see and hear Kerry in her crib.

In a minor form of protest, I brought down a Cub's seat cushion to protect my booty from White Sox cooties. Carter opened another bottle of Fourth Estate Pinot, which he poured in the dim light of the candle he was finally able to use. The music coming from the speakers was from the latest CD by Steely Dan — my choice, not his.

And then what I call "Carter's process" began. First, he swirled the wine in his pinot glass before he put his nose into the top of the glass to sniff the wine's bouquet. Next, he swished the wine around in his mouth and "chewed" it before he swallowed it.

Finally, his assessment: "This has elegance and a Burgundian flair. I detect dark fruit paired with floral notes and distinct taste of cherry cola."

I sipped. My take: it tasted good, but what can I say? I grew up in Omaha.

"When we catch the bomber, I'm going to thank him for this," he said.

"And why would you do that?" I asked.

"If he hadn't bugged every room in our house except this one, you would never be down here with me."

When Carter first arrived home, I showed him the bug detector and how David and I had discovered the devices. I admitted to him that I had not been setting the security system lately when I took Kerry out in the jogging stroller. He was upset, but he'd seen me struggle with all the paraphernalia and understood why I'd made that mistake.

I had omitted two small facts: the cameras in the apartment zeroing in on our back window and how close the bomber had to be to the same window to use the listening devices. If I told him either element, I was certain he would call the police and the bomber would disappear along with any chance of catching him.

Carter topped off his glass. "Using your previous bomber files, we now have all the background material for the R and D of the story."

Research and development is critical to a properly written investigative article. I already had that material in my files.

He snapped his fingers. "I almost forgot that I brought a surprise for you."

"Me?"

He nodded and handed me a *Chicago Tribune* press credential. It even had my picture on it.

I shrugged my shoulders. "I don't understand."

"Thanks to Micah, I'm going to interview the president on the 11th. I want you to be there, too, and have full access to the event."

YES!

I gave him a big hug. "Thank you so much for including me."

"I wouldn't have it any other way." He sipped more wine. "But we do have one other problem."

"We do?"

"Yes, we do. Sex."

"Honey, that's one area that has never been a problem for us."

"I understand, but what do we do now?"

"Now?"

"I can't perform properly in our bedroom with him listening."

Men!

They always worry about their performance. But he did have a point.

I took my ski parka off. "I guess I'll have to take one for the team. Try not to take too long or do anything fancy. Just the basics."

86

Friday morning, The Irregulars — minus Linda, who was still on bed rest — were at Hamlin Park. If the bomber watched the park, the noise from the cars and trucks on the heavily trafficked surrounding streets would make an audio pickup almost impossible. This gave me a chance to explain my plan to the rest of the group.

Margaret was in preschool. The rest of the kids were with Alicia Sanchez. We needed to concentrate on what we were going to do, and our kids would be a distraction.

"We need to act normally," I began. "We don't deviate from anything we do in our everyday lives. I have an inside source about the bomber's activities. When I hear from that person, we'll contact Tony Infantino and capture the bomber when he goes to the next clinic to blow it up."

"Sounds too easy," Molly said.

"I disagree," David said. "That's the beauty of the plan. This man seems driven to stop abortions. He is extremely careful, but my sense is that he might rely more on his own abilities than computers."

Cas clenched her jaw muscles. "How did you come to that simplified conclusion?"

"He appears to be a hands-on person. He's obviously comfortable with computers, so he could blow up the clinics from miles away, but now he's using a gun, which is up close and personal."

"I think we need to fool the bomber to make your plan work," Molly said.

"How are we going to do that?" he asked.

"You have a person who's going to tell you when the bomber's going to hit his next target, right Tina?" Molly asked.

"I do," I said.

"And the bomber can hear everything you say in your house."

"David and I are reasonably sure he can," I said.

"Why don't we have a meeting there and discuss trapping him somewhere else?"

"I don't understand," Cas said.

"You tell us you have a plan to trap him, maybe a week or so after we actually intend to catch him. He'll be fooled and not be watching out for us."

"He'll hear all of our plans and assume we're not on to him when, actually, we are," David said.

An intriguing idea.

If the bomber assumes we're focusing all our energies on a different target and time frame, he won't anticipate our trap.

"This is brilliant," I said. "Have you done something like this before, Molly?"

"Yeah, lots of times."

She began fiddling with her cell phone.

"Ah, Molly?" I said.

"What?"

"The times?"

"Oh, right. The farmers had me give the wrong intel to the bad guys I hung out with. They never suspected the farmers were actually going to do the opposite of what I told the bad guys."

"Disinformation," David said.

"Yeah, that was the word they used," Molly said. "Disinformation."

87

It was Friday afternoon. The president was going to be in Chicago in ten days, Monday, September 11. Kerry took her nap. I was on the computer going over my previous bomber notes when my mole contacted me:

He is going to strike next Friday, the 8th. The target is an abortion clinic on South Cottage Grove Avenue, on the South Side of Chicago. I learned he still has an ample supply of C4, but I don't know how he is going to plant the bomb.

Recently, I attempted to solve the entire problem, but he slipped out of my trap by only a few minutes. His two helpers weren't as lucky. You no longer have to worry about them.

They have been eliminated.

My hands shook as I read the message. The mole had almost ruined my chance at having the exclusive on the story by attempting to kill the bomber. The mole didn't succeed, but the bomber's two female collaborators had become collateral damage.

At least now we had only one bad guy to deal with.

It was time to try our system to foil the bomber. In the wine room, David had taped Kerry and me having several conversations. He had also recorded me doing things around the house when Kerry was with Carter. David had wired it so that when I started the recording the sound would go off and on for two hours.

I stepped into the wine room and called David.

"I hope this isn't a bad time," I said.

"Not at all," he said. "I was thinking about taking Margaret to the park after she gets out of preschool. Why?"

"My mole has given me the date the bomber plans to strike. It's next Friday. It's an abortion clinic on the South Side. The Irregulars need to meet with Tony and one of Carter's reporters at Dinkel's in an hour."

"Don't forget to start the audio recording when you leave."

"I have it here in the wine room. I'll text everyone else and turn it on when I leave."

88

An hour later, we sat in Dinkel's dining room. Since it was Friday, Alicia watched our kids. Margaret was still in preschool.

Before anyone arrived, I swept the room for bugs. I didn't find any and felt it was safe to tell them about the upcoming attack next Friday. Brittany Simon, the reporter Carter had assigned to the story, also joined us and sat next to me. Tony was there and made sure he grabbed a seat next to her.

I gave them a copy of the email I had received from the mole.

"What do you think?" I asked, after everyone had read it.

Tony locked his hands behind his head and leaned back in his chair. "That's not the target."

What?!

"It isn't?" Cas asked.

"Nope, gonna be Mittelman and his lab."

"And how would you know this?" Brittany asked.

"Obvious target is this women's clinic, but the NSA is picking up a lot of chatter that indicates Mittelman is the bomber's real goal," he said.

"And my mole is wrong?" I asked.

"Not sayin' that exactly," he said.

"Then what are you saying, exactly?" Brittany asked.

"Bomber knows the Chicago PD has limited resources," he said. "Was almost caught in Arlington five years ago. Figures out there has to be a mole in his organization. Taking advantage of that, mentions to his group the clinic is his target, knowing the mole'll tell us. But he's really going after Mittelman."

"He didn't count on the NSA finding out," David said.

"Didn't, because those guys are good at hearing stuff, especially since 9/11," Tony said.

"What can we do?" Cas asked.

"Feds are putting on the full court press around Mittelman's lab and have for the past week. They don't trust Hogan to do the job. Chicago PD has been assigned to help too."

This isn't good for our team.

"What about the target abortion clinic?" I asked.

"On next Friday, some of our people'll be at the clinic so they can arrest the bomber." He paused. "If he even goes there."

"I have an idea," Brittany said. "Why don't you have one of your people immediately begin to act like one of the clinic's doctors?"

"Too expensive," Tony said.

"Hear me out," she said. "When patients call the clinic, the office staff will say a new doctor is coming into the practice, and he'll be sharing night call with the clinic doctor."

"Brittany has a great idea," Cas said. "After business hours, send all the phone calls from the real doctor's answering service to a Chicago Police Department phone. When the bomber calls with a phony emergency, our own guy can go to the clinic posing as the new clinic doctor."

"I can set up a medical website for the new doctor and create a whole new identity for the decoy, one that'll withstand a thorough computer search," David said.

"When the bomber calls, he'll get the message that the decoy doctor is on call," Cas said. "If the bomber does an online check of the doctor, he'll have to believe our guy is real."

"Then your men can surround the clinic and arrest him when he shows up," Molly said.

"And when no one calls, we can blow off the whole operation and concentrate on Mittelman's lab, where the bomber's gonna do his thing." Tony hesitated. "But I like it. Clinic doctors won't be at risk. Captain'll be happy with that, and cost'll be minimal."

"Where are you going to be, Tony?" David asked.

"Been thinkin' about that. Might join you guys at the clinic on Friday."

"Why not be at Micah's lab?" Molly asked.

"Fed's top brass'll be there for that one. All chiefs and no Indians. Not much for lowly detectives like me to do."

"What will you do at the clinic?" Cas asked.

I knew his answer before he could open his mouth. "Tony is going to be the decoy doctor," I said.

89

"Only place for a rising star like me to be," Tony said.

"Then shouldn't you begin watching the building on Monday?" Brittany asked.

"Clinic closed for Labor Day."

"Then how about beginning on Tuesday?" she asked. "You might be lucky and take him down before he can bring the bomb in next Friday."

"*If* he brings it in, which no one thinks he will," he said. "Cost a lot of money to do a twenty-four-hour surveillance for even two days. It's killin' our budget to watch Mittelman's lab. But I can pop by in a doc's uniform once or twice early in the week, so if the perp is watchin', he'll think I'm the real deal."

"Since your funds are such a problem, maybe we can help you watch the clinic building, and I'll coach these guys on how to do it," I said.

"Huh?" he said. "Never considered that, but gotta a problem with it."

We waited.

"You guys aren't cops," he continued. "You can't be there."

"That's easy to fix," Molly said.

Tony gave her the hard cop-eye stare. "I said, you guys aren't cops. You can't be there. End of story. Got it, sweets?"

Molly stared back at him. He didn't blink. Neither did she.

I'd never seen her have attitude about anything. Now she did.

What's up with this?

"This isn't my first rodeo with stuff like this," she said. "I'll take care of it, okay?"

"How you plannin' on doin' it?" he asked.

"We'll sign a release to cover your ass," she said. "We get hurt, it's on us, not the Chicago PD."

"Like civilians do who go on a ride-around with cops in a black and white?" he asked.

"Exactly," she said.

"Gotta run it by the captain. He goes for it, I'll fax the papers for you guys to sign before we go any further with this."

"We'll have our lawyer check it before we sign it," Cas said.

"Linda?" I asked.

"For sure," Cas said.

Tony and Brittany left. The rest of us lingered around the table trying to figure out how we could structure a surveillance schedule around our daily parenting activities without the bomber knowing what we were doing. Safety had to be key. Our lives were at stake.

"The bomber watches our every move, right?" Cas said.

"With the cameras he has trained on our homes," I said, "that would be a reasonable assumption."

"And don't forget the GPS trackers on all of our cars," David said.

"Why don't we just remove them?" Cas asked.

"David and I talked about this," I said. "If we do that, it'll alert the bomber that we're on to him."

"And we don't want to do that," David said.

"So, what we have here is a great plan but no way to implement it," I said.

"XSport Fitness," Molly said, and then glanced down at her iPhone.

The rest of us stared at her.

"*And?*" Cas asked.

"We all go there," Molly said.

Cas softly banged her head in her hands. "God help us."

"That might be okay too," Molly said.

"Ah, Molly, could you expand on your idea a little?" I asked.

"Sure," she said, as she stared at her phone.

We waited. She read something from her screen and then sent a text.

She read the reply and looked up. "Where were we?"

"At XSport Fitness," I said.

"Oh, right. So, see, we all walk there, and by now, the bomber has to know that. That eliminates his GPS trackers, since we don't use our cars."

"I see where you're going with this," I said. "When it's one of our times to watch the clinic, we walk to XSport and drop our kids off. We then sneak out the back door and drive away in an Uber or Lyft."

90

Friday night, Carter and I were in the wine room. Kerry was asleep in her crib upstairs. We had the Nanit app on.

"I talked to Brittany," Carter said. "She told me about your meeting and your plan. I would like to hear it from you."

I told him the details.

"Thanks again for supporting me on doing this," I said, when I finished.

"It might be a terrific story, and you've waited over five years to finish it. I admit I'm worried, but if you insist on being there, this seems the safest way you can do it."

"Did Brittany also tell you that one of the cops is going to pose as the doctor?"

"She did. It's Tony Infantino."

I felt my face flush.

"She doesn't know about your past history with the detective."

Hold it.

This was too easy. Ever since I was blown up in Arlington, he had been overly concerned about my safety. And he hated Tony because he knew about our affair fourteen years ago. Now my husband seemed to be all in.

Something isn't right.

"Have you been talking to the FBI?" I asked.

"I have not directly spoken to the FBI."

"How about someone from the NSA?"

This time he didn't answer.

"But Brittany has," I continued.

"Yes, she has."

Gotcha.

I kept pressing. "The feds are certain the bomber will go after Micah and his lab."

"They are."

"Are they still picking up chatter about this?"

"Yes. In fact, it's increased."

"You think we're stupid for watching the clinic."

"I didn't say that."

"But you think it."

He remained silent.

I began to shiver. "Can we discuss this upstairs? I'm freezing in here."

"Would you like to relax instead and watch a couple of DVDs?"

"Sure. Which ones?"

"*The Day of the Jackal* and *The Manchurian Candidate*."

"As long as they're the original versions. I can't stand the remakes."

"You'll get no argument from me on that."

We went upstairs to the TV room and sat down on the couch. Since David had cleaned up the mess of DVDs and jackets, we had a reasonable chance that any movie Carter selected would be in its own jacket. He put on *The Day of the Jackal.*

The *Jackal* movie was set in 1963. In the film, the bad guy made a special gun that he disguised as a crutch. It made me wonder if terrorists ever watched flicks like this. Hopefully, modern security techniques would unmask a crude weapon like that.

The Manchurian Candidate involved a war hero, initially a good guy, who was brainwashed into being a bad guy. While dressed like a priest, he was instructed to assassinate a presidential candidate at Madison Square Garden.

President?

Darn it. Now I wouldn't sleep. All I would think about was a bad guy wearing a clerical collar and using a crutch, showing up at the United Center to shoot the president.

91

Two hours later, I sat up in bed wide awake. "That's it," I said.

Carter snoozed on his stomach. "What?" he said sleepily.

"Wait a second."

I went into the bathroom and turned on all of the faucets. As long as we whispered, the cascading water would cover what I was going to say. I beckoned for him to follow me into the bathroom.

"Molly suggested that we come up with a fake plan to divert the bomber's attention," I whispered in his ear.

"Say again?" he whispered back.

"Go with me on this. Monday, we have a meeting here at the house to discuss possible future targets for the bomber other than abortion clinics."

"But won't that be a problem because it's Labor Day?"

"I forgot about that. We'll do it on Sunday so it won't interfere with any holiday plans."

"Okay, so you have the meeting and he'll hear your plan."

"Exactly, and I think I figured out our *faux* target."

He waited.

"The President of the United States."

He raised his eyebrows. "You got this from those two DVDs."

"I did. I'll tell the girls and David that since the bomber is now using a gun, it's obvious to me he's going to shoot someone famous to bring national publicity to his cause."

"The president, when he comes here on September 11th."

"And the bomber is going to make a gun disguised as a crutch, or something like that, so he can sneak it into the United Center."

"You'll then make a carefully prepared list of measures to prevent this."

"Which of course we won't do at all."

"He'll assume you'll be totally immersed in these plans, and he won't suspect that you're planning to trap him two days before that."

"That's my plan, bubba." I leaned against his chest. "And I'm sticking to it."

"I hope it isn't too perfect a plan."

"How so?"

"You have to apprehend him on Friday, or there might be a bigger problem than blown up abortion clinics."

"I don't understand."

"You're about to give your killer a blueprint to shoot the president."

Honey, I hope you're wrong.

He climbed back into bed and fell asleep. I couldn't stop thinking about the events coming up, so I went down to my computer and wrote and printed the scripts for our meeting on Sunday.

We were going to discuss the bomber's case with the knowledge that he was going to hear every word we said. Our discussion had to sound spontaneous, but we couldn't afford to make any mistakes he might pick up on.

When I finished, I entered everything into my file. It wasn't until I went over my files that I'd figured out how to keep Tony from being blown up.

In every clinic bombing, the killer had hidden the device in the men's bathroom. If he did it this time, the police could have a bomb expert, possibly disguised as an orderly or nurse, find and defuse the bomb. When Tony went in later that night, the bomber wouldn't be able to set off the device. I hoped the bomber would then enter the building to see what went wrong.

And he would finally be arrested.

Part 4

92

We had an uneventful family weekend, except for the release papers Tony faxed to me on Saturday afternoon. I took them to Linda, and she okayed the content.

On Sunday morning, everyone came to my home right after breakfast. Carter hung out in the computer room working on his reporters' stories. The kids played in our main-floor family room. The adults would have to speak loudly over their noise when we read the scripts I'd written so we could make sure the bomber heard us.

Before they arrived, I partially closed the blinds so his cameras couldn't peer into the family room and see that we were reading instead of speaking spontaneously. The first item was for everyone to sign the release papers. David is a notary, so he put his stamp on each page after we individually signed. I would fax copies to Tony after everyone left.

Now we could begin.

"Here's how I see this," I began, waving my script so they would know I was starting. "I think the bomber is changing his method."

I nodded at Cas and pointed to the paper in front of her.

Cas read it and then spoke. "Why do you say that, Tina?"

"He recently shot an abortion doctor. I think he wants more publicity for his cause, and he'll stop the bombings and continue using other methods, like shooting doctors."

"Tina and I have discussed this at length," David read. "The bombings don't seem to be getting the bomber enough publicity, so we think he is going to change to a more aggressive method of protest."

"Jeez, bombing seems pretty aggressive to me," Molly said.

The rest of the Irregulars began thumbing through their pages hunting for what Molly had just said.

I walked over to her and leaned down. "That's not in the script," I whispered. "Don't ad lib."

She began to reply, but I stopped her by gently placing my hand over her mouth. "Don't say anything that's not written down here," I whispered again.

"Sorry," she whispered back.

"Does anyone have any ideas?" I asked.

Cas's eyes widened as she read her lines to herself before she said them out loud. "Didn't you mention last week that the president is coming to Chicago?"

"I did," I said.

"What if the bomber decides to shoot him?" she asked. "That would certainly get him maximum attention all over the world."

"It sure would," Molly read and then said.

"How do you think he would do it, David?" I asked.

He checked his script. "Are you guys familiar with the movies *The Day of the Jackal* and *The Manchurian Candidate?*"

A pause was followed by a murmur of yeses from everyone.

He raised his eyebrows behind his glasses as he read what he was about to say. "I think he could go in disguised as an old priest using a walker that is actually a dismantled gun."

"Do we tell the police?" Molly asked, sticking to her script.

"Yes, we do," I said. "I'll notify Tony Infantino about our concerns, and we'll let the police, Secret Service, and FBI handle it."

"What will we do?" Cas asked. "We don't have anything to do until they catch the bomber a week from Monday."

"It's about time I have a dinner party for the group," David said. "How about this Friday night?"

Which was the night we would be waiting for the bomber at the clinic he was going to blow up.

"What time?" I asked.

"Why don't we meet at my apartment at about seven?" he said. "That should give your husbands time to get home from work."

"That sounds fabulous," Cas said, reading her final lines. "I can't wait."

Let's hope the bomber buys into this.

93

Everyone left. After lunch, Carter took Kerry to Hamlin Park. I emailed my script to Tony, with a copy to Brittany and Carter. I also asked Tony if he'd received any feedback about the C4 comparisons from the FBI.

Then, I walked into the wine room and called Brittany.

"Brit, this is Tina," I said. "Gotta sec'?"

"I just read your email to Tony, and I think your plan is super," Brittany said. "And we need the FBI report about the C4 for the story."

"Can you get it?" I asked.

"Tina, *please*. It's Tony we're talking about here. I'll have a drink with him tonight and have the answer tomorrow."

"I assumed you were going to do that the last time we met."

"I sort of blew him off. It keeps him coming back."

"The dangling carrot."

"Whatever… But I've never done a stakeout. I don't think Tony is the person I want to give me instructions," she said. "There might be too many distractions. Could you give me some help?"

"Why don't I meet you near the clinic around two or so? We can check it out before the rest of the troops show up on Tuesday."

"But it's Sunday," she protested.

"Do you want to do this or not?"

She paused. "I'll see you at two."

I disconnected and texted Carter that I was going to XSport to try out our transportation system before I traveled to the South Side to scout out the clinic.

After calling for Lyft, I went out the back door of the club. The driver met me in the parking lot of Whole Foods, which was a block away.

It took half an hour to reach the clinic.

Brittany stood next to her car, a new red Lexus IS C convertible. She had parked across the street from the clinic. The Lyft driver dropped me off behind her car.

She eyed the driver. "Something I should know?"

I told her about the bomber's GPS device on my van.

"Smart move using Lyft," she said. "Do you think the bomber will tag my car too?"

"Good question. Let's check it out."

I searched under the fenders and bumpers. Her car was clean.

"This is really a nice ride," I said, visualizing myself roaring down Lakeshore Drive with the top down and the wind blowing my hair.

She smiled. "A present from my parents when I graduated from Northwestern last year."

Did you just emphasize "last year"?

Maybe I was wrong, but her tight designer jeans were enough of a statement about the differences in our ages.

I surveyed the South Side neighborhood where the clinic was located. Most of the dilapidated brick buildings were at least five decades old and in serious disrepair. The one-story abortion clinic had previously been a tire store, which had been out of business for several years.

"I don't see where we can watch that building without sticking out like a Packer's fan at a Bear's home game," Brittany said. "Any ideas?"

"Actually, I do." I turned around and pointed. "Right there."

"There" was a seedy apartment building behind us. It had a great view of the clinic. It was so disgustingly run down, it couldn't possibly have many permanent residents, so finding an available room wasn't going to be a problem.

Brittany's face blanched behind her glowing tan.

You've never seen anything like this, sweetie.

In the old days, I would have entered the three-story apartment building without a concern for my safety if it would have enabled me to get the facts for a story. But this time, I was a mommy. And I wasn't sure how Brittany would react if there was a problem.

I called Tony.

94

After parking his BMW behind Brittany's Lexus, Tony led us into the shabby lobby. The clerk was asleep, his head on the top of the desk.

Tony banged his fist on the wood counter. The man's head snapped up. He peered at us through heavy lids and rheumy eyes. His wrinkled skin looked like the pocket of my brother's baseball glove.

Tony badged him. "Need a room that faces the street."

"Full up, sorry," he said, his voice raspy from too many cigarettes.

You missed your last few dental appointments.

I stood off to the side, afraid the man's two remaining lower teeth might fly out when he spoke. Brittany stood close behind me.

Tony hit the desk again. "I need a room," he repeated, louder this time. "Got it, dude?"

"No need to get upset, detective." The clerk grabbed a set of keys off the rack behind him. "Follow me."

Brittany touched my shoulder. "I think I'll wait in the car."

"You want to help write this story?"

"For sure."

"Then get with the program. Breathe through your mouth and don't touch anything."

The desk clerk bypassed the rusty elevator, which probably hadn't moved since the White Sox last won a World Series. We followed the two men up the stairs. The stairwell reeked of a combination of sweat, urine, feces, cheap wine, vomit, and cigarettes.

I sniffed. "This is amazing," I said to myself.

"What?" Brittany asked from behind me.

I continued to walk up the creaky stairs. "This odor is always the same. When I had the police beat on the South Side of Chicago, the indigent patients in the ER smelled like this. I'll never forget it."

"Kind of like the desk clerk smells."

Why is your voice so far away?

I stopped on the first landing and glanced over my shoulder. Brittany was still on the first floor.

"I think it's revolting," she continued. "How can anyone live like this?"

"Suck it up, or go home and I'll write the story myself."

95

The clerk showed Tony four empty apartments on the top floor of the three-story building. He picked the last one on the right.

It was a musty single room. To the right of the door was an efficiency kitchen containing a rattling refrigerator and a lopsided kitchen table with no chairs. In the middle of the room was a dusty, overstuffed gray chair and, on the left, a saggy single bed. Two grimy windows faced the clinic. It smelled like the clerk slept in there.

He left. Tony pulled the grungy armchair up to the windows.

"You can set up here and watch the clinic," he said.

"And that's it?" I asked.

He shrugged his shoulders. "Am I missing somethin' here?"

"Cameras, computers, a way to communicate with you and the rest of the police department. I would say we're missing lots of things."

"Captain ran out of funds."

"And let me guess the rest. He doesn't think the bomber's going to show up here."

"You said it, not me, sweets."

"But..." Brittany broke in.

"No buts. You want to call me, use your cell phone. You got my number."

And with that, he left.

So much for serving and protecting.

"Asshole!" she screamed at his back. She turned to me. "We are so screwed."

"We'll figure it out."

I'd been in worse situations when I was with the Marines, but they always had my back.

Think.

The rancid smells of the room began to nauseate both of us, so I opened the windows.

Or at least tried to.

The windows must not have been opened since the last war the U.S. won. Brittany had to help me.

"Do we have to do this twenty-four hours a day?" she whined.

"I don't think we need to be here after the clinic closes." I pointed at the building. There were outside security cameras on each corner of the building. "They seem to have tight security."

"You're saying that if the bomber's going to get in, it'll have to be during the hours when the clinic's open."

"I am, just like he's done at the other clinics."

I pictured our setup.

"We need to see if there's a back door into this building," I said.

"What's wrong with the front door?" she asked.

"If the bomber starts watching the clinic building, he'll see us going in and out. Young white women in this neighborhood would stick out like an alcoholic having a cocktail in the Mormon Tabernacle."

"The same goes for my car. There aren't any new ones like mine parked outside." She paused. "You do realize Tony's probably right. No one, including Carter, thinks the bomber is really coming here."

"My mole was right before, and I'm a believer."

"But you were almost killed that time."

A valid point.

"There aren't many people who would want to be in this rat hole. We'll be safe in this room. What could happen up here?"

96

I rode in the backseat of an Uber car. I called Carter to tell him I was on my way back to XSport Fitness. "Have you talked to Brittany?" I asked.

"She just called me," he said. "Is the room as bad as she made it out to be?"

"Probably worse, but she needs to toughen up if she's going to last in this business."

"I agree, and I told her that when she began to complain."

"Thanks. She didn't seem to want to listen to me."

"She also told me about the lack of police tech support."

"I didn't expect them to help us. They use us when we can be of service to them, but other than that? Never."

"As members of the press, we're always on our own for stories."

"Any ideas?"

"What about David?"

"What about him?"

"He might be able to come up with the equipment you need."

"Honey, that's a great idea. I'll call him right away."

I did and explained the problem to David.

"I assumed they would have, at the very minimum, a way for us to communicate with them," David said, when I finished.

"Carter and I just talked about that. That's just the way it is."

"Well, we'll see about that. I'll call my friends at Hogan. I think we can come up with all the surveillance apparatus we'll need.

97

On Monday, Labor Day morning, Brittany texted me. She found a basement door in the back of the building that would shield our approach.

At 8 a.m. on Tuesday morning, the Lyft driver dropped Cas and me off in front of an abandoned Methodist church three blocks away from the clinic building.

David and Molly followed us in another Lyft. Our kids were at the XSport Fitness children's center. Margaret was in preschool. Brittany arrived in an Uber.

The girls didn't say anything as we walked through the grimy neighborhood. David lagged behind, weighed down by a carrier with his computer gear. Molly lugged a large bag, which I assumed carried the rest of his equipment.

When we reached the back door of the building, Cas stood motionless staring at it. We had to wait for Molly and David to catch up.

"Is this it?" David asked, when we walked in the back door of the building.

"Yeah, but see, it's not that bad once you get in the room," I said.

They followed me upstairs, and of course, it was way worse when we stepped into the room. David scanned the space, and from the stricken look on his face, I thought he was going to throw up.

He put his head down and began to hyperventilate.

Help him!

"David, would you like some assistance unpacking your computer gear?" I asked.

I knew he always did everything his own way. I hoped to shock him back to being able to function.

"I, ah, I'll do it," he said softly.

He kept his head down as he worked. I was afraid if he looked up he might throw up.

The slumlords who owned this crappy apartment had clearly never heard of Wi-Fi, so there was no direct computer access available. David solved this problem by using a MiFi apparatus he'd brought with him.

After he set up his equipment, he came to life. Working with his computers saved the day. He gave us the game plan and started with a digital camera.

"This has a telephoto lens," he said, as he locked the camera onto a tripod. "I want each of you to take a few pictures to get used to handling and focusing it."

While we did, he set up a bigger camera on a tripod.

"Do the same thing with the video camera. When you're done, I'll replay the shots from each camera to make sure you didn't screw up anything."

We were on our way.

98

For the next few minutes, we practiced shooting views of the clinic and the parking lot. When David was positive we knew what we were doing, he moved on.

"I'm going to turn the video camera on and focus it at the parking lot and two entrances," he said. "I'll leave it running twenty-four hours a day. The footage will simultaneously be relayed from here to my computer and then to the Hogan computers."

"What about Linda?" I asked.

"Great idea. I'll include her in the loop."

"What about this other camera?" Molly asked.

"If a delivery is made, snap a still picture of the worker's face and license plate and download it on the computer. The Hogan computers can research that person and the owner of the van or truck to make sure he or she is who they're supposed to be."

"What about a man entering the clinic or even walking close to it?" I asked.

"Again, snap a picture and send it on," he said. "We can't afford to miss anyone."

"Your company can do all this?" Cas asked.

"It has facial recognition software and access to data from most law enforcement files in the world. Hogan said we could access those computers until Friday but not after that."

"What about Tony, our phony doctor?" Cas asked.

"If the bomber does an online background check, he'll find a full history, including several medical articles the doctor supposedly has written."

"Your guys are good," Molly said.

"As you frequently say, this isn't their first rodeo."

The ever-present abortion protesters arrived about ten minutes before the clinic opened at 9 a.m. There were three of them. They pulled out folding lawn chairs and sat down, their posters at their sides.

Zooming in with the still camera, David snapped headshots of each one of the people and then downloaded the pictures into his computer.

"This is going to give us a chance to test the system," he said, as he sent the intel to the Hogan computers. "We need to know who these people are."

Three minutes later, David's cell phone rang. He put it on speaker. "The pictures you sent are three known protesters from the Chicago area," a female voice said.

David disconnected and gestured to me. "All we need now is our schedules."

"I'll take the first two-hour shift," I said. "Brittany, you're next, followed by Molly and, finally, David."

He held up a black phone. "There's one other item, and please don't tell anyone about it, okay?" he asked.

"No problem," I said. "What is that?"

"With this phone, we can monitor all the police frequencies so we'll know what's going on."

"Is that legal?" Cas asked.

David blushed. "No, that's why we shouldn't tell anyone we have it."

"Now all we have to do is catch the bomber," Cas said.

99

David had the last shift Tuesday afternoon. Wednesday morning, I opened the door to the apartment for the first shift.

Am I in the right room?

I sniffed.

What the heck?

Fresh flowers?

I sniffed again.

No, air freshener.

I surveyed the room. The floor and walls had been scrubbed down. The bed and chair were gone, along with the clattering refrigerator and the lopsided kitchen table.

This is pure David.

He'd hung pink drapes over the now sparkling clean windows. There was a camper's cooler plugged into the wall socket. I opened it. It was full of bottled water and fresh fruit.

He had even brought three new folding chairs with green cushions. Two of the chairs were in front of the windows. The third was by his computer setup.

The thing that still sucked was the lack of a bathroom in the apartment. The residents were supposed to use the one at the end of the hall. I had gone down there during my first shift and was so grossed out after I opened the door I didn't go in.

But not David. He'd hung up a key on the room's wall that said "bathroom." I wandered down to the end of the hall and unlocked the door.

Amazing.

He had done the best he could by scrubbing down the sink and toilet along with the floors and walls. He had purchased disposable toilet covers, handy wipes, and a bar of skin-freshening soap.

David would make someone a great wife.

Having him on our team was a real plus. Not only had he brought and hooked up all the equipment we would need, but we could use the bathroom when we wanted to without catching some incurable communicable disease. To have done all this, he must have stayed late, long after the clinic closed.

I sat down to watch the clinic. After a boring first hour, I called Tony's cell.

"Anything new?" I asked.

"Nope, but doesn't make any difference, because the bomber isn't coming there."

"Are you bummed to be missing the action at Micah's lab?"

"Massive cluster fuck out there. Don't have enough rank to get within three blocks of the building, so rather be anywhere but there."

"And you'll have a chance to be a hero here."

"Got that right. Bought some cool new doctor's duds at Barney's. Gotta look the part."

"I'm sure you will."

100

By 10 a.m. I was really bored staring out the window watching patients go in and out of the clinic. There wasn't anyone suspicious to snap a still picture of. The video was on.

I didn't have anything to do.

Or do I?

There was one place I wanted to see for myself: the men's bathroom in the clinic. I pulled a hoodie over my head to mask my features in case the bomber watched the clinic.

I walked down the stinky stairs, went out the basement back door, and jogged down two blocks before I crossed the street and made my way back to the clinic entrance.

As I approached the clinic's front door, the taunts from the anti-abortion protesters picked up in volume when they saw me, assuming I was coming in for an abortion.

Entering the clinic, I pulled back the hoodie and shook out my hair. I surveyed the waiting room. It was full of the women I'd watched walk into the clinic. The lady behind the desk evaluated me for a few seconds. "Sugar, in case you're here for a consultation about an abortion, you need to make an appointment first."

I leaned down so no one could hear me. "I just need to use the bathroom."

She pointed with her pen behind her. "Back there, down the hall, other side of the men's bathroom."

I stepped around behind the counter and followed her directions. I sniffed. As soon as the medicinal smells in the hallway hit my olfactory apparatus, I had to stop and shut my eyes.

Relax. This isn't Arlington.

Tell that to my brain.

As I walked toward the men's bathroom, I put my hand on the wall to support myself. The bathroom door opened, and a man stepped out.

Everything turned black.

101

The next thing I knew, there was something cold on my forehead.

"What the hell are you doin' here?" Tony whispered in my ear.

I opened my eyes. I was flat on my back in a bathroom. A wet paper towel was plastered on my forehead. When I saw the urinals on the wall, I knew which bathroom I was in.

"I was bored, so I decided to check out the men's bathroom," I said. "I walked down the hall and saw the bomber coming out of the men's bathroom. I guess it scared me, and I passed out. Did you see him?"

He laughed. "Wasn't the bomber. Was me. Went into the can to check out my outfit. Was me you saw coming out."

Leaning back, I saw that he wore a long white coat with a fake name, "Dr. L. Romano," stitched in large dark blue letters above the left front pocket. He wore a fake black beard. It looked kind of sexy.

I raised my arms. "Help me up, please."

Tony hesitated.

"For God's sake, I don't weigh that much," I said.

"Not too sure about that. Was tough enough dragging you in here. Back injury from lifting you up might not be covered by our workman's comp."

He walked around me a couple of times, and then his dark eyes lit up.

I've seen that look before.

He stood behind me, but I jumped up before he could put his arms under my armpits and hands on my breasts.

It still didn't stop him.

"Can lock the door." He glanced at his watch. "Got time for a quickie."

"Not in this lifetime."

"Your loss, sweets." He stepped back. "What do you think about my outfit and the beard?"

He had the whole doctor look going on: a heavily starched, long white coat with a stethoscope around his neck, several pens in the left front pocket, gray slacks, and highly polished, black Italian leather shoes. He caught me eying his matching dress shirt and tie.

"Robert Graham," he said. "Love his stuff. Got this at Sak's on Michigan Ave."

I said it before he could. "No, I can't see it."

He unbuttoned his white coat. "Didn't think so. And got enough room in here so I can wear a Kevlar vest."

"Do you think you'll need one?" I asked.

"Don't want to, but the captain insisted. Doesn't want to lose one of his studs."

Of course he doesn't.

102

I looked at his white coat again. "Who is L. Romano?"

"Louis is a cousin on my mother's side," Tony said. "Didn't want to use my name in case the perp checked up on me with my real name. Your boy David fixed it up on the website."

I dropped the soggy paper towel in the trash and began checking around. "Have you found anything?"

"You mean like a bomb?" Tony asked.

"No, Jimmy freaking Hoffa," I said. "Of course I mean a bomb. Why else would I come over here to search the men's bathroom?"

"Don't know. We used to do some pretty kinky stuff together. Remember when we almost got caught in the can at Joe's Stone Crab?"

I felt my face begin to burn with that memory.

"No, I don't," I lied. "Let's get to work. The bomber has hidden the previous bombs in the trash can, but maybe we should also check above the tiles in the ceiling."

He stood still.

"Tony, you're taller than I am. Push up the tiles and check in the ceiling."

"No can do."

"Why?"

"Not my job description. Bomb squad does that."

"We don't need a bomb squad in here. All we need to do is check around. If we find a bomb, we'll call them."

He still didn't move.

"Okay, if you won't do it, I will," I said. "Here, lift me up."

"Don't think so."

"Then let's start with the trash can."

He backed up toward the door. "I'll stand guard so some guy doesn't come in."

"Whatever."

I was about to lift the lid on the trash can before I fully comprehended why Tony had stepped out. What if the bomber booby-trapped the trash can last week before we even got in here?

I gently lifted my hand off the lid and tiptoed out into the hall to join Tony.

"Let the bomb squad do this," I said.

"Will on Friday afternoon, right before the clinic closes. Got it all covered, sweets."

103

Thursday afternoon, it was Brittany's turn to watch the clinic. I contacted my mole again to see if that person knew what the heck was going on, but I didn't receive a reply.

I was beginning to feel more than a little foolish, since it seemed that everyone with a badge and registered gun was busy surrounding Micah's clinic. I was positive they were laughing at the stupid moms and David who were watching the abortion clinic for nothing.

In half an hour, we were going to have a meeting of the Irregulars at Molly's house to go over our plans for Friday. David was in my kitchen baking chocolate cupcakes for everyone. He wanted them to be hot, which was why he was using my kitchen only three blocks from Molly's home. He didn't use Molly's kitchen because it was always too messy for him, and he said he couldn't work in there.

The heavenly aroma from the oven activated my salivary glands.

"That smells amazing," I said. "Do you want some help putting on the frosting?"

"No," he said.

"No?"

"I have a special way to do it."

Of course you do.

"Okay, fine," I said. "By the way, did you remember that Micah invited all of us to the United Center to hear him announce his discovery to the world?"

"I wish I could, but Saturday morning, Mary and Margaret are flying with me for a job interview in Palo Alto. Mary's off work for a couple of days, and we're taking a mini-vacation. We'll be back on Wednesday."

"I didn't know you were hunting for a job."

"Mary is missing out on too much of Margaret's growing up. It isn't fair, so it's my turn to become the breadwinner so she can have some mommy time."

"Why not go back to work with Hogan?"

"Eighty to ninety-hour work weeks and constant travel is the way of life with them. This is a small high-tech start-up company specializing in online cooking items."

Right in your wheelhouse.

"Will you guys have to move?"

"I hope not. That's one of the items I have to discuss with them."

"Negotiate hard. We can't do our stories without you."

104

Twenty minutes later, we sat in Molly's family room wolfing down David's cupcakes. I had given them the report about my visit to the clinic, along with showing them the floor plans of the clinic building that Tony had given me.

"Micah gave me tickets for all of you to attend his lecture on Monday, the 11th, at the United Center."

"Sorry," Molly said. "On Saturday, we're leaving for the Wisconsin Dells. My two older kids love the water parks. The little ones, not so much."

"I have three spinning classes to teach that day," Cas said. "There's no way I could get subs for each one of them."

"Guess I'll be going alone," I said.

"David, what about you?" Cas ask.

"We're going to the San Francisco area to visit some old friends."

He didn't mention the job interview, and I wasn't going to tell everyone in case he didn't get hired.

"All righty then, on to further business," I said. "Have you guys observed anything unusual at the clinic?"

"It seems to be a medical clinic, nothing more, nothing less," Cas said.

"The protesters sure are nice," Molly said.

"Nice?" I asked. "And how would you know that?"

"I talked to them."

WHAT?!

I felt my face burn. "You were supposed to stay in the room," I said.

"Yeah, but see, I get bored easily."

"Boy, is that a big surprise," Cas said.

"But anyway, it was hot, so I took them some bottled water. They, like, totally needed it."

My stomach began to churn. "You didn't say anything about the bomber, did you?"

"Not exactly."

"What does that even mean?" Cas asked.

"I did mention the other bombings to see how they felt about them."

We remained silent.

"They said firebombing a clinic might be okay if no one was injured, but to them, blowing up a doctor is unacceptable."

"How about shooting a doctor?" I asked.

"Same. They're not into hurting people."

"And your conclusion?" Cas asked.

"None of them are connected to our guy," Molly said.

105

On the way home from Molly's, I had time to call Tony.

"Anything?" I asked.

"Had the bomb guy go back into the clinic before it closed just to be sure everything is still clean."

My heart began to pound in my chest. "And?"

"Didn't find squat."

"I don't know whether that's good or bad."

"All it means is you have to pay close attention tomorrow."

"Don't worry. We will."

"Finally got the report back from the FBI lab comparing the C4 from Arlington with the bombings here. Confirmed a match."

"Not a big surprise. What about the C4 I took from Jamie's apartment?"

"Not back yet. Our lab guys are working it off the clock as a favor to me, and it's gonna take a while."

"What about the DNA sample I snagged from the shooter's bathroom? Did it match the bomber's DNA from Arlington?"

There were blood spatters in Arlington that couldn't be accounted for and presumably came from the bomber. If that DNA matched the sample from the shooter's bathroom, we had positive proof the Arlington bomber and the Chicago-area bomber/sniper were the same man.

"Not unless I'm the bomber and the shooter."

"What?"

"Was my DNA on the sink. Captain wasn't happy. Almost took me off the case after he saw the report. Hates to have us contaminate a crime scene."

"Sorry."

"Anything you forgot to tell me about the C4 on those trash samples you gave me?"

"Why?"

"Could somebody have planted it?"

I hesitated a few seconds to focus on that night.

"The cop who caught me said the alarm had gone off two times," I said. "I only set it off once. If it went off two times, then I guess anyone else could have triggered it the first time and planted the stuff I stole. Why are you asking about that now?"

"Tying up some loose ends on that case."

"Is there something you're not telling me?"

"Lots of things I'm not going to tell you, just like you do with me, but there's one difference…" he said. "When I catch your bomber, I'll give you an exclusive interview."

And I would put up with his BS to finish my story.

106

Friday night, a cloud cover obliterated the sun, which normally would have lit up the street until at least 8 p.m. To further complicate visibility, a light rain fell, and the ever-present Chicago wind blew off Lake Michigan.

Streetlights provided some illumination, but less than half of them worked. The multicolored blinking lights from the neon signs outside the three bars on the block didn't help much.

The clinic closed at 5 p.m. David had the last shift and was already in the room. Everyone else except Brittany rode together in a Lyft. She arrived in an Uber.

I noticed two empty bags neatly folded in the hallway outside the room. When we walked in, we found David behind his computer watching the screen.

I asked him about the carriers in the hallway.

"This is all going to be over soon," he said. "I don't want to leave Hogan's equipment here any longer than I have to."

From the stress lines on his face, there was no way he was going to watch the events unfold from the windows.

"Did you see the bomb squad guy?" I asked.

"A man wearing a scrub suit entered at 4:15. He just left. I checked his photograph against the Chicago PD database. He's one of theirs."

"Great. Anything else?"

"Not that I could see, and I'm pretty sure I didn't miss anything."

"Then we're good to go?" I asked.

"As good as we can be."

"When do the police arrive?" Cas asked.

"I talked to Tony this afternoon," I said. "His boss finally agreed to send a SWAT team. They're deployed in a garage two blocks away."

David looked up from his computer screen. "Why so far?"

"Not sure, but maybe they'll move in closer when the bomber calls the clinic."

The room was silent. At least no one said "if" he called.

David held up the police monitor phone. "Does Tony know we're going to monitor his transmissions with this?"

"You know me better than that," I said. "I didn't bust you out."

"Thanks for that, but I better begin to find the proper frequency or we'll miss everything."

He did, and we waited. Finally, a low-pitched woman's voice came on. "A man called the doctor's answering service at 17:32. As per our protocol with them, the call was transferred to me. He told me his girlfriend had an abortion earlier this week and was now bleeding."

Tony's voice came on. "Copy that. Anything else?"

"I told him I would contact Dr. Romano. I waited fifteen minutes before I called the man back. I told him Dr. Romano had called in and he would meet the man and his girlfriend at the clinic as soon as they could get there." The woman paused. "Looks like we're a go."

"Rollin'," Tony said.

Yes!

107

"You SWAT guys ready?" the woman with the low-pitched voice asked.

"We're moving," a male voice said. "The bomb unit just arrived. I'll deploy my men. When we're in position, I'll give you a heads up."

Everyone but David peeked out of the window.

"I don't understand why that lady cop acting like the actual answering service waited fifteen minutes to call the man back," Brittany said.

"I don't either," I said.

"It was my suggestion," Cas said. "Answering services have so many phone calls that they're forced to contact doctors in the order in which the patient's calls are received."

"And the bomber has done this before so he would immediately be suspicious if the usual system wasn't followed," David said.

"You got it," Cas said. "If the cop posing as the operator immediately called the bomber back, he would figure out something was wrong and disappear."

"Along with our story," I said.

I'd brought my binoculars, so I used them to scan all the buildings. There was the usual nighttime activity around the bars, but I didn't see anything suspicious.

I put the binoculars down. Molly picked them up. She busied herself by checking out the hookers walking on our side of the street.

The radio crackled again. "Infantino, we're in position."

"Copy that. Coming in."

"Boy, those SWAT guys are slick," Cas said. "I never saw them."

"Let's hope the bomber didn't either," Brittany said.

"How does the bomb work anyway?" Molly asked.

"C4 can be molded into any form and is inert without a detonator," I said.

"So without that thing, the C4 won't explode."

"Not a chance."

Because of the heavy mist and intermittent rain, the headlights from Tony's car were visible before I saw the car itself. He drove a new white Audi A8 that had been loaned to the Chicago PD by one of the auto dealers. Tony wanted to make himself look like a wealthy doctor.

He parked in the reserved doctor's parking slot at the side of the building. This space was partially shielded from us by some scraggly bushes.

He had a lapel microphone and earpiece, so he was in continuous communication with the SWAT team.

We could hear every word they said to each other.

"Everybody ready?" Tony asked.

"We're good to go," a male SWAT member said.

"Gettin' out of the car."

He opened the car door and stood up.

Suddenly, there was a call over the police radio: "Stand down! There's been an explosion at Mittelman's lab! Repeat: There has been an explosion at the lab! Officers are down!"

108

"Goddamnit!" Tony growled. "In the wrong fucking place! Missed everything." He paused. "Wrap it up and let's get outta here."

"Copy that," the same male SWAT member said.

"Tina, what's a detonator look like?" Molly asked.

"The only one I've ever seen was built into a pen and pencil set," I said. "But what difference does it make? We've wasted our time."

She pointed the binoculars at the clinic building. "Does it blink?"

"What are you talking about?"

"There's a green blinking thingy in those bushes by Tony's leg."

Bushes?

"Did anyone check the bushes?" I asked.

"I have no idea," David said.

"Can we call Tony on that phone?" I asked.

"Sorry, it's only a monitor," he said.

I knocked the camera out of the way and struggled to open the window.

"Cas, help me open this stupid window!"

She did.

"Tony, get out of there!" I screamed through the open window. "The bomb's in the bushes!"

Tony looked up at our room.

A red dot weaved around on his forehead. It stopped. A shot boomed out from somewhere to my left.

Tony's head jerked back and blood flew into the air. He crumpled to the ground between the car and the bushes.

Voices from the police monitor filled our tiny room. "Officer down! Officer down!" one voice screamed.

"Where did that fucking shot come from?" another voice asked.

"Did anyone see a muzzle flash?" a female voice asked.

No one's moving in to help him!

The device is in the bushes.

They're too far away!

The bomber will wait until the SWAT team gathers around Tony. And then he'll detonate his bomb.

It'll kill everybody!

I rushed out the apartment door and ran down the smelly stairs.

I talked Tony into this!

I ran toward him. The only sounds I heard were my feet pounding on the cement and my rapid breathing. I felt like I was alone, running in a dark, rainy tunnel.

The blinking green light in the bushes was my goal. I sprinted straight toward it.

C4 needs that detonator to work.

I got to Tony first. His head was covered in blood. I wanted to reach down to help him.

No time!

I ripped the branches of the bush out of the way. There was a slim black box with the blinking green light on top of a much larger brown brick.

The light stopped blinking and turned red.

Do something!

I grabbed the box and threw it as far as I could. There was a brilliant flash of light in the misty night. It was followed by a thunderous boom.

109

The acrid odor from the exploded detonator hung in the damp air. The rain fell harder. I turned and squatted down by Tony. He was flat on his back. His head was at a weird angle. He didn't move.

I don't know what to do!

I reached out toward him. Cas ran up to us.

"Do not move his head," she instructed, which was exactly what I was going to do.

I pulled my hands back. She dropped down on her knees and stabilized his head and neck with one hand. She opened his mouth and checked his airway with the other.

Her voice was matter-of-fact. "Put pressure on his wound."

"What?!"

She sounded like a school teacher. "Put pressure on his head where he was shot."

I did. Blood oozed through my fingers. A copper odor enveloped us.

Bile erupted into the back of my throat.

"How hard do I press?"

Her voice was calm. "Hard enough to stop the bleeding."

I felt a hand on my shoulder.

"Let me help you with that." A SWAT officer knelt down beside me and placed a pressure dressing on the side of Tony's head.

"We need an EMT," Cas said. "If he stops breathing, we'll need to bag him."

Stops breathing?!

Several SWAT members deployed around us. They faced away from us, their guns pointing toward the buildings across the street.

"Lady, this area isn't secure," the cop said. "We don't know where the shooter is. Neither of you should be here."

Cas ignored his statement. So did I.

"We have a problem," she said, her voice still annoyingly calm. "He just stopped breathing. We need to bag him."

She didn't seem all that excited. I felt like I was about to pee in my shorts.

Two EMT techs ran up. They pushed the cop and me out of the way.

"GSW to the right fronto-temporal area," Cas said. "He just ceased spontaneous respirations."

The EMT techs pulled out equipment.

"What about his neck?" one tech asked.

"I'll stabilize it. You bag him."

"Done."

The tech shoved a device in Tony's mouth. He put a mask with an attached bag over Tony's nose and mouth.

Cas held Tony's head steady. The tech squeezed the bag. Tony's chest moved up and down. The other tech put a body board next to Tony. Blood soaked through the pressure dressing.

"Bag him three more times, and then we move him to board," Cas said.

"Got it."

Cas continued to stabilize Tony's neck as the two men slid Tony on the board.

Cas strapped Tony's head and neck to the board and secured it.

The tech continued to use the apparatus to breathe for Tony. Cas grabbed a pair of scissors from the tech's belt and slit both of Tony's sleeves. The tech applied a blood pressure cuff to Tony's right arm and pumped it up.

"Ninety over sixty. Pulse 144."

"Need an IV," the second tech said.

My pulse felt like it was twice that high, but they were calm in a sea of madness.

Cas swabbed something on Tony's left arm. She wrapped a tourniquet around his muscular bicep. The tech handed a needle to her. She quickly inserted it. The tech secured the needle with a strip of tape and then hooked up plastic tubing to an IV bag.

"Check his pupils," Cas said.

The tech wiped blood out of Tony's eyes and flashed his light into them.

"Divergent gaze. Right pupil sluggish."

"He needs a neurosurgeon right now," Cas said.

It was the first time I sensed tension in her voice.

"Let's move!" the first tech said.

They picked up the board with Tony secured to it and put him on a gurney. Cas held the IV bag.

I turned around and threw up into the bushes.

110

"I'm sorry?" I said to another EMT tech, as he unwrapped a blood pressure cuff off of my right arm. "It's my ears. They're ringing so loudly I can't hear you."

I sat in an ambulance. I couldn't stop shivering. I kept asking about Tony, but no one knew anything.

Tony might die because I got him into this.

There was total chaos outside the vehicle.

"I said 'nice throw,' lady," he said, as he helped me wipe Tony's dried blood off my hand and forearms. My top and shorts were soaked, too, but they were a lost cause.

He reached up and removed more blood from my face. "Not much I can do about your hair," he said. "Shower will help that."

"Not sure how his blood got in there."

"In all the excitement you probably touched your hair." He looked at me. "Like you just did."

I quickly lowered my hands from my head.

A SWAT team member walked up to me. "One of our guys said you threw the detonator almost two hundred feet in the air before it exploded." He paused. "Thank you for saving all of us."

Another SWAT cop came up. "Ma'am, you have real balls, but if you don't mind me asking, what the hell were you thinking?"

"I wasn't. I guess that's why I did it. How is Tony?"

"Sorry, I don't know."

"Did you catch the bomber?"

"Didn't catch the bomber or the shooter."

"Don't you think they're the same person?"

"I don't think. Not my job. The detectives do that, especially with what's going on at lab."

"God, with all this excitement I forgot all about that. What happened? Is Dr. Mittelman okay?"

"There was a bomb somewhere in the lab. It was detonated one minute before Infantino got shot. I don't know anything about who was injured out there."

"So there are at least two people involved in doing this?"

"Again, it's not my job to speculate, but our bomb guy says a device can be set off by a cell phone, so the bomber could have done it from here before he shot Tony."

"Where did the shot come from?" I asked.

"No one saw a muzzle flash, so it'll be up to the shooting team to figure it out."

Cas walked up, covered in Tony's blood. The tech handed her a wet towel. She used it to clean herself up and then she hugged me. "Thanks for helping me with Tony."

"All I did was get in the way. How is he?"

"You pretty much saw it all. He has an intracranial GSW. It's what's going on inside his head right now that matters."

I touched the scar on the right side of my head. "How well I know."

111

A mass of humanity and vehicles jammed the street, making our return to the stakeout apartment a struggle. In addition to the police and rescue units, there were fire trucks and other emergency vehicles blocking the way. A cloud of smoke from the exploded detonator hung over the street, the stench of the spent explosive still fouling the air.

There was already a yellow crime scene tape across the front door of the building. Three uniformed cops, who didn't appear happy, guarded it. One of them held a clipboard.

Cas stood next to me. I wanted to call Carter, but my cell phone was upstairs in my backpack.

"We need to get in here," I said to the cop in the middle.

"Not happening," he said.

"Please. I need my cell phone."

His response was to cross his arms in front of his chest. The other two followed his lead.

"They're with me, officer," a low-pitched voice behind me said. "They're material witnesses." She pointed at Tony's dried blood on our clothes. "I need to interview them in there."

I turned around and saw a woman about my age with short, curly ash brown hair holding up a gold detective's shield. The brown leather jacket and black slacks she wore didn't hide an athletic figure. She held up her credentials to the cop holding the murder book. He checked her in. She gently shoved Cas and me past the three officers into the lobby before they could object further.

She stopped. We did too. She held out her right hand.

"I'm Detective Jan Corritore."

I shook her hand. Cas did too.

"I'm Tony's partner," she continued.

"But..." I began.

"Being a woman?"

"Well, yeah."

"Tony and me, a skirt, for a partner. Hard to figure, but it works."

She urged us forward. "I'm running this investigation and need all the help I can get."

"We'll do whatever we can," I said. "Where are my friends?"

"Still upstairs with one of my detectives," she said. "Follow me."

We walked into the room. A male detective talked to Brittany and Molly. David wasn't there.

"I got this, Nick," Corritore said.

He left. I introduced Detective Corritore to Molly and Brittany, who immediately took out her cell phone.

"What are you doing?" Corritore asked.

"I'm going to send out a tweet about what just happened. Then I'll take a couple of pictures and post them on the *Tribune* Facebook and Instagram accounts."

"I'm not sure how smart that is right about now," Corritore said.

"It's breaking news, and I have the exclusive," she said.

Before Corritore could say anything else, I yanked the cell phone out of Brittany's hand. "Last time I checked, this was our story."

"You can write it for the paper's print edition, or the online version, but by then it'll be old news. You guys probably never used social media back in the day."

She reached for her phone. I held on to it.

"Call your boss," I said. "Tell him what happened and that I'm fine. I'll call him when Detective Corritore is done talking to us."

I handed her the phone. Carter would freak out, but there was no other way.

"If he okays the social media, then do it," I continued. "But just so you know, 'in the day,' as you put it, we had all the facts before we wrote one word."

She took back the phone and began punching in numbers. "*Whatever.*"

112

"Where's David?" I asked.

"I'm pretty sure he's still in the bathroom," Molly said. "He got kinda sick when Tony was shot, and then, when the bomb exploded, he really freaked out and ran out of the room."

I turned to Corritore. "I'll be right back."

"I'm going with you," she said.

We went down the hall to the bathroom. Cas was right behind us. The door was locked. Behind the closed door, we heard someone retching.

I knocked softly. "David, are you okay?"

The toilet flushed. The faucet was turned on, followed by splashing.

A few seconds later, the door slowly opened. David had a towel in his hands. To say that his face was ashen was a gross understatement. He looked like was going to die.

"I am so embarrassed," he whispered, as he folded up the towel.

Putting my arm around his shoulders, I gave him a hug. "Let's go sit down, okay?"

David hung up the towel and leaned on me as we walked back down the hall. I noticed Corritore inspect the bathroom before she closed the door.

"Don't use this room," she said. "It's now part of the crime scene."

David sat down in the chair by his computer. Once he was there, the color returned to his face. The familiar surroundings of his equipment seemed to revive him.

Corritore took over. "I need to know everything you people remember," she said, taking out her small notebook and a pen. "Tina, you go first. Set the scene for me. Where was everyone positioned?"

I walked to the window. "I was right here. Molly was to my right with the binoculars. Cas was to my left. Brittany was next to Molly. David was back there with his computer." I turned around. "Actually, where he's sitting right now."

"Why weren't you with everyone else, David?" Corritore asked.

"I, ah, didn't want to watch," he said softly.

"Got it," Corritore said. She motioned with her hand. "Keep going, Tina."

"Molly saw the detonator. I realized what was happening. I yelled through the window at Tony to get out of there, but before he could, he was shot. I saw him fall. I ran to him, picked up the detonator, and threw it as far as I could."

"The shot might have come from one of these buildings," Corritore said. "But so far we haven't come up with much. What else do you remember?"

"I yelled at Tony about the bomb. A red laser dot appeared on his head." I took in a deep breath. "And then he was shot."

113

"That was the sequence," I concluded.

"Anything else?" Corritore asked.

I shut my eyes and relived the scene. "I heard a gunshot to my left. As I ran out the door, I remember hearing someone yelling and footsteps behind me."

"That was me behind Tina," Cas said. "David screamed at us to stop. But before that happened, Molly spotted the detonator. We opened the window. Tina yelled at Tony. He looked up at us. I saw the red dot, too, and then Tony was hit. Tina turned around and ran out the door. I would have been right with her, but I had to dodge David, who was standing right behind me."

"David, I thought you were at your computer?" Corritore asked.

"I was, but when I heard Tina yell at Tony, I ran to the window to see what was wrong," he said. "I was behind Cas, and she bumped into me when she ran to the door. I guess it must have been me who screamed at them to stop." He put his head down. "I honestly don't remember doing it."

His face turned white. I was afraid he would need to go back to the bathroom, but he swallowed a couple of times and seemed to rally.

"I looked out the window and saw Tina running toward Tony," he continued. "Cas was behind her. Tina reached down in the bushes and grabbed something, which she threw in the air. There was a bright flash of light and then a loud explosion." He stopped and took in a deep breath. "I… I thought everyone had been killed, and I got sick. I don't know much else, because I spent the rest of the time in the bathroom until you came and got me."

Corritore turned to Molly and Brittany. "Did you guys leave the room too?"

"No, we stayed here," Molly said.

David suddenly stood up and wobbled out of the room. Through the open door we could hear him dry-heaving in the bathroom.

"Poor guy," Molly said.

"I wish we could do something to help him," Cas said.

"Catching the bomber might take care of it," I said.

Corritore went over her notes. "Okay, one more time," she said. "Tina, are you positive you heard the gunshot come from your left?"

"I am. Now that I think about it, the shot was so loud it seemed like it was close to me, like on a firing range."

She pulled out her gun. "You guys stay here."

"Where are you going?" I asked.

"If that gunshot came from your left and was that loud, the suspect might still be hiding in one of the rooms on this floor."

She radioed for backup.

114

Corritore opened the apartment door.

"Shouldn't you wait for your backup?" I asked.

Her voice was firm. "This guy ambushed Tony. He would do the same thing for me if our roles were reversed. When they get here, tell them where I am."

She ran out the door to the first room on our left. She shouted, "Police!" and crashed the door open.

One minute later, she repeated the process in the next room. Nothing happened.

There was one more room and the bathroom still to be searched. She knocked on the bathroom door.

"David, are you okay?" she asked

There was a pause. "I just need to sit here a while," he said softly.

"I'll meet you back in the room," she said. "I have something to do out here."

I turned to Cas. "Her backup isn't here, and there's only one room left. She needs help."

I took the Glock out of my backpack and chambered a round. Cas reached into hers and pulled out her Taser and the wasp spray.

We joined Corritore in the hallway. We stood in front of the last room at the end of the hall. If the killer was still here, he was in this room.

Corritore eyed my gun and Cas's weapons.

"We're gonna be your backup," I said.

"Okay, but stay out here in the hall," she said. "You are civilians. I do not want you getting hurt." She glanced at Cas's wasp spray and shrugged. "I have no idea what you do with that, but whatever it is, don't point it at me."

"What if you need help?" I asked.

"You stay here!"

She took in a deep breath and kicked the door open. She barged inside.

"Police!" she shouted, moving to her right.

We wanted to help, but we waited in the hallway. Through the open doorway, we watched the detective cover the room with her flashlight. There was a form on a chair by the window.

Corritore ran to it with her gun in front of her. It was a white lab coat draped over the chair.

She nudged it with her gun. "It's from a laundry company in Arlington, Virginia." She turned to us. "You guys know anything about this?"

"I do," I said. "It's a message to me from the bomber. He wants me to know he did this."

Corritore holstered her gun and found a light switch on the wall. She flipped it, but the ceiling light didn't go on. She shined her flashlight up at it. The bulb was missing.

"The shooter wasn't taking any chances on someone coming up behind him and turning on the light," she said.

Through the open window, she studied the spot in the parking lot where Tony had fallen. "This is where it happened."

"How can you be so sure?" I asked.

"The smell."

I sniffed. Even in the hallway, the pungent odor of fresh gunpowder faintly permeated the air.

"Where do you think he is now?" Cas asked.

"Best guess is that as soon as he fired at Tony he split. No one would notice anyone leaving with all this confusion."

"But what about the bomb?" I asked. "Wouldn't he wait to set it off?"

"I wouldn't," she said. "I would shoot Tony and set the bomb off with my cell phone. Or have the device on a timer, guessing at how long it would take for the SWAT team to get to Tony."

From the hallway, I looked at the chair and the window. "Doesn't appear to be a hard shot," I said.

"Couldn't be more than thirty or forty yards," Corritore confirmed. "It's a perfect kill zone."

"But Tony was still alive when the EMTs took him," I said. "The other doctor he shot isn't. Hard to believe the bomber missed."

"He didn't exactly miss," she said. "Let's hope and pray Tony makes it."

115

We reentered our room. Corritore's backup finally arrived. She sent them down to the room and called for the CSI team.

Molly stood and stared out the windows. David took down his computer equipment. One of his carriers was already full of cyber gear. Brittany was gone. I retrieved my cell phone from my backpack and called Carter.

He picked up immediately. "Are you okay?"

"I'm fine."

"Brittany told me her version of what happened. What's yours?"

I told him everything, just as I'd related it to Corritore.

I finished. He didn't respond.

"I'm sorry," I continued. "I shouldn't have done what I did, but I couldn't help myself."

"I understand why you did it, but I've already taken the liberty of editing the story. It will be reported that after Infantino was shot, it is believed that a member of the SWAT team discovered the bomb in the bushes. They threw the detonator into the sky before there was a terrible catastrophe."

"Carter, that's not what happened."

"I know it, and you know it, but the bomber doesn't. David might be wrong about the bomber."

"What do you mean?"

"The bomber might be extremely unhappy if he finds out that a woman who almost killed him five years ago outsmarted him again. He missed killing you in Arlington, but he had a second opportunity tonight. I don't want him to have a third chance. The story is true. The detonator was thrown and a catastrophe was averted."

"There's one problem. Brittany wants to splash this all over social media."

"She told me, and I okayed it."

"Are you crazy? We don't have all the facts!"

"All she will post is exactly what I just told you. No more and no less."

"Why are you doing this?"

"I have to assume the bomber will monitor all forms of communication. My hope is that he will read this on one of them and it will buy time to get you out of there and home safely."

"Okay, I get that." I hesitated. "Do you hate me for doing what I did, especially since it was Tony?"

"I know I wouldn't have had the courage to do what you did, regardless of who you saved." His voice was suddenly hard. "But promise me that this is the last time you will ever do something stupid like this. You could have gotten yourself killed."

I didn't respond. Instead, I began to sob.

116

I walked with Cas to the church where the Lyft driver had let us off. Behind us, Molly helped David carry his computer equipment in the two carriers.

"I have one question," I said to Cas, while we waited for a Lyft to take them home. I was going to take a different one to the hospital. "You didn't seem at all excited while you took care of Tony."

"I wasn't," she said.

"How is that even remotely possible? I jumped from planes and have been shot at in a war zone, but I have to tell you, my heart was racing, and I didn't know what to do next. Help me understand that."

"Years of training. I had to be focused, regardless of whether or not he was someone I knew. His life depended on me doing my job. If I screwed up, he was going to die."

"I could never do that."

"Scary part is that I loved it. I miss that adrenaline rush. It's addictive."

The Lyft driver arrived. We had a group hug, and the three of them left.

I called Hannah and Micah, but they didn't answer.

Unexpectedly, Carter drove up. He slammed on his brakes and jumped out of the car. He ran to me and grabbed me in a tight embrace.

"I'm so glad you are safe," he whispered. "I can't stop shaking."

He leaned back and surveyed my blood-stained hair and clothes. He hugged me again.

When he released me, I looked into his eyes. Tears flowed down his cheeks. I started crying too.

Finally, I stopped and stepped back. "How did you get here so fast?"

"I was already in the van when you called."

"Who's with Kerry?" I peeked into the van. "You didn't bring her down here, did you?"

"Of course not. Alicia came to the rescue again."

"We need to give her a bonus for this."

"Already done."

"What about Micah?"

"He was not in the lab when the bomb was detonated. Several FBI agents and policemen were wounded in the blast. So were many Hogan security guards and clinic staff members. The tally is thirty-four so far."

"Any of them killed?"

"None."

I thought of my experience in Arlington.

"Serious injuries?"

"I don't know."

"How did the bomber get a device inside a building that has been completely surrounded for at least a week?"

"A question that all of the FBI higher-ups are asking of their minions. There's a lot of finger pointing at this point, but the simple answer is that no one knows."

"We won't figure it out standing here," I said. "I have a job to do."

"It's hard for me to say this, as the news editor of this story, but it doesn't seem very important to me right now."

"It is to me. I want to write the story of Tony's injuries."

Carter let go of me and pulled my laptop out of the back seat of the van. "You'll need this."

He handed it to me, along with a raincoat I could use to cover my blood-stained clothes. "I'll drop you at the hospital. It'll be safe there, and I want you away from this turmoil."

"Is Brittany already there?"

"She is."

"I hate to admit you were right. Having her on this story has been a real help." I paused. "Even if she is using social media to report it."

I climbed into the passenger side of the van and cancelled my Lyft ride.

Carter dropped me off in front of the Stroger Cook County Hospital ER.

It is one of the busiest emergency rooms in the United States. The mob scene at the entrance, with all types of patients coming and going, reflected that.

Even with all the chaos around me, it was the first time I'd been alone since Tony was shot.

He's in there because of me.

I stood with my backpack in one hand and my laptop in the other. And I began to cry again.

This time for him.

I started to pray.

I don't know what else I can do.

117

I wasn't sure how long I stood there, but eventually, I went inside and found Brittany sitting in the surgery waiting room.

As soon as the hospital smells assaulted my nose, I began to freak out. I held on to the chair next to her and shut my eyes. The PTSD attack lasted less than a minute.

"Are you okay?" she asked.

"I don't do well in hospitals," I answered, when I could finally talk.

"Why?"

I told her. When I got to the part about my brain bleed, her face turned white and she began to breathe faster.

"Oh, my God! Carter never told me about your injuries. No wonder you want to catch this guy."

I sat down next to her. "How is Tony?"

She glanced at the clock on the wall. "He's been in surgery almost five hours."

I scanned the room. "S.R.O."

Standing room only.

"You got that right."

Every rank of police officer, including the commissioner, was crammed into the small, nondescript windowless room.

I pointed at three police officers and an elderly couple. "Tony's brothers and his parents."

"What about them?" she asked, as she pointed to four stunning young women, each standing alone.

"It's Tony. I'm surprised there aren't more of them here."

While we waited, Brittany wrote the edited draft of the shooting on her laptop. I absentmindedly picked at the clotted blood on my shorts.

Tony's.

I had dried blood under my fingernails.

More from Tony.

Bile rose in my throat, but I gulped it down.

Ten minutes later, one of the trauma surgeons came out from the operating room. His green scrub shirt was soaked with sweat. I prayed harder, this time that something hadn't gone wrong during the operation.

118

Everyone stood up. The police commissioner waved at us to sit down. We did. He walked over to the doctor. They shook hands and put their heads together for a quiet conversation. The commissioner stopped talking. The surgeon nodded. The commissioner led the doctor to Tony's parents. More conversation. Another nod.

Finally, the doctor faced the room. "I'm Dr. Michael Morrison. I'm a neurosurgeon, and I just finished operating on Detective Infantino. The Commissioner suggested that I brief everyone in the room, and I have the family's permission to inform you about what happened."

My stomach began to churn.

"The bullet entered in his right fronto-temporal region approximately three centimeters above and one centimeter behind the lateral edge of his orbit." The doctor pointed to an area on his own right temple before he continued.

"The missile traveled on a downward path and exited one centimeter above the medial aspect of his right eyebrow. There was profuse intracranial bleeding which was difficult to control, but once I was able to do that, I found there was surprisingly minimal damage to the patient's right frontal lobe. My guess is that he was turning his head when he was shot, which caused an oblique downward trajectory of the bullet. His right frontal sinus was also fractured. Dr. Gerald Simons, one of our ENT specialists, reduced the fragments and endoscopically drained the sinus." He paused and took in a breath.

"In summary," he concluded, "Detective Infantino is one lucky man. If he hadn't turned his head a few centimeters before the bullet's impact, he could have been blind in his right eye, or dead. He is now in a medically-induced coma and will be for at least forty-eight hours or until the swelling in his brain decreases."

I can relate to that.

The doctor abruptly stopped talking. The commissioner stepped forward.

"At this point, I think it would be inappropriate for Dr. Morrison to take any questions," the commissioner said. "I'm sure he is exhausted and needs to check on his patient."

He studied the room and the cops under his command before he spoke again. "I want the man who did this. Every resource we have will be available to you." He paused. "Get to work and find the bastard who shot Detective Infantino."

The room rapidly emptied except for Tony's family and the four women, who continued to stand off by themselves.

I gripped Brittany's arm. "I'll write this part of the story."

"But..."

"I need to do this. For me. Go home. Send what you've written to Carter."

She walked away. I opened my laptop and began writing the copy about Tony's injuries. When I finished the first draft, Carter would do a Q and A with me, insisting that I have at least two sources to substantiate each fact, especially the medical ones. I would then rewrite the piece, and he would edit it. I would argue with him. We would go back and forth until the story was acceptable to both of us and he sent it on.

It's going to be a long night.

119

At 3 a.m., I climbed out of the Lyft and walked to the apartment building behind our home. In my backpack I had the Glock, a flashlight, the lock pick gun, and the torque wrench.

If the bomber was in his room, I was going to stop him once and for all. After everything he'd done to me, and now to Tony, holding him so the cops could arrest him wasn't an option.

I want to finish this.

The front door lock wasn't any more of a problem than it was the first time. I took the elevator to the third floor. I stopped in front of 3C and put my ear up to the door.

Nothing.

Taking in a deep breath, I let the lock pick and torque wrench do their magic. I put my equipment into my backpack and took out my Glock and a flashlight.

I opened the door and held the gun and flashlight in front of me. The room was empty. All the computers and cameras were gone.

I moved around the tiny apartment, but there was nothing else there. I sniffed. The odor of cleaning products was still present but not as strong.

Walking over to the window, I stared down at our dark and peaceful home. That was when I saw it. There was a yellow Post-it note stuck to the window.

There was writing on it: *I cannot be stopped.*

I ripped the note off the glass, crumpled it up, and threw it on the floor.

It was hard to disagree with him.

Part 5

120

The Saturday morning sunlight seeped through the bedroom blinds and woke me up. I heard Carter in Kerry's room putting her down for her morning nap.

I tiptoed down the stairs to the kitchen. The morning edition of the *Tribune* was on the table. The two stories, about the attempted bombing of an abortion clinic and the shooting of a Chicago detective during the attempt, were in the local news section.

The facts about the shooting and attempted bombing were correct, except for one: I was the one who threw the detonator before it could ignite the C4 bomb and kill everyone around it. In the story, as per Carter's plan, the hero was believed to be an unnamed SWAT member. Brittany's byline was on it.

The other story, about Tony's injuries and subsequent surgery, was totally factual, and my byline was on it. We hoped the bomber wouldn't even read it, but to be safer, I used my married name of Taylor instead of Edwards and my initials, C.E., instead of Christina.

Carter walked up behind me and hugged me. "What do you think?"

"For the most part, I like what Brittany wrote. My story is pretty straightforward."

He sat down across from me in the breakfast nook. "Tough night."

"Worse for Tony. Have you heard anything while I was asleep?"

"Nothing. Are you going to see him?"

"I hadn't considered it, and I don't see what purpose it would serve."

"He might want to thank you for saving his life."

"Honey, he's in a medically induced coma. Been there, done that, but then, I was the one who was zonked out. I don't need to see any of that again."

"There's still a story out there."

"There is, but the bomber seems to always be one step ahead of me. I might not be smart enough to write it."

He waited.

"One thing I don't understand is how he planted the bomb in Micah's lab while it was surrounded by lots of competent law enforcement people."

"That's why there's still an ongoing story, because the feds can't figure it out either."

"Where was the device hidden?"

"It was in Micah's private bathroom."

"Suggesting it's my bomber."

"I would agree."

"I understand why Brittany's story and mine are in the local news section. But why isn't Micah's story on the front page?"

"The FBI spiked the story. It won't be published."

"What? Why?"

"The president is coming to Chicago in two days to share the stage with Micah. The FBI and the Secret Service don't want any publicity about the attempt on Micah or his lab."

"So they're not worried about Micah?"

"No, the president is their only concern." He paused. "That said, I can't envision how the bomber would be able to slip any type of weapon or bomb into the United Center with the FBI and Secret Service on full alert to protect the president."

"I think he'll try."

"What are you suggesting?"

"The bomber wants to bring the issue of embryonic stem cell production and abortion to the front page of every newspaper in the world, right?"

"We have always assumed that to be true."

"Attempting to blow up or shoot Micah won't have the same impact as trying to do the same thing to the President of the United States in front of thousands of people and the media."

"You think the bomber is going to be there."

"Call it my reporter's intuition."

I can feel it.

121

It was early Sunday morning. I felt the need to run in the neighborhood with Macy Gray singing into my ear buds. I no longer felt like someone was watching me, and I wanted to listen to music so I could concentrate.

I'm missing something.

Each time I tried to figure it out, I saw blood spurting out of Tony's head and my concentration evaporated.

Why did Tony ask me about the C4 on the trash I stole from across the street? What did that have to do with any of this? He could give me the answer when he woke up.

If he woke up.

When I returned home, I went down to the computer room and called Linda.

"Gotta problem," I said, after I asked about how she was feeling.

"Give it to me," she said. "It's not like I am doing much, resting at home waiting to have this baby."

"Before Tony was shot, he received the report from the FBI lab about the C4 from the bombing in Arlington and the ones here. He said they all matched."

"So what's the problem?"

"After he told me that, he asked if I thought someone had planted C4 on the trash samples I stole from the "industrial spies" across the street."

"That doesn't make sense."

"That's why I called you."

"Tell me exactly what happened that night."

"I stole garbage from their trash can. I gave a sample to Tony. The Chicago PD lab found C4 on that trash, which confirmed there might be a terrific story across the street, so I kept working it."

"Did Tony say anything about the comparison of those abortion clinic samples to the C4 you stole from the industrial spies' trash?"

"I didn't ask because there was no reason to. The bomber's C4 and the 'industrial spies" C4 are would be totally different."

"What if the C4 from the trash didn't match the rest of the industrial spies' C4 they used in their plot at O'Hare?"

"It had to."

"Walk me through the night you stole the trash."

"I lifted the lid from one of their trash cans and gave some of the garbage to Tony. The end."

"Think, girl, there has to be more. Go over exactly what happened in that alley."

I did.

"Did you say the cop said their security system went off twice that night?"

"He did, but I think he was wrong. I set it off, but only one time."

"What if someone else set it off before you did?"

"I considered that, but why would anyone do that?"

She paused. "To smear different C4 on the industrial spies' trash."

"But that doesn't make any sense to me."

"It does if someone wanted to keep you interested in investigating the industrial spies."

Huh?

"Could it have been Micah?" I wondered.

"Micah?"

"He wanted me to help save his family from the 'industrial spies.' To do that, he had to keep me involved in pursuing their story."

"But here's the problem with that. Unless Micah stole C4 from another source — which, by the way, is a federal crime — the only C4 he had access to would have come from the industrial spies. If he did smear C4 on the trash, it would be from the same batch they had, which was not a match, right?"

Uh-oh!

122

"What if it was the abortion clinic bomber who coated the trash with C4?" I mused.

"Why would you suggest that?" Linda asked

"When I was blown up in Arlington, Carter maintained the bomber was actually my mole."

"I'm totally confused."

"Carter thought the bomber, masquerading online as the mole, initially contacted me to entice me into writing a story that would make national headlines."

"If he's right, and the bomber is your mole, you have a big problem."

"I'm not sure I want to hear this."

"And with good reason. By exchanging emails with your mole, you have given him the opportunity to hack into your computer."

Not good.

"Your mole emailed you that the bomber was going to strike at the South Side clinic?" she continued.

I had a sinking feeling in my stomach. "He did."

"And, using that intel, you made plans to set a trap to catch the bomber."

"I did."

"And, by doing that, he used you to lure Tony to the clinic where he shot Tony."

"But why did the bomber want to murder Tony?"

"Maybe Tony discovered something that proved the bomber and the mole are the same person."

"Could the bomber hack into Tony's Chicago PD computer through my computer?"

"I could do it, so it would be fairly easy for the bomber to do it too."

"Can you hack into Tony's Chicago PD files to see what the bomber might have discovered?"

"Of course I can. I'll call you right back."

It took eight minutes.

"I have Tony's files on the screen in front of me. He sent the C4 sample from the trash to the FBI lab right after you gave it to him. He later sent the C4 from the three bombings here to compare them to Arlington."

"And?"

"Like he told you, the C4 from each of the abortion clinic bombings here and in Arlington matched." She took in a breath. "What he didn't tell you was those C4 samples also matched the C4 from the trash."

"The trash sample didn't match the 'industrial spies' C4?"

"It did not, and Tony figured that out by comparing the original FBI report with the one he just sent in."

"And I asked him to do that." I felt my throat tighten up. "And the bomber learned Tony knew that information by hacking into the police computer through my computer."

Can this get any worse?

"I accessed all of Tony's notes about the case. He guessed the C4 on the trash of the 'industrial spies' had actually been put there by the abortion clinic bomber, but there was no indication he knew the bomber and the mole were the same person.

"That's the reason the bomber tried to kill Tony, to stop him from figuring it out."

"And from finding out who the bomber actually is."

Maybe Carter was right and the mole and the abortion clinic bomber are the same person.

And if he is, I've been duped from the beginning of the abortion clinic bombing story.

Some investigative reporter I turned out to be.

123

It was 10 a.m. on Monday. I handed the attendant my parking pass and pulled the van into the reserved parking area of the United Center's enormous parking lot. The outside temperature was in the mid-nineties.

Carter was already here to begin the president's interview. Kerry was with Alicia.

Having lived in D.C., I wasn't surprised by the frenzied activities associated with a visit by POTUS to our city. There were hundreds of security people mingling with the people who were coming to hear the president. At least four SWAT teams were visible. I was positive there were snipers on the roof of every nearby building.

But what surprised me was the presence of people protesting embryonic stem cell research. How did they find out the president was here to embrace that research when he previously had been outspoken against it?

Obviously somebody alerted them, because they were lined up across the street from the United Center and numbered in the hundreds. They waved signs and chanted various slogans opposing embryonic stem cell research, but for the moment, they seemed under control.

I wondered if any of them would get inside.

There were no supporters waving signs or chanting for embryonic stem cell research. Their side must not have gotten the memo about what the president was going to say today.

The cavernous building held at least twenty-three thousand people, most of them still in the parking lot with me. By the time I made it to the priority security line, I was sweating profusely, partly because of the Chicago heat and humidity but more so because I was worried about the president and Micah's safety.

Is the bomber somewhere in this mass of humanity?

If the bomber was there and he detonated a device inside the United Center, not only would the president be killed but so would several thousand others, including my husband and me. The body count could be ten times higher than 9/11. It would be the worst catastrophe in modern American history.

I scanned the people around me. There were over one hundred priests scattered in the crowd. They were in the regular lines waiting to enter. Some leaned on canes. Several sat in wheel chairs. And a few leaned on walkers.

The parking lot began to look like Saint Peter's Square as more priests arrived. If the Catholic clergy were here to protest, they might do it as soon as the president opened his mouth to introduce Micah. My bomber might not have to do anything to stop the president's speech. By protesting inside, the priests could do it for him.

As I moved forward, I put myself in the bomber's place. What would I do to disguise myself?

Penguins.

I pictured a waddle of penguins in the parking lot. A casual observer couldn't tell one from the other, because they all looked alike.

Just like the priests in their black suits and white clerical collars.

If the bomber is here disguised as a priest, how will I ever spot him?

124

If the bomber wasn't going to blow up a C4 bomb, he might use his new method of choice, a sniper rifle. I remembered the *Day of the Jackal*. Was life going to imitate art if the bomber, disguised as one of the priests, was here to shoot the President of the United States using a homemade gun he had hidden in a walker?

Once I reached the front of the line, I handed my purse to a guard. My backpack was still in the van. I stepped through the security arch. A second guard scanned my priority pass into his computer. The results flashed on the screen. The guard checked them. The line suddenly stopped moving.

"Ma'am, come with me," he said.

"Is there a problem?" I asked.

He stood up. "Ma'am, please, let's not make a scene."

"Why would I do that? I'm a taxpaying citizen here to listen to a speech by the leader of the free world."

He took hold of my arm. "This way, please."

"I am not moving until you tell me what's going on."

Another guard joined him. He grabbed my other arm. "Might want to rethink that one."

They escorted me inside to a room about twenty feet away from the priority entry door in the United Center. The guard holding my purse dropped it on the only table in the room.

The female FBI agent who had interrogated me at O'Hare sat at the table. Security monitor screens hung on three of the walls. A large computer was on the table. My picture was on the screen.

"Mrs. Thomas," she said. "It seems like our paths keep crossing."

Her blond hair was way shorter than mine. She wore a white blouse, a cheap blue suit, and unstylish black shoes. She had an ear bud in her left ear and a bulge under her coat from the handgun on her right hip.

"Is this about Arlington? If it is, that's old news, so it's about time you guys got over it."

"It is your recent involvement at O'Hare and the events that led up to it that we find more troubling."

"Should I contact my attorney?"

"There is no need for that," said a male agent who entered the room. He walked up to me. "At least not yet."

He wore a blue suit and a wrinkled white shirt with a dark tie. He also had an ear bud and bulge from the gun he wore on his right side.

"Is that some sort of threat?" I said. "If it is, I want to talk to my husband. Oh, sorry, I forgot. He's busy interviewing POTUS, who might be unhappy if you interrupt them."

The male agent leaned into my space. "We're going to watch your every move. If you even twitch, we'll escort you from the building so fast you won't be able to blink before you're outside."

I felt heat begin to rise in my face.

"We wouldn't let you within twenty miles of this location except for a Presidential Order making us do so," the female agent added.

I clenched my hands into fists, but I kept quiet.

"The Director is not happy about this," she said.

It must be tough for you guys to take orders you don't like.

I relaxed my fingers. "May I go to my seat?"

She handed my purse to me and pointed to the door behind me.

125

I stomped into the concourse and stopped. That little encounter made my blood boil.

Jerks! I'm not the bad guy here.

Several people bumped into me as I stood motionless, still seething about what the FBI agents said to me.

Move before you get run over.

It was like a Bull's basketball game, absolute chaos. People streamed in every direction. More priests walked onto the main floor of the arena. I didn't know there were this many in the Catholic Archdiocese of Chicago.

It looked more and more like there was going to be a massive protest against embryonic stem cell research.

Poor Micah. All he wants to do is cure people.

The overwhelming odor came from sweat exuding from the people who had stood in the baking heat waiting to enter the building. The familiar cement smell of the United Center was present, too, but the food aromas were missing since the concession stands were closed.

I sat down at the end of the fourth row of the section and put my purse on my lap. I decided to text Carter to see if he was done with the interview.

I took my cell phone out of my purse and turned it on.

No service. Maybe the Secret Service had the NSA block all cell phone transmissions so the president wouldn't be interrupted.

I scanned the arena and saw the same two FBI agents standing to the left of the stage. They watched me. I glared back.

I checked out the main floor of the arena again. There were security personnel everywhere. There was no way the bomber got in with any weapon larger than a paperclip.

Unless it's one of the priests and he has a gun hidden in his walker.

Dignitaries walked out on the stage. Our two U.S. senators, all of our Illinois representatives in Congress, and the mayor chatted with each other like they were buddies, even though most of them despised each other. Micah and Hannah hadn't come out, so I assumed they would enter with the president.

Lots of big hitters.

I wondered how Carter's interview had gone with the president. I said a prayer that the leader of the free world, all of these dignitaries, and the rest of us in the crowd would live through this event.

126

The lady sitting next to me, according to the pass hanging around her neck, was a reporter from *USA Today*. She was becoming increasingly upset by my constantly turning around to watch the priests behind me.

"Do you have a problem?" she asked.

"I'm, ah, looking for someone," I said.

She glanced at my name tag and read my name. "I remember you," she sneered at me. "You're the reporter from the *Washington Post* who caused an abortion clinic to be blown up."

I felt my face begin to burn. "That's not exactly what happened."

"How did you get a priority pass? I heard you were blackballed from our industry."

I wanted to tell her I'd recently written a front page piece for the *Tribune,* but I was still a leper in her newspaper world — and to many of my former fellow reporters too.

I stood up, my face burning even more. I looped the strap of my purse across my chest. "Excuse me. I have to use the restroom."

I have to stop this before the bomber strikes.

The only people I could count on to help me were the two FBI agents. There was no other option.

I hurried up to them. "You have to help me. The man who has been blowing up abortion clinics is here to kill the president."

"Yeah, and Michael Jordan is going to make another comeback in this building," the female agent said.

The male FBI agent pointed at the crowd. "Just exactly which one of these people is your killer?"

"I think he's dressed like a priest."

"Think?" the female asked.

"I don't know that for sure, but I know he's here."

"If he is dressed up like a priest, is he going to use his rosary beads for bullets?" the male agent asked. "Or maybe they're really tiny bombs."

"This isn't funny," I said.

"See those teleprompters in front of the podium?" asked the female agent. "Notice anything about them?"

I hadn't seen them at all. "No, I guess not."

"They're the ones the Secret Service use when there might be a threat to POTUS. They're bulletproof and positioned for his maximum protection."

"I didn't know they had anything like that."

"Neither does your bad guy," he said. "Why don't you be a good little girl and sit down until this is over? You've caused enough distraction already. Just let us do our jobs without your usual interference."

The president's speech was scheduled to begin in twenty-one minutes.

I have to do something!

127

Clearly, it was futile trying to get law enforcement to believe me, since I had no proof. I needed to buy time to get some.

"I have to go to the bathroom," I said to the FBI agents.

"Better hurry," the female agent said. "We wouldn't want you to miss the president's speech."

I rushed to the women's restroom. I went in and exited in less than thirty seconds.

He's here! I can feel his presence!

The outside doors into the arena were still open as more people streamed in.

Think logically. If he isn't going to blow us up, he might use a sniper rifle.

The bomber had shot the abortion doctor from apartment 3E. When the bomber shot Tony, the gun he fired was on the third floor too.

Third floor?

Was the bomber here on the third level of the United Center?

And then it hit me: *The Manchurian Candidate!* In the movie, the sniper, dressed like a priest, fired his rifle from an elevated suite in an arena like the United Center.

In a suite.

Dressed like a priest.

This has to be it!

I scanned the upper levels of the auditorium. All but one of the penthouse luxury boxes in the three hundred tier were illuminated and rapidly filling up with people. One suite was dark. It was the elevation where the priest had been in the movie.

I scanned the auditorium main floor again. Turning around, I took a breath and began to push my way back through the crowd that was still coming in. Over my shoulder, I saw the FBI agents scanning the crowd. They were no longer watching for me. I wished the Irregulars were here to help.

It's up to me.

128

Two guards stood in front of the escalator to the three hundred tier. They checked my priority pass and waved me on. Fortunately, the pass guaranteed me access to every level.

The crowd rapidly thinned as people crammed into the open doors of the luxury boxes to get to their seats before the speeches began.

There was a "Closed for Repairs" sign on the door of one of the suites. Two orange cones stood in front of it. I moved one cone and turned the door knob. The door was locked. I pawed around in my purse for my lock pick, but I'd left it in my backpack, fearing it wouldn't pass through security.

Maybe the suite really was closed for repairs and that was why it was dark.

I have to get into this suite to be sure.

There was a short, squatty female janitor standing off to the periphery of the crowd. She leaned on a long broom, waiting to begin the clean up after the festivities were over.

"Excuse me." I waved at her. "Here, over here."

She left her cart and walked over to me. "Help you, ma'am?"

"Yes, you certainly can. I'm with the *Chicago Tribune.*" I showed her my priority pass. "I'm supposed to cover the speeches from this suite. Have you seen anyone going in?"

"Only person going in or out of this suite has been the plumber. Some idiot plugged up the toilet, and it overflowed early this morning. A freaking mess. He's been working on it all day, but he hasn't been able to fix it, so management decided to close it off."

"Have you seen an elderly priest using a walker up here?"

"With the size of this crowd, I probably woulda' missed Elvis with his guitar, but I'm positive I haven't seen any priests like that." She paused. "Actually, I haven't seen any priests on this level at all."

"You're sure?"

"Yeah, priests kind of stick out, especially up here with all these rich and famous people."

"Thanks."

She went back to her cart. I was so sure the bomber would be here dressed up like a priest.

Now what?

I watched big hitters enter the suites. I didn't see any priests.

Priests?

Why were all these priests here? Who alerted them to come?

That's it! I underestimated you.

The bomber had toyed with me from the beginning in Arlington, pushing me into writing his anti-abortion story. The hundreds of priests in the building were a smokescreen. He wasn't dressed like a priest, but he could be disguised as someone else.

I looked at the female janitor. What people are nearly invisible at events like this?

The workers.

Like a laundryman entering an abortion clinic, they are all around, but we never notice them because they are part of the background.

I have to get into that suite.

129

I slipped into the open door of the suite next to the one I needed to enter. This one was crammed with people.

On the left side of the room was a mirrored bar with crystal decanters and stemware. There were six black leather barstools in front of it. They were full.

Sitting on a hardwood floor in the middle of the room was a modern black leather couch. Two matching black leather and chrome chairs were placed perpendicular to it. They were full too.

There was a low glass and chrome coffee table in front of that grouping. On the opposite wall was a long table full of food. The aroma of BBQ, Chicago dogs, and pizza drifted in the air. The smell of industrial cleaning agents, expensive perfumes, and sweat filled the noisy room.

I pushed past the mass of people congregated around the booze and food and walked further into the room. The cacophony of noise from everyone talking irritated my ears.

The opposite end of the suite opened out to the expansive arena below. There were two rows of seven padded bleacher seats in front of the end of the suite. The seats were full. There was only one way to get into that next suite.

I edged my way to the end bleacher seat next to my target suite. Taking in a deep breath, I sat on the low railing between the two suites. When I saw that no one was watching, I lifted my legs and moved them up and over the railing.

I quickly moved back into the dark, empty suite. In the gloom, I could make out a similar décor to the suite I'd just been in. Except for one thing. There was no food or alcohol. Only the stench of a backed-up toilet filled the room.

I walked around the suite.

No one here.

I was out of ideas. If the bomber was in the United Center, he'd beaten me again.

Something hard nudged me in the middle of my back.

"I'm sorry you're here," a male voice said from behind me.

I recognize that voice...

I turned around.

The man wore a janitor's green jump suit. He held a funny-looking rifle. It was pointed at my chest.

It was David John.

130

My voice cracked when I spoke. "David? What's going on? You're supposed to be out of town."

"I am here to do God's work," he said.

His black glasses and New York Yankees hat were gone. So was his red beard.

"In a janitor's suit?"

He smiled, but his lips thinned out into a tight line. "You gave me the idea from the DVDs. I hoped you would alert the FBI and Secret Service and convince them I was here disguised as a priest with a rifle. You know, keep them busy and allow me to finish what I started so long ago."

My mind whirled. "I don't understand."

"You haven't figured it out?"

"I'm here chasing the bomber who tried to kill me in Arlington and is now terrorizing Chicago, but... You, David? Bombing?" I stared into his green eyes, and it hit me. "You're my mole?!"

"I always was. It was the only way I could push you into continuing to write my story." He quickly scanned the arena. "I'm sorry you figured I would be in here. It's a complication I hadn't counted on."

I didn't know whether to laugh, cry, or get angry, but I knew I had to think clearly or lots of bad things were going to happen very soon.

He motioned with the rifle. "Back up," he ordered.

I did. "What are you going to do to me?"

"Tie you up so you can watch. After I leave, you can report to the world why I did this."

"You can't do this. There has to be another way. I'll write an article showing why you feel the way you do. I promise I'll give you the means to go public with your side of the issue."

"Been there, done that, and it's never worked." His voice hardened. "By pulling the trigger, I will show the president and this international group of reporters that our cause cannot be stopped. Then you can write the full story."

Carter and I always laughed at movies where the bad guy tied the good guy's hands in the front and not the back.

Hands bound in front give me a chance. In the back, I'm screwed.

Holding my arms in front of me, I prayed David would instinctively secure them there.

"Okay, tie me up, but you can't kill the president," I said.

He took off the belt from his jump suit and used it to bind my hands together in front of me.

Yes!

He arched his eyebrows. "The president? Why would you say that?"

"He's here, and he's about to announce that he's going to support embryonic stem cell research."

"I can see why you're confused, but don't you remember the original *Manchurian Candidate*? Poor, crazy Raymond didn't kill the presidential candidate. He killed his stepfather and his mother."

No!

He was going to shoot Micah and Hannah, not the president. The vision of their four children without their parents flashed into my brain.

I can't let this happen.

He turned me around and pushed me toward the empty seats in the front of the suite.

"Now what?" I asked, trying to sound calm despite my heart nearly beating through my chest.

"You are going to sit there and watch me shoot a man who kills the unborn babies he creates in a petri dish."

"What about Hannah?"

"Poor dear. If I have time to get off a second shot, she'll be collateral damage."

131

I was taller than David, and he was a pathologic clean freak. *Two things in my favor.*

"I have to go to the bathroom," I said.

"You can do that after I have completed God's mission," David said, shoving me in the back against the seats at the front of the suite.

"I really need to right now."

"Sit down and shut up."

I turned around and faced him. "If you don't let me use the bathroom right now, I am going to pee on the floor. I apologize if I splash urine on your shoes."

Hail to the Chief blared over the loudspeakers.

"The president is coming," he said. "There is no time for this foolishness."

"Oh, really? Watch me."

My hands were bound, but that wasn't stopping me. I reached under my skirt and pulled my panties down.

His eyebrows shot up.

Shaking the panties free from my foot, I pulled my skirt up to my thighs, spread my legs widely, and began peeing. The stream of urine splashed on the hardwood floor and my feet. It splattered on his legs and shoes.

He started hopping up and down.

"Stop that!" he wailed.

I continued to pee. He spun around and turned his back to me trying to avoid the gush of cascading urine.

Now!

Using my height advantage, I looped my tied hands over his head and moved the belt down to his throat. I tugged backward as hard as I could, nearly lifting his feet off the floor.

He dropped the rifle and clawed at my tied hands. He gurgled as he struggled to breathe. Pulling harder, I leaned back as far as I could so his feet were no longer touching anything.

He kicked his legs and flailed his arms. The only sound coming from his airway was a strangled wheeze.

The crowd began to roar.

The president is coming!

Unexpectedly, the belt dropped to the floor. With the tension released from the now-untied belt, my hands flew upward, and I staggered backward. He bent forward with his hands on his knees and struggled to pull air through his swollen vocal cords.

I reached down for the rifle. He saw me move and dove for the weapon. So did I. He got to it first. I jumped on his back. The rifle was trapped under him. He struggled to pull it into firing position.

I grabbed his red hair with both hands and slammed his forehead and nose on the floor. There was a loud crunch. Blood gushed onto the floor, forming a bright red puddle under his face. He gurgled as he tried to inhale. I felt him relax under me.

You're not gonna shoot anyone, buster!

132

The noise resounding through the United Center was deafening. Leaning on the back of David's head, I used it as a support to help me stand up. I glanced over my shoulder and saw the president waving at the crowd. Micah and Hannah stood to his left.

Suddenly, David rolled over and grabbed the rifle's barrel.

"You bitch!" he hissed.

Still on his knees, he thrust the stock of the gun directly into my abdomen. Instantly, I was struck with an abdominal cramp of frightening intensity.

He jabbed me with the stock again, harder this time. Searing pain doubled me over. It felt like something in my belly ripped apart.

Adrenaline surged through my system. I fought through the pain.

This little wimp isn't going to beat me.

He jumped up, pushing past me. "I will not be stopped!"

He brought the rifle into firing position to acquire Micah, his first target. I jerked the rifle barrel down and smashed him in his now-broken nose with my elbow.

His eyes bugged open and more blood flew all over me. He lurched backward. His arms wind-milled, and the rifle flew from his grasp. I picked it up and pointed it at his chest.

Blood from his face dripped on the floor. "You won't shoot me," he smirked. "I know you. You can't do it."

He laughed.

I hate men who laugh at me.

He moved toward me and reached out to grab the rifle.

"You don't know me at all."

I aimed at his center mass and pulled the trigger. The bullet hit my intended mark and knocked him off his feet. He fell backward over the coffee table and rolled to his side.

The noise in the United Center was so loud I could barely hear the shot, and I'd fired the rifle.

He groaned. Crawling to his knees, he reached into his pocket and pulled out his cell phone.

He laughed at me again. "You should have known I had a master plan."

There's a bomb in the building too! He's going to set it off with his cell phone.

Thousands of people are going to die!

I pulled the trigger again and again, but his specially-made sniper rifle was a single-shot weapon.

The rifle's empty.

"Bet you wish you had these," he said, reaching in his pocket and pulling out a handful of bullets.

He struggled to his feet and began to dial the cell phone. The crowd stopped yelling. The president began to speak.

Do something!

I swung the barrel of the rifle like I was hitting golf ball with a driver. I hit my target, catching him flush on the side of the head with the gun's stock. It sounded like I hit a hollow pumpkin.

He crumpled to the floor.

Kicking the phone away from his hand, I smashed it again and again with the butt of the gun. I kicked the remnants of the phone away from him.

"Bet this wasn't part of your master plan, smart guy."

I staggered over to the railing and dropped the rifle into the next suite.

My legs gave out. I fell against the empty seats.

And then, there was blackness.

133

I opened my eyes. A woman wearing a white lab coat over a green scrub suit held on to my right arm.

"Where am I?" I asked.

"In the United Center's first-aid station," she said.

The smell of alcohol irritated my nose as she swabbed my arm with a wet cotton ball.

I struggled to sit up.

"Hold 'er, girl," she said. "I really need to get this IV started."

"What happened to me?"

"I think something happened to your abdomen. You got a midline scar. Did you have surgery before?"

I waited for a searing wave of pain in my belly to pass.

"I was blown up five years ago. My bladder and liver were ruptured."

Her face blanched. "Oh, shit." She turned to someone behind her. "We need a surgeon right now!"

She turned back to me. "This is gonna sting a little."

I felt her jab my arm as she started the IV.

"Great," she said, as she applied tape over her handiwork.

"How did I get here?"

"A man covered with blood staggered out of one of the three hundred-level suites. A janitor saw him. She called security.

They checked inside the room and found you passed out. They carried you down here."

My head began to swim.

"I feel dizzy," I croaked. "My husband is here with the president. Call him."

I'm tired. I think I'll take a nap.

Her voice sounded far away. "Stay with me, sweetie."

"Better start another IV," I heard a male voice say.

"Might need a subclavian," the female said. "Her pressure is dropping."

Could you guys quiet down? I want to go to sleep.

I felt hands pushing on my tummy. "Her abdomen is tight," the male voice said. "She's got at least one unit of blood in there."

I went to sleep.

Part 6

134

When I woke up, I blinked a couple of times and found myself staring into Carter's blue eyes.

"I'm glad they called you." I blinked again. "Am I still in the first-aid station?"

"No, you're at the MidAmerica Hospital," Carter said.

What? Why?

I tried to sit up but was slammed by lower abdominal cramps. I stopped moving. Out of the corner of my eye, I saw a unit of blood dripping into the IV in my right arm.

Been here before.

I nodded toward it. "Looks like I had a little problem."

"You could say that. The surgeon told me you were hit in the abdomen. That blunt trauma tore scar tissue in your liver and bladder and caused extensive internal bleeding. Thank God, the surgeon was able to stop it."

I gently ran my fingers over my belly. "The last time a surgeon operated on me I had a big bandage and staples. Why not now?"

"The surgeon used a scope and was able to cauterize the bleeders without totally opening your abdomen."

I digested that information.

"Huh," I said.

My mind was foggy from the pain meds.

"Huh," I said again.

Carter held my hand.

"What day is it?"

"Wednesday morning, actually."

"I've been out for a while."

"You have."

"Where is Kerry?"

"With Alicia. She has been since this happened. I've been here with you."

He squeezed my hand.

"Looks like I've come full circle," I said.

"Do you mean with David?"

"How did you know it was David who did this to me?"

"The FBI agents told me."

"Well, they were right. It was David. And this is the second time I've had abdominal surgery because of what he did to me. I can't wait to write this story."

My husband didn't say anything.

"I said, 'I can't wait to write this story.' "

"About that."

"Carter, I am going to write this story! I have to. He's tried to kill me twice! I can't have risked my life for nothing."

I had pain and brain fog, but not so much that I couldn't comprehend what my husband was saying to me. "The Secret Service, right?"

"The Secret Service, the FBI, the CIA, and every other federal agency that deals with anyone potentially making an attempt on the president's life."

This was the end. I was never going to write the bomber's story. I could bitch and moan, but it wouldn't do any good. It was over.

I didn't know whether I wanted to cry or laugh at the absurdity of the situation. Instead, I shifted around in bed and became aware of the irritating hospital smells. I braced for a PTSD attack, but it didn't happen.

Huh?

Maybe David had finally knocked it out of me.

"How did the interview go?" I asked.

"Really well. The president provided a lot of material."

"What about the speeches?"

"The parts I heard were well-received. I didn't hear them all, because the FBI agents came and pulled me into the first-aid station to see you."

"Did all those priests protest?"

"When Micah began his talk, they stood up but remained silent. When he announced his discovery of the cure for MS, the audience erupted with cheers and the priests sat down."

"Now what?"

"You won't be allowed to write about David, so no one will ever know what he intended to do or what actually transpired."

"Except me — and David."

"Indeed."

135

"What about my friends?" I asked.

"The FBI told me you can tell them everything, but if they breathe one word of it, they will risk federal prosecution," Carter said.

"Have you told them what David did to me?"

"No, I thought you should do that. I told Cas you had a touch of food poisoning and were admitted to the hospital to receive IV fluids. She told Molly and Linda the same thing."

Though my abdomen was aching, my mind was clearing.

"I miss Kerry. When do I get to go home?"

"The trauma surgeon wants to recheck your blood count tomorrow morning, and if it's back up to acceptable levels, he will discharge you."

"That's a relief. Is Kerry okay?"

"She misses her mommy. I wanted Alicia to bring her up here to see you, but Linda suggested I not do that."

"Linda? I thought you talked to Cas."

"I did, but Linda called me just before I walked into your room."

"Why?"

"She's on the OB floor. She had an emergency C-section about the same time your surgeon was beginning your case. You were in the OR the same time she was."

"Small world."

"It is, isn't it?"

"I want to see her."

"I knew you would, but your doctor nixed that until tomorrow."

"One question. What did she have?"

"A boy."

"Name?"

"I forgot to ask. I was a little addled by all of this."

"One more question."

He waited.

"David. Did they catch him?"

"No, they didn't."

"He's still out there."

"But you don't have to worry. There are two police officers stationed outside your door. You are totally safe in here."

136

Carter left to relieve Alicia and take care of our daughter, but the nurses and lab people kept bugging me. The old joke about not being able to sleep in a hospital was true — again. It bugged me over five years ago, and it was worse this time. I couldn't wait to go home and hug my husband and Kerry.

And sleep in my own bed without any interruptions. At least the hospital smells were masked by the flowers that had been delivered. They were from my parents, my brother, and Carter and Kerry.

And the President of the United States. He not only had someone send flowers, but he included a handwritten note of thanks. And he arranged for the two guards, this hospital, and the room I was in. It didn't seem possible, but it was even nicer than the one Linda was in the last time I was here to visit her.

Sniffing the aroma of the now-familiar fragrance of the room, I remembered what Molly had said during that visit to Linda. I could detect cedar and sandalwood, maybe even roses.

Lying back in bed, I shut off the lights and thought about David. His planning had been meticulous, even to the point of using the cameras and audio to follow everything I did. I shut my eyes and tried to relax.

But that doesn't make sense.

Why did David need the cameras and listening devices? He was in on all of our meetings. He knew exactly what we were going to do. I yawned, suddenly overcome by exhaustion.

I'll think about that tomorrow.

The cloying scent in the room began to intensify, and my nose began to burn. I blindly reached out for the nurse's call button to have someone come up and fix it. Groping around in the dark, I couldn't find it, but I found something else instead.

It was a man's hand.

137

"At last, we finally get to be alone," the man said. "I can't tell you how long I've waited for this moment."

It wasn't David's voice.

I sat straight up, which caused intense burning in my abdomen. "Who are you?"

"Tina, I'm devastated that you don't recognize me," he said. "Have I changed that much?"

I stared at the man in the darkness of the room. He was short, slender, and completely bald.

And then it came to me.

"You're the lab tech who's been drawing my blood. You did with Linda too."

"You are correct, but I was once so much more than a lowly laboratory technician. I used to be one of the most famous and sought after physicians in the world." He moved closer to my bed. "But then that false story you wrote about me took that all away."

Who is this guy?

"I can see by the look on your face that you still don't remember me." He held out his wrist. "Take one more sniff."

"I don't have to. It smells like you took a bath in that stuff."

"That would be a very expensive bath, for sure. It is still the most expensive cologne in the world. It's Clive Christian No. 1."

He flipped on the room lights. I was no longer uncertain about who the voice belonged to.

Dr. Mick Doyle stood next to my bed.

138

"It can't be you!" I said. "You're still in prison."

"Correction," Doyle said. "Was in prison. You've been so busy with your new life that you completely forgot about me. If you knew I had been released, you might have been more alert."

"But it can't be you! You don't have an accent."

"The other prisoners who made me their bitch while I was incarcerated didn't like it. They literally beat it out of me." He stepped closer. "It's time for me to keep my promise to you."

I whipped my head around, searching for a weapon, but the quick move caused a burning pain to radiate through my abdomen.

"Dear girl, you shouldn't do that. As a physician, I can assure you that it will cause severe pain."

I had to barter with him, hoping to stall him until someone came into my room to save me. "You've been to prison once. You don't want to go back. Let's be reasonable here."

"Reasonable? I'll tell you what would have been reasonable. For you to tell the truth in the story you wrote about me. It was all lies."

"I can write a retraction."

"And what about my fourteen years in prison with the monsters who ravaged me on a daily basis? Can you fix that too?"

He glanced at his platinum Piaget, similar to the one he wore the last time I saw him over a decade ago.

"I'm sorry I'm going to have to cut this short, but I must finish up before the drugs that I put in the coffee of the two police guards in the hall outside wear off. I've been watching you and your friends all this time, trying to decide what would be the best way to kill you. When I heard that you were here in this hospital, I knew I had the solution."

I held up my trembling hand. "How did you hear that?"

He raised his eyebrows. "I assumed you knew, since you visited my apartment behind your home. I was watching through your back window. Listening, too, but I have those men who used to live across the street from you to thank for that. I used their listening devices to monitor you and your friend's and husband's conversations."

"There was no way you could have known I was in that apartment."

"I had a security camera in one of the computers that recorded your visit. I moved out the next day. I had all the information that I needed and didn't want you to realize I was the one watching you."

"It wasn't David's apartment?"

"Oh my, no. He was much too busy blowing up buildings and shooting doctors to have time for that. And from what I observed, you two were so close that he knew every move you were going to make anyway. You thought you were a smart journalist. What sweet irony that you won't be able to report this story."

I had been so fixated on Jamie and the abortion clinic story that I completely missed this third, equally real, threat in my neighborhood: Dr. Mick Doyle.

139

"But you had at least one helper," I said.

"Those women never existed," Doyle said. "The disguises were useful until your friend Cas got a good look at me as I entered that apartment. I was afraid that if she saw me again, she would realize I wasn't a woman, so I put my wigs away."

"But my mole said his group had killed both of them, and David was the mole. Were you two working together?"

"Never. In prison, I created a plan to get even with you and had to find a way to implement it, so I learned all about computers. I hacked into David's last mole response to you and added that. Clever, don't you think? The perfect way to confuse things a bit more. Oh, that and the Post-it note I stuck to the window for you."

He reached in his pocket and pulled out a syringe and knife. "This injection won't hurt at all, but it will paralyze you so you can't move while I slice you up with this." He waved the blade close to my face and then reached down for my arm.

I inched backward in my bed and cocked my fist. "Not in this lifetime, asshole!" I screamed as loud as I could, hoping a nurse or someone would come running in to see what was happening.

I beat you before. I'll do it again.

As another searing pain went through my abdomen, I saw a red dot unexpectedly appear in the middle of Doyle's forehead.

A window to my left broke. A small black dot replaced the red one. The back of his head exploded against the large flower arrangement behind him.

140

I was moved to another posh room while the CSI unit processed the crime scene in my old room. Detective Jan Corritore sat on one side of me. Carter was on the other, holding me in his arms.

Corritore closed her spiral notebook and put her pen in her jacket pocket. "I guess that's about it. I've been asking you all the questions here. Do either of you want to know anything?"

"Where was the sniper when the shot was fired?" Carter asked.

She pointed over her shoulder. "In the hospital's hotel across the street. The shooter checked in the same day you did, Tina, and checked out before we could find him or her."

"Any fingerprints in the shooter's room?" Carter asked.

"It was wiped clean. No shell casing. Nothing."

"What about the bullet?" I asked. "Will you be able to identify it?"

"The medical examiner said the bullet exploded when it blew through Doyle's skull. Nothing was left except a few small metal fragments."

"Sounds like a pro," Carter said.

"That's what Tina told me before you arrived," Corritore said. "She thinks it was a terrorist, but I gotta wonder about David John."

"That doesn't make sense," I said. "I know how hard I smashed his face against the floor. I doubt he'll be able to see out of his swollen eyes for a month."

"Possible," she said.

"Fourteen years ago, Doyle funneled his profits to the Vakili Corporation, which was a front for terrorists," I said. "He was one of them, so he had a lot of information about how their system worked. I think he got tired of prison and opted to roll over on his terrorist buddies to get an early release."

"I guess he was willing to take the chance that they might not find out he ratted them out," she said.

"But it seems as if they did," Carter said.

"If that's true, thank God they went after him when they did," I said.

"I'll call the feds and see if they have any insight into any of this." She patted my knee. "You've had a rough time of it lately. I'm glad you're okay."

"No more so than I am, Detective," Carter said. "I think Tina is done writing dangerous stories."

Corritore stood up. "I'll check on you in a couple of days, if that's okay."

"You can check on me every day," I said. "Right now I feel like I need that."

She stepped out and Carter wrapped his arms around me again. "I love you so much. I'm so glad you're safe."

"Me, too, honey. Me too."

141

Carter had brought my laptop to me. He knew journaling was the way I'd processed my emotional problems when I was blown up in Arlington, and he realized this was what I needed to do now.

First, I went over all my files on David's story. It took me a couple of hours and several emails to various agencies to give me the entire story.

Next, I reviewed my old files on Dr. Mick Doyle. I'd lied to Corritore about the sniper being a terrorist. I did it to cover for David. He was a bomber and a killer, but he was also my friend, and I was sure he was the shooter who had saved my life.

The cameras and listening devices weren't his, so he knew from the start I was in danger from another source. He saved me from Doyle. When I needed him most, he was there for me. He had proven himself to be a Hamlin Park Irregular.

The world needed to know about him, even if the only place his story would ever be published would be in my private journal, the one I started five years ago to deal with PTSD after he blew me up.

A Bomber.

A Killer.

And a Friend.

By

Christina Edwards Thomas

Have you ever run into someone in your neighborhood who looked completely harmless — like a leprechaun? I did. He was a man who became my friend and running companion.

And who saved my life.

He also detonated a bomb in an abortion clinic in Arlington, Virginia, five years ago, which nearly killed me. I was in the building when he blew me up. But he didn't know me then…

Part 7

142

Thursday morning, I was discharged from the hospital. I called Carter and told him I wanted to see Linda and her baby before he picked me up.

I was still in my room when Cas and Molly walked in.

"How are you feeling?" Cas asked.

"Better," I said.

"You must have had a really bad case of food poisoning," Molly added.

I opened my mouth to correct her, but Molly kept talking.

"Wow," she said. "This is even nicer than Linda's room."

"POTUS did it for me," I said.

I saw the blank look on Molly's face.

"The President of the United States."

"IKR," she said.

Now, I had the blank look. I shrugged my shoulders.

"I know, right? I use it all the time when I'm texting."

"Good to know."

"When do you get to go home?" Cas asked.

"My doctor just discharged me," I said. "Because of my previous emergency surgery after David blew me up in Arlington, the doctor wanted to keep me here an extra night."

"David?" Cas asked. "What's he got to do with this?"

"Why don't we go down to Linda's room? I want her to hear this, and I want to see her baby."

I told the nurses I would come back to get my stuff. The three of us took the elevator down two floors to Linda's room.

I entered her elegant postpartum room with Cas and Molly right behind me. I walked up to Linda's bed. She held her newborn in her arms.

"He is *so* cute," I said. "What's his name?"

"We finally decided on Jason."

"We" decided?

I was certain Howard didn't have a vote in the name game. Linda's parents were a different story. They would be the major donors to Jason's financial future, which gave them naming rights.

It's what family money does.

Linda looked like she'd been up all night scrubbing the floors of the hospital with an old toothbrush.

"You feeling okay?" Cas asked.

"This emergency C-section was way harder than the other way," Linda said. "I'm having excruciating abdominal pains, both from my C-section incision and the gas building up in my as yet non-functioning bowels, so I need to walk in the hall."

"I had the same thing after I was blown up," I said. "Before you do that, there's something I need to tell all of you about David and the truth about why I'm here."

I told them everything about David and what had happened between us at the United Center.

143

"Wow," Molly finally said.

"Unimaginable," Linda said.

"Who would've thought?" Cas asked.

"Not me, that's pretty obvious," I said.

"I can't even begin to tell you how many laws he's broken," Linda said.

"Yeah, about that," I said.

I told them about the gag order from the feds forbidding us to tell anyone about David.

"So, we can't ever talk about this?" Molly asked, after I finished.

"You can, but then your family will get to visit you in a federal prison," I said.

"Then this is the only time we should talk about this, right?" Cas asked.

"It is. Right here, and right now. I'm going to tell you guys what the FBI told me in exchange for not publishing David's story."

"I want to go first," Cas said. "With such tight security around Micah's lab, how did David sneak the bomb in there?"

"Initially, he helped the Hogan Company set up security in Micah's lab. That's when he did it."

"Made it easy for him," Cas said.

"It did. Planting the bomb in the bathroom was his signature to let the world know he was responsible. He hid the bomb in the ceiling so it wouldn't be discovered before he was ready to detonate it."

"And you said there were C4 bombs hidden in the United Center too," Linda said. "How did he get them in there?"

"The same way he brought in pieces of his sniper rifle. When he found out the president was coming to Chicago, he got a job working night security in the United Center. With his background at Hogan, they were thrilled to hire him. He hid the C4 high enough in the roof that the bomb dogs didn't find them. He waited to assemble the rifle until the moment he needed the gun."

"Why did he shoot Tony?" Molly asked.

"The FBI lab sent a report to Tony that the C4 residue from the other abortion clinic bombings matched that found on the trash I stole. Tony realized the only way it could have gotten there was for it to be planted by the bomber. David hacked into the Chicago PD computers and discovered where Tony was headed in his investigation. He shot Tony before he figured out David and the bomber were the same person."

"Why did David plant the C4 in the trash you stole?" Cas asked.

"To push me into writing about what Micah was doing in his lab."

"Then the world would reject Micah's embryonic stem cell research," Cas said.

"That was David's plan."

144

"How did he shoot Tony and blow up the bomb in Micah's lab when he was in the room with us when both things happened?" Molly asked.

"David had the final shift, which gave him time go into the last apartment on our floor, assemble a special sniper rifle, and attach it to a moveable tripod," I said. "The tripod was controlled from his computer. The view from the rifle's scope was displayed on his computer screen. He fired the weapon using his computer one minute after he detonated the bomb in Micah's office bathroom, which he also did from his computer."

"But if he was this good with his computer, why was the bomb next to Tony on a timer?" Cas asked.

"He shot Tony and planned to detonate the bomb when the SWAT team arrived to save him. He wanted to ensure a maximum killing field, but the view through the rifle's scope was too small to allow him to see well enough to do that. His only option was to set the detonator on a timer and guess about how long it would take the SWAT team to get to Tony."

"That's why you had time to grab the detonator and throw it away from the C4," Cas said.

"It was, but the timer was also the reason David freaked out," I said. "He never anticipated you or me running downstairs to help Tony. He was afraid we were going to be blown up along with the SWAT team."

"As we ran down the stairs, David went crazy yelling at us to stop," Cas said.

"Yep, he saw what happened and got sick and ran to the bathroom," Molly said. "Brittany saw him do it too."

"You guessed he did it because he thought Cas and I had died," I said.

"So did Brittany," Molly said.

"But you were wrong," I said. "He used that time to dismantle the gun."

"When did he do that?" Cas asked. "Detective Corritore returned to the room with both of us. Where was the gun?"

"Still in the shooting room. Our first move after we returned to our room was to go down to the bathroom, where we heard David throwing up. He opened the door and returned to the room with us. I saw Corritore check the bathroom after he stepped out. She never did again."

"How did he take down the gun and remove it without being seen by any of us, including a trained police detective?" Cas asked.

"When we were back in our room, Corritore began questioning us. The answers became graphic. None of us were surprised when David became queasy and went back to the bathroom where we heard him dry heaving."

"Or thought we did," Cas said.

"Exactly, but he didn't go directly to the bathroom. He grabbed one of the computer carriers he'd left outside the room. He packed the dismantled rifle into the bag and then hauled it into the bathroom. He shut the door and hid it in the bathroom."

"Then, we came out of our room to check the other rooms for the shooter," Cas said.

"But he stayed in the bathroom while we did that," I said. "While Cas and I watched Corritore rush into the third room, he snuck back into our room with the rifle components in the computer carrier. He also carried the second empty computer bag into the room so that none of us would think twice about what he was doing."

"How did he get the rifle to the car?"

"I think I helped with that," Molly said.

"You did," I said. "When we left, he said he needed help with his computer equipment. He carried the dismantled gun and some of his equipment in one bag. You hauled the rest in the other."

145

"Do we know who David really is?" Molly asked.

"Or if that's his actual name?" Cas asked.

"He always wiped down anything he touched — except for the DVDs he picked up in my house. According to the FBI, the prints on the DVD cases matched the partial print on the wall of the clinic in Arlington, Virginia. And I had his blood on me when I was admitted to the hospital. That matched the blood found in Arlington too."

"So?" Cas asked. "Who is he?"

"The FBI agents think he's a priest who morphed into an increasingly violent abortion protester."

"If he had stopped after shooting Tony, it could have been the perfect crime," Linda said.

"But he didn't, and he won't."

The Hamlin Park Irregulars looked at each other.

"Do you mean he's still out there?" Cas asked.

"Before I shot him, he told me his plan was to shoot Micah and, if he had time, Hannah. Then he was going to detonate bombs in the far end of the building above the stage. I shot him in the center of his chest, but it didn't kill him, because he wore a Kevlar vest."

"How do you know he's still alive?" Molly asked.

"Internal security cameras outside the suite recorded a man in a janitor's outfit holding his head and staggering toward the escalator. The outside security cameras showed the same man climbing into a white minivan."

"And he's disappeared," Cas said.

"Not exactly."

I told them about Dr. Mick Doyle.

This time my friends really freaked out.

Linda hugged Jason closer to her chest. "That happened here?" she asked. "In this hospital?"

"Two floors up," I said.

"I always thought that lab tech was creepy," Molly said.

"And you would be right," I said.

"And you think David fired the shot," Cas said.

"I'll never know for sure, but — strange as it sounds — I think he did."

"Did he ever work for Hogan?" Linda asked.

"He started to work for them five years before the bombing in Arlington. The job gave him the perfect cover to convince us he was a real security expert. It also gave him access to all national security databases so he could easily monitor what they knew about him."

"With that computer access, it would have been impossible for any law enforcement agency to ever catch him," Linda said.

"At least we don't have anything to worry about ever again," Molly said.

"What do you mean?" Linda asked.

"Our little leprechaun guy will always be out there to protect us. Kind of a green insurance policy."

"If he has time when he's not bombing abortion clinics," I said.

146

I saw Cas glance out of the window in Linda's room. She quickly walked out to the nurse's station before she even had a chance to hold baby Jason.

What's this all about?

I saw that Linda was beginning to get uncomfortable. "Molly, why don't you help Linda walk around in the hall?" I asked. "I'll watch Jason."

They left, and I slowly picked up the baby, trying to avoid any stress to my sore belly. I walked around the room with him, and when I looked up, I saw Cas talking to a doctor.

He was at least a foot taller than the diminutive Cas. He had a long angular face with swept-back graying hair that curled over the collar of his button-down crisp white shirt. His patrician air gave me the feeling that he was a Ralph Lauren model masquerading as a physician.

He was hot, but it was Cas's demeanor that grabbed my attention. My Taser-using, Raid-spraying pit bull had morphed into a giggling teenager. Gone were her twitching jaw muscles, replaced by a wide smile — something she rarely exhibited. Unexpectedly, she gave the doctor a hug that lasted a little longer than I thought it should have.

Whoa, baby.

From the hall, Linda and Molly witnessed the entire episode. Linda glanced at me and raised her eyebrows. I motioned for her to bring Molly back to the room.

When they reentered, I pointed at Cas and the doctor, who were still chatting. "What do you make of that?"

"I'm not sure," Linda said. "Maybe they were close friends from when she worked here."

"I hope that's all they were, but I've never seen her act that giddy."

"Flirty might be a better term. When she saw him, her face lit up like a new author whose book has been anointed by Oprah."

"She doesn't do that with Joe, that's for sure," Molly said.

My abdomen ached, so I handed Jason to Linda. "Should we ask her about this?"

Linda began rocking him. "Let's hope this is an association from another life."

"And if it's not?" Linda asked.

"Maybe we'll have a story we don't want to write," I said.

147

A group of physicians wearing long white coats got off the elevator.

"Hey, guys, isn't that the doc with the expensive sunglasses we saw the last time we were here?" Molly asked.

"You're correct," Linda said. "It's Dr. J. Randall Fertig, Howard's mother's breast cancer doctor."

"Right, the guy who cures all his breast cancer patients," Molly said.

Fertig saw Cas talking to her doctor-friend and ripped off his sunglasses. He glowered at the doctor. That look made the hairs on my neck stand up.

There was pure hatred in Fertig's black eyes.

Suddenly, the other doctor looked up and saw Fertig staring at him.

Uh-oh.

The doctor glared back at Fertig.

Man, these two doctors really don't like each other.

It looked like the beginning of an old-fashioned gunfight that started with a stare-down. If looks could kill, one of the doctors would be dead.

I heard a "ding-dong" about a possible storyline in my brain. But after almost being killed chasing stories the past few weeks, I wanted to shut it down. What sane person wouldn't?

The answer? Me.

I keep trying to suppress it, but I am an investigative journalist and a sucker for a great story, and until I could prove to myself this wasn't worth pursuing, I would work on it with my friends.

And it wouldn't be dangerous. A doctor would never try to harm me or any of the Hamlin Park Irregulars just because we were working on a story about him.

Or would he?

Look for Book 3 in the *Hamlin Park Irregulars* series

— *bada-Boom!* —

to learn the answer to Tina's question.

Here is an excerpt: it will be published in the late fall of 2018.

"Landed over there," I heard the young police officer say, as I walked up to the scene of the car crash.

The cold early morning Chicago wind blasted in from Lake Michigan, but the stench of smoldering rubber tires and spilled gasoline, mixed with the odor of burned human hair and skin, still fouled the autumn air.

"Must have bounced off the bridge abutment," he said. "Only way it could have landed behind the car."

He pointed to a scraggly, misshapen bush on the side of Kennedy Freeway about twenty feet behind the doctor's mangled car. The vehicle had been totally incinerated in the blaze, and only the smoking metal carcass remained. Even the tires had been vaporized. It was impossible to identify the make of the car.

"Can't say I've ever seen that before," Detective Tony Infantino said.

I had called Tony, my friend and ex-lover, to meet me so I would have a way to get close to the yellow crime scene tape.

I tugged on Tony's arm. "What are you guys talking about?"

"Stuff about the accident."

The cop put his head down and walked toward his patrol car.

"Tony, what's going on?" I demanded.

"Doc came roaring down the Kennedy going over a buck-twenty."

"*How* fast?"

"Over a hundred twenty miles an hour, according to the accident investigators. No problem for a big car like that. Ran directly into the cement bridge abutment. Never hit his breaks."

"What kind of car was it?"

"According to the DMV registration, it was a Bentley."

"You're sure there wasn't a malfunction of the car?"

"Doubt it."

"But it could have happened."

"Could, but doesn't explain why he wasn't wearing a seat belt and the air bags didn't work."

I pointed at the charred remains of the vehicle. "Does a car usually burn up like this?"

"Only if there's an accelerant in it."

"Accelerant?"

"Cans of something, probably gas, in the back seat and the trunk. Car hits the bridge. Bada-bing: fire is first. Becomes a blaze. Then *bada-BOOM!*: gas tank explodes."

"Terrible way to die."

"Dude was a crispy critter. Wasn't much left of him. Be a quick autopsy."

"That bad?"

"Worse. They couldn't tell who was driving the car."

"Then how was the body ID'd?"

"His head."

"His head?"

"What that rookie cop was talking about. At first, they couldn't find it, so the EMT guys put what was left of him in a body bag and took it downtown."

"But his head was missing?"

He nodded. "When he hit the bridge, the doc went headfirst through the windshield."

"If he went through all the way, why was he burned so badly?"

"His whole body didn't quite make it all the way through the windshield."

"What did?"

"His head."

"That doesn't seem possible."

"In high velocity impacts, bodies frequently get trapped in broken windshields, like the doc's did. EMT's pried what was left of his shoulders and the lower part of his neck back out of the glass, but his head was gone."

"Where did it go?"

"Cop found it an hour ago stuck in the bush over there. Pieces of glass from the shattered window cut it off."

~

Acknowledgements

It has been said that you aren't really a writer until you've published your second book. If you have finished this book, then I guess that makes me a "real" writer, so I thank you.

It is also said that writing is rewriting, and I can attest to that, especially for the second book of this series. I never dreamed finishing this book would be harder than the first.

The reason it was? I'm not good at keeping track of the facts from *boom-BOOM!*, like the color of Tony's BMW or how many blocks away Molly lives from Tina.

But Nancy Cohen is. Without her, this book would have been a mess. Thank you, Nancy, for keeping my facts correct, helping with the story structure, and watching for misplaced commas and grammar mistakes.

Thanks to Shannon Baker, who continues to point out the places in my books that I didn't research properly (like police procedures). Shannon is a terrific author, and her books, especially her latest, *Dark Signal*, are a great read. The protagonist of her series, Kate Fox, is different from Tina Thomas, but they share a Nebraska upbringing, meaning they understand Husker football and Scott Frost. GBR!

Louis Romano is a fellow writer I met in Cabo San Lucas. He has encouraged me throughout my writing journey and understands what it is to be a newbie writer. Check out his latest book, *Exclusion: the fight for Chinatown.*

My new cast member is Jen Maher. She does my online advertising, something I would never attempt on my own. If you need help, she can do it for you, too, at Jen Maher Consulting.

I am so sorry to admit that I didn't publicly thank Ana Magno in the first book. Ana created the covers of the first two books, and I think they're amazing. I'm looking forward to the next one for *bada-BOOM!*

And the Professor, Rich Krevolin. He edited my first book, then called *Front Window*. Through the many initial edits of all the books, he has never discouraged me, gently pointing out my many missteps. He is a true Renaissance man; a writer of books, poetry, screenplays, and plays, director and producer of movies and documentaries, painter, professional storytelling consultant, college professor, and actor. Check him out online. He has done it all.

To my son-in-law, Jeff Taylor, (Carter Thomas in the books) and my daughter, Tina, (the protagonist in the Hamlin Park Irregulars series): Thanks for providing the inspiration and the setting for these books during the time you lived in Chicago. Readers, you can check out *boom-BOOM! by Dr. Wally Duff, the video book trailer* on YouTube to see Jeff and Tina's home in Lakeview, Chicago and the real Hamlin Park.

And to Kerry Taylor, who is a two-year-old in the books. She is now eighteen and attends Scripps. Unlike her language skills in the books, she speaks perfect English and writes far better than I ever will.

To Macy and Nick, Kerry's sister and brother. Thanks for waiting your turn. You will make an appearance later in the series.

And there is a Fourth Estate wine — two varietals, actually — a pinot noir and a chardonnay. It's Tina's other passion. Check it out on fourthestatewinery.com, especially the "about us" section and "delicious pairings." In that latter section you will find my wife's recipe: Mindy's Roast Chicken with Mashed Red or Sweet Potatoes. Try it, with the Fourth Estate Pinot Noir, of course.

To my son, James E. Duff, and his wife, Julia Morrison, who have provided expert advice about the content and pacing of my books. Their indie movie, *Hank and Asha*, won many film awards including the Napa Film Festival. It's a wonderful comedic love story with a truthful ending. Watch it: hankandasha.com.

To Brittany Simon, the reporter in the book. She is actually Brittany Haynie, who is married to Luke Haynie and mom to new guy on the block, Jetter.

And to my lovely wife, Mindy, who never complains when I leave her alone to immerse myself in writing these books. For your patience with me, your first literary shout-out will come in the next book, *bada-BOOM!*, a role which will be even more fleshed out in your favorite book, the fifth one in the series (currently titled *Love Changes Everything*, but I might fit a "boom" in there somewhere…).

Finally, a little bit about me. I continue to be a full-time otolaryngologist — a fancy name for a nose picker — husband, father, grandfather, magician for birthday parties, exercise nut, and a golfer, which makes me nuts.

The next book, *bada-BOOM!*, has a strong medical tilt, delving into the treatment of cancer of the breast and how competitive doctors and their wives are with each other, something I have too much experience with.

If you want to discuss *boom-BOOM!*, *déjà-BOOM!*, *bada-BOOM!*, or any of the other upcoming books in the Hamlin Park Irregulars series, please contact me at hamlinparkirregulars@gmail.com or www.hamlinparkirregulars.com.

93760075R00226

Made in the USA
Lexington, KY
18 July 2018